Susan stared at the cheerful room with a sad look on her face. "How was he killed?"

Kathleen looked around, making sure they were alone before she answered. "He was strangled. Probably last night. When the back doors of the van were opened this morning, dozens of balloons flew out. . . ."

Susan had seen the mylar balloons, shaped and colored like stars, Christmas trees, wreaths, balls, ornaments, even decorated gingerbread men. "Weren't they tied down in some way?"

"They are usually. But whoever put Z in the bottom of the van just stuffed him in. When the door was opened, the balloons took off into the sky and there he was . . . colored ribbons tied around his neck."

'TIS
THE SEASON
TO BE
MURDERED

VALERIE WOLZIEN

FAWCETT GOLD MEDAL • NEW YORK

For Margaret Cooper, Connie DeMott, and Miriam Rinn with thanks for allowing me to be a part of the best writing group ever.

A Fawcett Gold Medal Book
Published by Ballantine Books
Copyright © 1994 by Valerie Wolzien

All rights reserved under International and Pan-American Copyright Conventions. Published in the United States of America by Ballantine Books, a division of Random House, Inc., New York, and simultaneously in Canada by Random House of Canada Limited, Toronto.

Library of Congress Catalog Card Number: 94-94402

ISBN 0-449-00741-3

Printed in the United States of America

BVG 01

ONE

J<small>ED</small> H<small>ENSHAW</small> <small>WAS ADMIRING HIS WIFE THROUGH HALF-</small>
closed eyes. Candles on the mantel, logs blazing in the fire-
place, and hundreds of sparkling Christmas-tree lights made
the emerald earrings he'd given her that morning twinkle
and shine as she ... "What exactly are you doing?" he
asked, suddenly puzzled by her behavior. "You can't still be
wrapping presents—Christmas is over."

Susan's hair fell over the earrings as she glanced at her
wrist. "Not for thirty-seven minutes, it's not. Besides, I finished wrapping presents about this time last night. I'm just
sorting wrapping paper."

"Hon, my mother doesn't even save used paper anymore."

"I said sorting, not saving. For recycling. I know the
tissue and glossy papers go in the recycling bin, but the
metallic is garbage. I suppose this tissue with tiny stars
should be thrown away—I think they're plastic." Unaccus-
tomed to her new bifocals, she squinted at the gaudy sheets.
"And I have no idea what this bag is made out of ... Is it
Mylar plastic, or maybe aluminum?" She waited a few minutes before continuing. "Jed, are you listening to me?"

A slight snore answered her question.

She tried again, a little louder. "Jed?"

"I think I had too much to eat," Jed mumbled, and

1

buried his head under a needlepoint pillow shaped like an angel.

More like too much wine, eggnog, and brandy, but Susan kept the thought to herself. She leaned back against the coffee table and examined the messy room. She loved every minute of Christmas, from the champagne that she and her husband shared at midnight on Christmas Eve to the inevitable chaos left behind by opening presents and the daylong entertaining of family, friends, and neighbors. But now, their guests had gone home, and her children were busy. Chad, sixteen, was upstairs, duplicating new rock cassettes that he would exchange for friends' copies of their new acquisitions. Chrissy, home from her freshman year at college, was out with old high-school classmates.

Susan, deciding to let her husband sleep, gave up and stuffed the piles of wrapping paper under the couch. She seemed to hear a pitcher of eggnog calling her from the refrigerator. Or was it fruitcake? Or that Kentucky-bourbon cake Kathleen had brought to dinner? Maybe the Jamaican black cake she had made for the first time this year?

She should have a small slice of each one she decided, entering her kitchen. She deserved the calories. She had to clean up this mess. And it would make her task just that much easier if she finished off this plate of pecan crescents. As she reached out her hand, a large open mouth appeared from under the table.

"Clue!" Susan recognized the year-old golden retriever bitch that had been lurking nearby since Susan began her annual baking binge the day after Thanksgiving. "Haven't you had enough? You're going to need to go on a diet!" She patted her puppy on the head, knowing that, in this case, she was the pot calling the kettle black.

She shared the last few cookies on the plate with Clue, and then got down to work. She filled the sink with soapy water and washed her grandmother's cut-glass goblets. They dried on a linen towel while she emptied and refilled the dishwasher. The three-tiered cake plate was a cinch for her and Clue to empty, but a pain to wash, and she was startled when her daughter appeared in the room.

"Chrissy! I had no idea you were home!" Susan tightened her grip on the slippery crystal.

Clue was jumping around and tearing at Chrissy's new, purple suede boots. The pretty girl knelt down and rubbed the animal behind the ears and tossed an envelope to her mother at the same time.

"I found this on the floor of the front hall. It looks like someone stepped on it. The name is a little hard to recognize, but it says something Henshaw. Maybe a late Christmas card."

Susan glanced at the writing and didn't recognize it. "I'll open it later. It's probably from a neighbor. An invitation that someone had a child deliver. It'll wait until my hands are dry." She smiled at her daughter. "How was your evening?"

"Super. Has anyone fed this animal tonight?" Chrissy asked, offering a glazed apricot to Clue.

"People have been feeding her all day long. Clue's breakfast was a candy cane stolen from the Christmas tree; her brunch was some gingerbread cookies and a cup of eggnog that I left too close to the edge of the table; for lunch she had more than a taste of everything you and I and everyone else had, from turkey to plum pudding; and tonight, one of Chad's friends brought over a box of gourmet dog treats for her, and she consumed it, box and all—I suppose that was her dinner. And she's still begging. I don't know where she puts it all."

"In this fat stomach," Chrissy said, patting the animal's belly. "I'm thirsty. Is there any seltzer in the refrig'?"

"Probably," Susan muttered, wondering what was clanking against the wall of her dishwasher. She hoped it wasn't something fragile.

Chrissy sliced cold turkey to accompany the seltzer. Susan had boned the bird and stuffed it with an exotic dressing of chestnuts, fruit, and Grand Marnier. She put down the plate she was drying and joined her daughter. Like many cooks, she enjoyed the leftovers more than the original meal itself.

"How did you think the day went?" she asked her daughter.

"You mean Mrs. Davies and Mrs. Cutler, don't you?"

Susan frowned. "Do you think it was a mistake to invite them? They didn't seem to have much fun." Susan always included friends and neighbors who were going to be spending the holidays alone when she planned the family's Christmas dinner. This year Gillian Davies and Alexis Cutler had been their guests. Both women were recently single; both were mothers spending the holiday alone for the first time; and both lived on the same street. Aside from that, they had little in common that Susan could find. Except that they were giving parties the same evening. Susan had received invitations to both.

"They're rather stressed-out, aren't they?" Chrissy answered her question. "That's sometimes a symptom of living in the suburbs. I think an urban lifestyle can be much healthier, don't you?"

Susan had momentarily forgotten that her lovely daughter had gone off to college a charming innocent only to return home, less than three months later, a jaded sophisticate. Just goes to show what eleven thousand dollars put in the right place can do, Susan thought, hiding a smile. "It's certainly difficult to be a single mother in the suburbs," she said, thinking that she was agreeing with her daughter.

"But that's the point, isn't it?" Chrissy asked. "They were fine as long as they were mothers; the problems started when their kids left home. Empty nest. Like you'll be when Chad leaves for college in two years. But you'll have Dad, of course. So it will be easier for you."

"Did you think either of them had a good time?"

"They're a little competitive, aren't they?"

"I didn't notice."

"The way they were trying to prove what good mothers they were with Bananas. And talking about how happy they are these days—I thought they protested just a little too much, didn't you?"

Happily for Susan, who didn't want to ruin her holiday mood by gossiping about neighbors, Chrissy immediately lost interest in the topic. "Have you tried out your Christmas gift yet?" the girl asked, picking at a drumstick with her fingers. "There's a packet of decaf beans with it."

Susan started guiltily. Chrissy and Chad had gotten together and very generously given their mother a new, imported cappuccino machine this morning. Susan adored good coffee—her old machine had died recently—and she had planned to express her appreciation by starting to use this gift immediately after dinner. But she'd forgotten.

Dinner had been a little chaotic. As usual, Kathleen and Jerry Gordon had come over, bringing their preschool son with them. As much fun as it was to have a small child around at Christmas, Bananas, overexcited by the day, had kept his parents (both exhausted after a late night spent constructing a very complex HO train set) as well as Alexis and Gillian busy trying to assemble Lego versions of farm equipment, castles, and boats. He had spilled apple juice on the cashmere sweater that was a present to Chrissy from her grandmother, had burst into tears when asked to use his fork rather than his fingers to eat mashed potatoes, and when left alone, had fallen asleep on the floor under the Christmas tree, with Clue obligingly serving as his pillow.

Susan had thought about the cappuccino then, but the doorbell had rung, and two couples they'd known for years had appeared, bearing gifts and a large bottle of brandy. Clue, who insisted on greeting all the Henshaws' guests, had leapt up; Bananas's head had hit the floor; and by the time everyone was settled in front of the fire with a balloon glass of the brandy, Susan had completely forgotten that she intended to use her children's gift.

"Why don't we try it now? I'll go get it." Susan hurried back to the living room, chagrined by her omission. It was such a lovely present. . . .

She was back in her kitchen in minutes, the box held high in her hands. "I hope you and Chad know how much I love this," she began.

"Enough to offer me a midnight snack?" Her son had left the sanctuary of his room. As usual these days, only hunger could draw him out. Happily for his continuing relationship with the rest of the family, he was hungry more often than not.

"Take anything you want," his mother offered. "There's leftover everything. From soup to nuts."

"We didn't have soup."

"No, it's just an expression," Susan said, trying to talk and read the directions that came with her new gift at the same time. These glasses were really bad; the instructions looked like a foreign language. She was immediately glad she'd kept the thought to herself; it was a foreign language. She turned the paper over and found the directions in English, shaking her head at her own stupidity. She leaned back against the tile counter and started to read.

A few minutes later, she gave up. How could it possibly take thirty-nine steps to produce one cup of espresso topped with steamed milk? It was simpler to make beef bourguignon. Chrissy had set up the sleek, black gadget in the middle of the counter. It looked like a bomb. How did it steam the milk? she wondered. "I think we should grind the beans first. The directions say 'until fine.' "

"I'll do it," Chad offered.

"What do you know about grinding coffee beans?" Chrissy asked him, grabbing the small electric grinder from her brother.

"Oh, sure, Miss College Freshman. I saw how you were sniffing the wine at dinner as though you'd become some sort of fancy connoisseur in the three months since you left home."

"I'm—"

"We all know you're dating the heir to the grocery fortune of the Northeast. You've told us often enough. . . ."

Chrissy wasn't about to allow that to pass without comment. "He's not the heir to the grocery fortune of the Northeast! He's a member of the family who owns only the most famous gourmet shop in New York City. . . ."

"And don't forget those branches in the Hamptons, Westport, and Chicago. . . ." Chad smirked.

"Okay, you two. It's Christmas for a few more minutes. Couldn't you at least wait to argue until after midnight?" Susan was becoming exasperated with her children. They had always squabbled, but Chad had seemed lonely when his older sister left for college and, only a week ago, so happy that she was coming home that Susan had hoped things were changing for them. They had been fighting since Chrissy walked in the door.

"You're just upset because your girlfriend didn't come over today—" Chrissy began.

"Shut up, you." Chad evidently wanted to say more, but a glance at his mother kept him quiet. He grabbed a handful of fudge off the counter and slammed out of the room. Susan fiddled with the machine until she heard him stomp up the stairs, then she turned to her daughter. "What girlfriend?" she asked.

"You don't know?" Chrissy may have learned a lot in her first semester of college, but apparently she still believed her mother to be mentally deficient.

It was Christmas. And she had been given this wonderful present. Susan smiled as she spoke. "Would you be betraying any confidences if you told me about her?"

"I can't believe you don't know. Everyone was talking about her tonight . . . ," Chrissy started.

"Who?" Susan decided a simple question might be the best way to get a simple answer. She was only asking for one name, for heaven's sake.

"Courtney Sawyer." Chrissy poured beans into the grinder.

"Howard and Betsy's daughter. How does he know her? She's been away at boarding school since seventh or eighth grade. I don't think I'd recognize the child."

"You wouldn't if you still think of her as a child," Chrissy agreed, pressing the switch and grinding the beans. "Are you ready for these?" she asked, sniffing the fragrance.

"Pour them in there," Susan said, pointing. "And tell me exactly what you meant by that last comment. She's Chad's age, isn't she?"

"Do you know the expression 'sixteen going on thirty'?"

Susan was beginning to understand why Chad found his sister so irritating. "Yes, I've heard it," was all she said, pouring water in one container, milk in another, and pressing what she hoped was the correct series of buttons in the proper order.

"Well, that's Courtney. From what I've heard, her party is going to be something."

"What party?" Susan asked, wondering if that bubbling

noise was normal or if she should unplug the machine before it exploded.

"The one the Lindgrens were talking about!" Chrissy
reached over and pressed another button on the machine.
"The salesman at Bloomingdale's showed me how to use
this—it's not difficult."

The Lindgrens had been one of the couples who spent a
considerable part of the afternoon in front of the Henshaws'
fireplace. Susan thought back over the conversation. "I
don't remember any talk about Courtney."

"Mother, what were you doing? Daydreaming?"

It wasn't often that Susan got to hear herself quoted by
her children, and she had to work to resist smiling. That is,
she did until she heard the rest of Chrissy's story. "Mrs.
Lindgren was talking about some caterer the Sawyers had
gotten for Courtney's party and how this caterer was in the
middle of some sort of nervous breakdown or something and
screwed up all their plans. They were very upset about it."

Susan could imagine, but she let her daughter continue
without interrupting.

"So that's how I heard that Courtney is going to have
some sort of fancy-schmancy, sweet-sixteen party—honestly,
I don't know what's happening to the suburbs. The impor-
tance placed on the rituals of childhood is almost repulsive.
And hiring some catering company with a strange name and
then complaining about it all evening . . ."

"What name?"

"I don't remember exactly." Chrissy looked puzzled.
"Something to do with plants. I thought it sounded more
like a florist than a . . ."

"The Holly and Ms. Ivy?" Susan asked, interrupting her
daughter.

"Yes. Dumb name, don't you think? Why are you getting
so upset?" Chrissy looked at her mother curiously. "What's
wrong?"

"It's probably nothing." The scent of coffee was beginning to fill the kitchen. "What exactly were the Lindgrens
saying about The Holly and Ms. Ivy?"

"You should probably call them, if you really want to
know. I just heard that whoever was in charge of reserving

the place where the party was going to be held had screwed up. Is that the caterer's job?"

"The Holly and Ms. Ivy is more than a caterer—they're really a party planning service. They do everything, from sending out invitations to arranging for people to park cars. Everything. In fact, I've hired them to do my New Year's party this year."

"Mother! Why?" Chrissy looked as though her mother had admitted to an exotic sexual perversion. "You love giving parties!"

"I just thought I'd try something different this year," Susan said. "And you know I had the flu right after Halloween, and it took me such a long time to feel well. I really wasn't right until Thanksgiving. . . . And I'd heard such good things about The Holly and Ms. Ivy that I thought it might be interesting to have the party done by someone else." Susan wondered if her daughter realized that she was just making excuses. She wasn't really sure why she had decided to turn the Henshaws' annual New Year's Eve party over to someone else—maybe it was just that she had been offered the opportunity at a moment when the idea was particularly appealing.

Apparently these were not burning questions to Chrissy; she was more interested in the cappuccino. "That's done, isn't it?"

Susan poured two tiny cups of coffee, squirting steaming milk on top. "Want some sugar or artificial sweetener?"

"I can get it. You know, it isn't like you to hire a caterer. Is anything wrong?" Chrissy asked the question when her back was to her mother.

Susan stirred sugar into the drink. The question surprised her. She wasn't accustomed to concern about her life from her daughter. Usually it was the other way around. She was relieved when Jed's entrance eliminated the need for her to respond.

"Do I smell coffee?"

"Decaf cappuccino. Do you want some?"

"I'll get it," Chrissy offered quickly.

"Thanks. But I hope no one will be offended if I take

this upstairs and sip it in a warm bed. It's been a great Christmas, but I'm beat."

"Me, too," his daughter agreed. "And I'm going into the city tomorrow to see that exhibit at MOMA, so I have to get up early."

"I don't think the museum opens till—"

"I want to hit the after-Christmas sales at Bergdorf's and Saks first. Good night."

Jed and Susan exchanged smiles. "She's growing up," Susan said.

"But she's still the best shopper in the family," Jed said. "Who else would even want to think about shopping the day after Christmas?"

"I suppose," Susan said, not bothering to admit that she had plans of her own for tomorrow. There was this great duffle coat that she expected to be on sale at Saks. "I'll take Clue out for a last walk and be right up."

The dog had a vocabulary that wouldn't impress the scorers of the SATs, but it worked for her—and *walk* was right at the top of the list. Susan had a hard time getting the leash attached to the collar of the happily prancing dog, and she should have learned by now to put her coat on first. By the time they were outside, Susan and dog were both more than a little irritated. But the Henshaws lived on a large block, and by the time they were halfway around it, both dog and owner were happy and content.

Bows on wreaths and evergreen swags fluttered in the breezes. Candles twinkled in the windows. Electric lights outlined Tudor paneling and circled hundreds of evergreens and small deciduous trees. Santas waved, and angels trumpeted from lawns and on roofs. Fragrant woodsmoke swirled from chimneys and out windows. . . .

But something looked wrong. There was heavy smoke coming from the side of JoAnn Kent's house. Susan tugged on the leash and ran up the driveway toward the large split-level, dog following happily. Clue seemed to feel that there was nothing like a midnight jog to cap off the holiday.

Susan arrived at the front door and banged on it as hard as she could, her fists smashing the large pine cone wreath that hung on the dark green enamel. "JoAnn! JoAnn!

There's a fire!" She couldn't for the life of her remember the name of the attractive, blond stockbroker who was Mr. Kent. She would just have to assume that he would hear the word fire and respond. "Fire! Fire!"

The door opened so quickly that she almost fell inside. "Susan, for heaven's sake! What are you yelling about? The fire's out!" JoAnn Kent, trim and chic in a black velvet cat suit, tiny crystal angels dangling from each ear, was standing before her.

"Your house . . ." Susan tried to catch her breath. "Your house is on fire."

"That's just the kitchen fan. It's still smoky in there. Someone left the small oven on after the goose was taken out, and the fat started to burn. Then the curtains caught fire. The whole room is a mess, and believe me, I'm going to sue the pants off The Holly and Ms. Ivy for it." She glared at the dog who was bounding up and down. "Can't you keep that monster under control?"

"Clue! Stop jumping! She's still a puppy. She'll calm down soon." Susan pulled on the leash, jerking her dog off the other woman. "There's really no fire?"

"There was, but now it's just smoke."

"You said something about The Holly and Ms. Ivy. . . ."

"Don't tell me you were the person who recommended those idiots to me! I've been wondering just who I had to thank all day long!"

"No, I don't think. . . ."

"Sure! You wouldn't admit it now! Not after they ruined my Christmas dinner and practically burned down my newly remodeled kitchen! Now I'm going to have a large glass of Scotch and go to bed!" JoAnn looked down at her holiday attire. "After I pick your dog's fur off my clothing!"

Susan could only be glad that JoAnn had slammed the door before noticing that Clue was chewing up the large satin ribbon that had been decorating one of the pair of topiaries placed on either side of the door. "Come on, sweetie, time for bed."

Clue trotted happily all the way home, ribbon hanging from her mouth.

TWO

SUSAN TRIED TO STAY IN BED THE NEXT MORNING. IT WAS
Boxing Day in England; she had decided to adopt that tradition and take the day off, sleeping late before doing some
leisurely shopping. And she really gave it her best shot.

There was a crisis with a client at the advertising agency
where Jed was executive vice president, and he needed to
be on the seven A.M. train into Grand Central. Since his
wife wanted to sleep in, he hadn't turned on the light in the
bedroom, dressing from the glow of the fixture in the ad-
joining bath. He'd only dropped his shoes once, knocked
his cappuccino cup (happily empty) off the dresser while
feeling around for his wallet, pulled an electric candle out
of a window checking on the weather, and squashed his
wife's feet when he sat on the bed to put on his socks. Susan wondered if it was a sign that they had been married
too long when she found herself wondering if it was absolutely necessary for them to kiss good-bye. But she was
sleepy, and the thought did not keep her awake for more
than a second or two.

Then she slept for a few more minutes before Chrissy
stuck her head inside the door. "Mom? Are you asleep?"

Would she deserve a Mother's Day card if she didn't answer? Did she even get a Mother's Day card last year?

12

Cursing her own integrity, she answered, "Good morning, Chrissy. What can I do for you?"

"I need the train schedule. I'm going to the city, remember?"

"It's in the kitchen by the phone—exactly where it always is."

"I looked there."

"Look again." The second word was hardly out of her mouth before she was asleep.

She expected Chad to be next, but he didn't usually lick her nose. "Lie down, Clue." Jed hated the dog in bed with them. Susan, who remembered the days when both her children would pile under the quilt on the weekends, was happy to have company. She drifted back to sleep, with Clue's head propped on her hip.

"Bye, Mom. We'll call for a ride if we get back late."

We? Late? A ride where? Susan decided she would worry about it later. It was her day to sleep. She stretched her toes to the bottom of the bed and buried her nose in the pile of down pillows at the head. She loved sleeping late. The warm quilt, the soft cotton sheets, the smell of chocolate scorching . . . She sat up in bed. "Chad!"

"It's okay. I picked it up!" Her son's voice came faintly up the stairs.

Susan thought for a moment. Clue eyed her, apparently wondering what the choice would be between staying here asleep and getting up for a brisk walk. Either way, the dog would be happy, but Susan remembered the temperature outdoors and pulled the blankets up over her shoulders. Chad was sixteen. He wasn't going to let the house burn down.

She closed her eyes, only to open them almost immediately. How could she have forgotten about the fire last night? What had she been thinking of? She couldn't take the day off—she had to find out what was going on with The Holly and Ms. Ivy. And if it might wreck her New Year's Eve party.

She rolled over in bed and pulled open the drawer in the nightstand by her side. A moss green notebook was tucked in the drawer, a tiny silver pen marking her place. Susan started to skim the filled pages, wishing a cup of coffee would magically appear. A compulsive list maker, Susan read columns of things to do, food to bake, presents to buy—all work that had gone into making yesterday a success. Somewhere in the middle of all this were two different lists: one, of things she wanted to get done after the holidays were over (starting, of course, with losing the same ten pounds she was so familiar with); the other, of subjects she had discussed with Gwen Ivy during the planning for her party this Saturday.

Susan mulled over her first meeting with Gwen Ivy while she searched. They had run into each other in front of the cheese counter at Dean and DeLuca the week before Thanksgiving. Susan, still reeling from the flu, had been feeling foggy and having a difficult time making her selection when she noticed a familiar figure ahead of her.

Gwen Ivy was well known as half of the most famous catering and party-giving company in Connecticut. They were located in Hancock, and Susan had often gone to parties in the city, been asked where she lived, and when she replied, the unvarying response was something like "Oh, that's where Holly and Ivy are located, isn't it?" This was usually followed by wondering whether Susan had ever hired this famous team. She always answered that she loved planning her own parties, much to her companion's disappointment. She had been thinking about all this at the cheese counter when she realized she was staring at the caterer. And she wasn't the only person in the room doing so.

Gwen Ivy was chic. Her blond hair, pale almost to ivory, was cut in a geometric helmet from which an assortment of unique earrings dangled. She was not so much clothed as draped in layers of fabulous fabrics, which she peeled on and off as the seasons dictated. On that particular day, Gwen was wearing burnished suede boots that contrasted nicely with layers of forest green and camel wool. Earrings of carved amber matched a wide cuff of the same material on her wrist. Susan had noticed the wrist particularly since it was near the list Gwen Ivy held. That shopping list was keeping Susan inside this overheated store, wearing her heaviest wool melon coat over a mohair sweater set that she had chosen this morning for its warmth. She began to feel like she might faint . . .

"Are you okay? Maybe we should sit down?"

Susan realized that Gwen Ivy was speaking to her. "I don't feel very well," she admitted. "It's hot."

"It is. Why don't we get something cool to drink? Over there," Gwen Ivy suggested, taking her elbow gently.

"What about your packages?"

"We'll take care of them for Ms. Ivy." A helpful clerk had appeared at their side, leading them to a seat and eyeing a hovering waiter to clear the table immediately.

"You live in Hancock, don't you?" Gwen Ivy asked, after they had ordered two iced coffees.

Susan, busy taking off her coat, nodded.

"I thought I'd seen you around. You're famous for investigating murders—and you were at the Malloy's party last weekend, weren't you?"

"Yes. You did the catering. It was wonderful." Susan was feeling a little better. "Do you give out recipes? The chèvre pastries were wonderful."

"We don't usually, but if you look in the latest Junior League cookbook, you'll find something you might recognize—just add a half cup of pignoli nuts."

"Thanks."

"And maybe you'll give me your recipe for paella? I've heard it's wonderful."

"Of course. I learned it in a class I took years ago at the New School." Susan stirred a spoonful of sugar into the tall glass of caramel-colored liquid. "You heard about my recipe?"

"That and more. Your parties are the talk of the town."

Susan felt well enough to smile. "I always enjoyed giving parties."

Gwen Ivy leaned a little more closely toward Susan. "Is there any reason that you said that in the past tense?"

Susan shook her head. "I had the flu this fall, and I can't seem to shake it. Nothing is as much fun as it used to be."

"Are you having a large crowd for Thanksgiving?"

"Not this year. We're going to a friend's home. But I'll start baking for Christmas soon, and I have to get busy

planning our annual New Year's Eve party." And that's
when the idea struck. "I never really understood why people hire caterers—until now. I mean, Christmas cookies are
fun, but I just can't get excited about a big party."

"Well, you could call off the party and take a vacation."
Gwen Ivy paused. "Or you could hire The Holly and Ms.
Ivy to organize everything." She raised well-tended eyebrows. "Sometimes a break is what people need the most—
and I'd love working on a party with you."

And that's how it happened. Susan looked down at the
list she had finally found. Instead of being a list of things
she had to do, this year it was a list of things she expected
someone else to tend to. She didn't know how things usually went with other caterers, but working with Z Holly and
Gwen Ivy had been a lot of fun.

Z, as he called himself, was as boyishly charming as
Gwen was chic. They had explained that they were the
founders and co-owners of The Holly and Ms. Ivy (having
agreed on the name after consuming two full bottles of
Moët brut), and that they were thrilled to have the
Henshaws' business. As Gwen had put it, "Doing a party
for you will really make our reputation in this town."

Flattered, Susan had made this list, examined menus,
ripped out ideas from magazines, consulted numerous times
with both Z and Gwen, prepared a guest list, written a
check, and then got on with her preparations for Christmas.
It had been delightful. Of course, that would change immediately if The Holly and Ms. Ivy turned out to be incompetent. And burning down your employer's kitchen would
surely be considered incompetent. It was certainly no way
to encourage future business. And what exactly had Chrissy
been saying she'd overheard about Courtney's party?

Susan leapt out of bed so quickly that the dog had to roll
over to keep up. "Chrissy!" she called out.

"She's gone. Didn't you hear her?" Chad yelled up the
stairs.

"No. I didn't," Susan answered, thinking she would have
to speak with her daughter about this. "Would you walk
Clue, Chad? I have to—"

"Mom! I'm on my way out the door. The guys are waiting for me."

"Where are you—"

"Skiing. A whole bunch of us are going up north for the day. Don't you remember? I told you about it last Friday as well as yesterday. You really don't pay any attention to me now that the college kid is home, do you?"

"I—" Susan heard someone honk impatiently in her driveway. She wondered how many of her neighbors were also having their sleep interrupted by her children. "Go ahead and have a wonderful time," she urged in as pleasant a voice as she could manage, biting her tongue before it could recite maternal warnings about frostbitten toes and broken limbs. Chad wasn't listening anyway.

The front door slammed, and she ran to the window in time to see a red Jeep skid up over the curb and out of her driveway, narrowly missing the antique Jaguar XKE that was the much-loved transportation of her friend Kathleen Gordon. Chad waved vaguely back toward the house, and he was off.

Susan wondered if he had remembered to take his new gloves. She looked down at Clue, and Clue looked up at her. "Be glad you're spayed. It will save you hours of worry."

Clue wagged her tail, perfectly happy to be agreeable until after her morning walk and a big breakfast.

"Just let me get dressed, and we'll hit the sidewalk," Susan said, avoiding the *w* word. She glanced out the window while going through her dresser, expecting to see Kathleen's car parked in the drive. Except for fresh skid marks, the macadam was bare. Susan opened her mouth and then shut it. She really had to stop chatting with the dog. She pulled a cotton turtleneck from the drawer and slipped it over her head. Jeans, a heavy V-neck wool sweater, wool socks, and fur-lined boots completed her outfit. She dressed for weather rather than for style—a good thing, since she hadn't done any laundry since the beginning of last week. Her underwear drawer in particular looked a little empty. And it seemed to be getting emptier.

"Drop it, Clue!" Susan ordered in what she was coming

to think of as her obedience-class voice. Surprisingly, the retriever opened her mouth and dropped Susan's expensive ivory silk bra on the floor. Only to grab it up again as Susan reached for it. The puppy was barely one year old. Susan was in her midforties. Experience would lose to enthusiasm and reflexes. Her only chance was superior intelligence.

"Let's go for a walk, Clue," Susan called over her shoulder, striding from the room. She didn't look down until they were in the hallway.

It had worked. Clue, mouth empty, was panting with excitement. Susan attached the dog's new leash to her collar, opened the door, and headed out into the cold.

The sky was gray, and the air smelled like snow. Susan smiled, thinking of how happy that had made her children when they were young and had received sleds and skis for Christmas. Then she frowned. Chad and Chrissy were away from home, one in the city, and one in the mountains. A storm would be more threatening than exciting—at least for their mother until they were both safe at home. Clue was tugging on the leash, trying to start down the street. Susan obediently trotted behind, pleased that they were heading toward the Kents' home. Checking in this morning would be the neighborly thing to do. Besides, she had to know what was going on with her caterers. And it looked like she was going to hear the story from the horse's mouth. Parked in the drive of the Kent home was the distinctive forest green van of The Holly and Ms. Ivy. Sitting in the driver's seat was Gwen Ivy. Susan hurried over.

"Gwen! Hi!"

The cap of blond hair turned slowly, and Susan gasped. Gwen Ivy had a hideous black eye. She grimaced and greeted Susan. "Hi, yourself. Merry Christmas a day late. Although I certainly wish it were Halloween. I'd like to hide this thing behind a mask."

"What happened?" It was out of Susan's mouth before she realized that it might be rude to ask.

"I ran into Santa's fist."

"What?"

"Really. I had to go over to a client's home where we'd

left some large trays that we need for a dinner this evening. And I ran into their Christmas display: a life-size Santa, sleigh, and reindeer—all cast in bronze. I was impressed with it in the daytime—it's almost a work of art. But last night, I ran into it while my hands were full of trays, and all I saw were stars."

"I don't think I know that particular display," Susan said.

"Well, it's something to avoid in the dark."

Neither woman said anything for a few awkward minutes. Then both spoke at once.

"I suppose the—"

"Actually, Z and I had this argument—"

"He hit y—"

"No! No, of course not. I got upset, and I was running away." Gwen Ivy touched her eyelid gently, and Susan waited for her to continue. "I ran into that damn Christmas decoration. I should have been looking where I was going. It was my own fault."

Susan wondered why Gwen was so anxious to assume responsibility for her injury, but she didn't think this was necessarily the time or place to ask a bunch of questions. Her feet were getting cold, and Clue was making breakfast of another ribbon from the Kents' decorations. She looked up at the windows, wondering if JoAnn was watching.

Gwen noticed her concern. "They're not home. I rang the bell, and no one answered."

"So why are you here?"

"To collect the money that the Kents owe me—and to present them with this. I was just making it out."

Susan stared at the pink sheet of paper in the other woman's hand. "What is it?"

"A bill for all the equipment we lost in the fire. We are not going to eat this one, believe me. The Holly and Ms. Ivy have moved way beyond that type of thing. We'll take them to court over this. . . ." To Susan's surprise, she chuckled. "Or else we'll threaten to send your dog over to deal with them."

Susan looked down. Clue had finished with the ribbon, and the plant it had been tied to, and was gnawing on the bottom of the pristine marble urn. "Clue! No! Stop that!"

The dog didn't pause. Susan pulled on the leash, dragging the eighty-seven-pound dog away from what it seemed to consider to be a justly deserved breakfast.

"Didn't you tell me you were starting obedience classes a few weeks ago?"

"We're working on 'heel' and 'stay,' not 'don't eat the planter,' " Susan answered.

"I once dated a man who had a golden. They'll eat anything. I was taking a lot of cooking classes then. The poor animal got all my disasters—lived to a ripe old age, too, I'm told."

"Do you have time for a cup of coffee?" Susan asked, impulsively.

"Not unless you come over to my place and have it with me while I work."

"Fine with me, but I have to take Clue home first and give her some breakfast."

"I'll just put this in the mailbox and head on over. The coffee will be ready by the time you get there."

"Great!" Susan agreed, ordered her dog to come, and headed home.

THREE

"DOES THIS MEAN YOU AND JED DIDN'T GET MUCH SLEEP last night?" Kathleen was standing at the bottom of the stairway, Susan's silk underwear dangling from a finger.

Susan grabbed the bra before Clue could steal it again. "The teeth marks are the dog's. I wasn't wearing it at the time. And Jed left for a meeting before I was up this morning. Want some coffee?"

"Definitely." The two women had been friends for almost ten years. Kathleen wasn't a bit hesitant about leading the way. They'd solved eight crimes together. Confirmed caffeine fiends, they were on their third automatic coffeemaker. "I gather you forgot that we were planning to do a little postholiday shopping this morning."

"I did not. I just had some other things to do first." Susan didn't really enjoy shopping after the holidays, but she had to make three returns today. Jed and Chad had both been given sweaters that didn't fit, and Chrissy wanted a black turtleneck rather than the color Susan had spent hours choosing just three days ago. And there was that coat waiting for her at Saks. "Didn't I see you drive by here earlier?"

Kathleen nodded, spooning sugar into her coffee. "I had to drop Bananas off at the Rogers'. He's spending the morning with Ruthie. He was thrilled. She's his first crush.

He keeps repeating her name and giggling." She peered into a tin decorated with a leaping reindeer. "Oh good, shortbread. I love your shortbread," she enthused, taking a few of the small rounds, biting one in half, and then frowning.

"Is it okay?" Susan asked.

"Wonderful as always," Kathleen assured her. "I was just wondering about whether or not I should have left Ban this morning."

"You're not jealous, are you?"

"Heavens no. I'm thrilled that he has a good female friend. Most of his companions are tough little boys. This will be good for him. I was thinking about Ginnie Rogers. She may not need company right now."

"Why not?"

"She's supposed to be giving some sort of dinner party tonight for people from Andy's company, and the entrée hasn't shown up yet."

"Shown up?"

"Ginnie hates cooking. She's been ordering at least parts of meals from some catering company for the last few years. She was telling me about them . . ."

"Not The Holly and Ms. Ivy?" Susan asked, taking a cookie and popping it in her mouth.

"I don't know."

Susan sighed. Everything had seemed to be going so well. "Even if it's not, I have to go over to their offices and talk with Gwen. Do you want to go with me? It won't take long, then we can hit the stores together."

"Gwen?"

"Gwen Ivy. She's the Ms. Ivy of the group. If you have the time, just let me feed Clue and grab my coat. I'll explain on the way."

Kathleen smiled. "Fine with me as long as you don't mind if I eat a few more of these. They're my favorite."

"Eat away. I sure don't need the calories." She looked enviously at her friend's figure. No matter how much Kathleen ate, she didn't gain an ounce. The fact that she still had female friends showed what a good person she was.

"Why are you going to talk with Gwen Ivy? I thought you'd finished planning for Saturday night weeks ago."

Susan was busy looking at her reflection in the gloss finish on her refrigerator. She was dressed to walk the dog. Was she too casual to go downtown? Oh, well, it was the day after Christmas; no one would expect her to be a fashion plate. If Kathleen was driving, she could put on lipstick and blush in the car. "What? I thought so, yes, but evidently The Holly and Ms. Ivy are having some problems. What's that?" She looked down at the dark green envelope Kathleen had in her hand.

"I don't know. Looks like an unopened Christmas card or invitation. It was sitting here on the table."

"Oh, someone tossed that in the mail drop last night. Go ahead and open it. I have to go to the garage to get Clue's breakfast. I don't know why Jed keeps buying dog food in such huge bags." She wandered off to the attached garage.

When she returned to the kitchen, Kathleen was still sitting at the table, a card in her hand.

"Greetings or good news?" Susan asked, pouring a large portion of kibble into a bright red, ceramic dish.

"Neither."

"Well, what is it?"

"I don't know. It's probably someone's idea of a joke. I'd forget all about it."

Susan was surprised by the seriousness of Kathleen's voice. "What does it say?"

"See for yourself." Kathleen handed the missive over.

Susan took the envelope and the heavy, cream, bond notepaper inside, and read the spiky writing while Kathleen peered into the half-dozen glass cookie jars that lined a shelf of Susan's built-in pantry.

"What do you call these little thumbprint cookies?"

"Little thumbprint cookies. What else? You don't think this is serious, do you?" Susan waved the small sheet of paper in front of her friend's face.

Kathleen shrugged. "No. I'd ignore it, if I were you. It's probably just a bad joke."

Susan replaced the paper in the envelope, tucking it behind the wall phone out of Clue's range, and frowned. "It looks like a woman's writing, and it's on The Holly and Ms. Ivy's stationery," she said slowly.

"It looks like the writing of an art major to me," Kathleen said. "And if you think Gwen Ivy wrote it, why don't you just ask her about it? Maybe it's just a bit of bad taste."

Susan idly patted her dog on the head. She didn't relate bad taste to Gwen Ivy. "Maybe I will," she agreed, doubting it.

"Then we'd better get going, hadn't we?"

Susan tossed a cookie to her pet, grabbed her purse, and followed Kathleen out of the house, stopping only to readjust some dried white roses on the large, blue-spruce wreath hanging on her front door.

"Pretty," Kathleen said absently, pulling her keys from the large embroidered purse her mother-in-law had given her for Christmas.

"I can't get the flowers wired in properly. They keep slipping."

"I don't know much about it. We just order our wreaths from H.E.C. They look nice and traditional, and they smell wonderful."

Susan stopped worrying about the note and concentrated on her Christmas decorations. Using a variety of natural materials (reindeer moss and bayberry collected at their cottage in Maine last summer, living herbs like rosemary topiaries and miniature trees, and faux mushrooms that looked remarkably real), her house smelled as good as it looked. The wreath set the theme, and she had spent a lot of time making it. It had remained perfect for two days, but had been shedding ever since. She plucked an end of the deep bronze ribbon from the doorway and headed into the car.

"You're not having an affair, are you?" Kathleen asked, thinking about the note as her engine roared to life.

"Of course not."

Kathleen decided not to ask any more questions. Affairs were things that friends could talk about whenever they wanted to—and not before. She waited a few discreet minutes, and when Susan didn't continue, she changed the subject.

"What's worrying you about Gwen Ivy?"

"Well, for one thing, she has a black eye."

"How does she explain that?"

"At first she gave me some silly story about running into a Christmas decoration. Kind of a seasonal walking into an open door. She knew right away that I was skeptical, and she told me the truth—or maybe part of the truth."

"What?"

"She said that she had an argument with her partner, and that she ran away into the arm of some sort of huge Santa decoration."

"Why is that more believable than the first story?"

"The argument."

"You think Mr. Holly hit her?"

"Z."

"Excuse me?"

"He calls himself Z. His name is Zeke Holly, but he calls himself Z."

"You don't think he hit her."

The car was stopped at a light, so there was no need for Susan to speak quite so loudly. "I don't think he's the type of man who would hit anyone, and I am not having an affair with Z."

"I didn't think . . ."

"Then why did you look at me like that?"

"That note is pretty strange. You must admit that. People don't usually send anonymous notes accusing people of being involved with men other than their husbands for no reason at all," Kathleen said flatly, peering out the window at a stopped car blocking her way. "Doesn't that woman see that the light is green?"

Susan chuckled. "Read her license plate." The letters and numbers on the rear of the BMW station wagon said MOMOF 9. "The poor woman is probably taking a well-deserved nap."

Kathleen honked gently. "I hate to wake her up, but the trucker behind me looks like he's going to smash the wreath on his grill into my trunk if we sit here any longer."

"He's probably a father of nine who spent yesterday napping."

Kathleen chuckled and put her car into gear as their way was cleared.

Susan looked at her friend and started to speak. "I . . ." She stopped.

"I'm your friend, and I'll talk with you about anything, but I don't think the fact that I opened that note means we have to speak about it at all," Kathleen said.

Susan smiled. "We turn right at the next light."

"Haven't I heard that Z and Gwen are a couple?"

"Probably. I know a lot of people think that."

"But they're not."

"No." Susan wondered if she had spoken the one word a little too loudly.

"What sort of menu did you finally pick out for New Year's Eve?" Kathleen tactfully changed the topic.

Susan grinned. "I'm not telling. It makes me hungry just to think about it. Have you ever had quail? Oh, wait! Turn left here. It's in that black building with the green roof and red trim down that drive there." Susan pointed to a huge old two-story, cedar-shingled building. Yards and yards of white-pine roping were draped from all the old wooden gutters, held in place by large bunches of variegated ivy and red bows.

"Some place," Kathleen said, following her directions.

"It was the carriage house of the largest estate in town— the home burned and the rest of the buildings were torn down decades ago. It's been used by a lot of different companies over the years. Chrissy took ballet here when she was six years old. And Chad had origami classes up in the hayloft one summer. A squash club owned the building before that. But The Holly and Ms. Ivy remodeled about five years ago, and they've been here ever since. Wait until you see the inside."

Kathleen steered her car into the small but empty lot next to the carriage house. "Smells wonderful," she commented.

"The entire first floor is kitchen. You won't believe it," Susan assured her, leading the way up the brick path to the front door.

They didn't have to knock. They were greeted at the door by Gwen Ivy. She was wearing green dark glasses. A dark green apron covered her clothing; flour covered the apron. Kathleen and Susan followed her into the long, brightly lit room.

"Wow." Kathleen stopped for a second and stared. The original mahogany woodwork, the hardwood floors, and brass hardware remained. The rest of the building had been extensively remodeled. The room was divided into nearly a dozen different work areas, each one with an identical green Garland stove, a large industrial refrigerator-freezer, generous counter space, racks containing pots, pans, and equipment as exotic as fish steamers and duck presses. Green-shaded lights hung over each space. An elegant curved stairway rose to the second floor at the rear of the room, and it was to this that Gwen Ivy led her guests.

"This is truly unbelievable," Kathleen said, as they walked between the pristine workstations.

"That's the way it was designed to be. The offices are upstairs, and everyone who comes to do business with The Holly and Ms. Ivy has to pass all this. It's even more impressive when my chefs are working." She glanced down at her Swatch. "They'll be here in just a few minutes. You'll see."

"What were you cooking?" Susan asked, as they passed the workstation closest to the stairway. She counted eight large bowls sitting on the counter, covered with green-and-white linen cloths.

"Just setting out some *birnbrot* to rise. It's a Swiss holiday bread filled with fruit—mainly pears—and kirsch. The dough has been in the refrigerator overnight. Someone else will take care of it now. Come on up. I made coffee."

"You do the cooking for The Holly and Ms. Ivy?" Kathleen asked, as Susan peered over the banister at the recipe lying next to the bowls. *Birnbrot* sure sounded good. She wondered how difficult it would be to make.

"Not much anymore. When we began, Z and I did all of it." She glanced back at the kitchen area as she opened the door to the offices. "Those were much simpler times though."

"How many people work for you now?" Kathleen asked.

"During most of the year, about twenty. But this is our

busy time; right now, we have almost forty people. We get chefs in training on their vacations from cooking schools, but most of our temporary positions are for untrained people. Truck drivers and the like. A lot of this business is just lifting and toting. Our office is this way."

"You and Z share an office?" Kathleen asked.

"Z and I started this business in a phone booth at Grand Central Station, and we've stayed close ever since."

Kathleen glanced over at Susan, who was peering at photographs that lined the walls.

Gwen noticed, too. "Those are our credentials—photographs taken at parties we've given," she explained.

"I guess that type of reference means a lot in your business," Kathleen commented idly.

"References mean everything in our business. We're good, but we're expensive. People who hire us want their parties to be the best, and they want them run as smoothly as possible. If their neighbor gave a perfect party and they saw our trucks out front, they'll call us when they're entertaining."

"That's why you have such a distinctive logo."

"Exactly. And why everything is color coordinated. Dark green ivy twining around a sprig of holly is printed on everything we do."

Kathleen and Susan exchanged looks. It had also been on the note Susan had received.

"Come on in," Gwen suggested, guiding them into a small room overflowing with an antique partners desk, four chairs, and file cabinets around the walls. "We have a more impressive space where Z works with clients, but I feel more comfortable here. Have a seat. There's coffee, if you'd like some."

"We'd love it." Kathleen answered for both of them.

Gwen poured three mugs of the steaming brew and set a plate on the cluttered desk in front of them. "Have some cookies. We get the rejects up here. Oh, everything is fine," she added, seeing Susan's startled look. "No poison or anything. We're giving a traditional English tea party this afternoon for some people over on Tollhouse Road. You know, cucumber sandwiches, Dundee cake, seed cake . . ." She peered at the large plate. "These are jam tarts, shortbread, almond bars, Victoria sponge sandwiches, and Prince Albert cakes—all either broken or misshapen."

Kathleen picked a raspberry-jam tart, and Susan chose a crooked rectangle of cream, sponge cake, and lemon curd. They munched happily for a few minutes before anyone spoke. "Did you catch up with the Kents?"

"No, I had to leave the bill in their mailbox. I decided to head back here. I don't want the entire town wondering about this eye." She gently touched the purple skin. "You're probably wondering why I lied about how I got it."

"I . . . ," Susan began.

"It's just what we were talking about before. The reputation of The Holly and Ms. Ivy is very important. I didn't want anyone to know that Z and I were arguing. It was entirely personal. It had nothing to do with the company, but it could still be damaging to us."

"Of course. You always seem very together," Susan said.

Gwen leaned back in her chair before answering. "We are. We started this business twelve years ago."

"That's when you met?" Kathleen jumped in to ask, helping herself to a piece of plum cake at the same time.

"No, that's when we graduated from college. I was a psychology major, and Z was American studies."

"Well qualified to do nothing in fact," Susan said. "I know. I was English lit."

"Yes, but I had always loved to cook, and I'd taken cooking classes up on Cape Cod the summer between high school and leaving for college. Then I worked at a cooking school for three summers, so I had a skill. And Z . . ." She paused for a moment. "Z had style."

"Style?"

"Style," Gwen repeated. "His clothing, his writing, everything about him said style—and that's pretty unusual on a college campus. His dorm room was actually decorated, and he gave parties. Real parties. Not just passing-around paper cups and buying a keg. He had a theme. He sent out handwritten invitations. He decorated. And at the last party of our senior year, he asked me to cook for him. He called it the penultimate party. You know, the next to the last, assuming that graduation would call for a real blowout, but with families. I was living in an apartment on campus, so I had a kitchen but almost no equipment. And that was true of all my friends. Most college students don't buy a large *batterie de cuisine*. But I begged, borrowed, and improvised enough to create a huge pot of *boeuf bourguignnone* and another of ratatouille for the vegetarians. I created loaves and loaves of braided bread made from twining egg, whole wheat, and rye batters together. I cut up tons of salad stuff, and Z tossed it in vinaigrette. And for dessert, Z and I made everyone three jam-filled crepes—raspberry, apricot, and damson."

"Sounds fabulous," Susan said. Kathleen was busy trying to remember the last party she'd attended in college. She thought it was the one where her date threw up on her. She had kept her stomach steady with handfuls of popcorn and Fritos.

"It was," Gwen said. "And we had a great time doing it. After the fifth or sixth guest said that we should go into business, we started to listen."

"You said something about a phone booth," Susan reminded her.

"Starting to listen was one thing; deciding to go ahead was another. We knew that we loved giving parties, but we were also acutely aware of how little we knew about business. And we didn't have any cash. So, after exams and three days before graduation, Z and I took the train down to New York City, looking for financial backers."

"You went to banks?" Kathleen asked.

"We weren't that naive. I went to visit a venture capitalist who was distantly related to someone who had been at the party. Z went to see a wealthy aunt." She shook her head. "It was some day. I was turned down immediately, of course. I didn't even know how much money to ask for. I spent the rest of the day wandering around Bridge Kitchenware and the Broadway Panhandler and feeling depressed. By the time I was scheduled to meet Z at the station to return to school, I was in a stew, wondering if I should go to graduate school, or try to get a job cooking in a restaurant, or what. Z was waiting at Grand Central Station." She smiled at the memory. "When he saw me coming, he got up from his seat and just beamed. His aunt was not only going to give him the money to get started, she was giving us our first job."

"Lucky you," Susan commented.

"More than we knew at the time. His aunt died recently, but she was an old-time society dowager, and she was giving a wedding shower for a daughter of one of her wealthy friends. We prepared an elegant spring dinner party for three dozen of her nearest and dearest in the large kitchen of her prewar apartment. I look back on it now and know that it was a miracle that everything went so well. We certainly had our share of disasters that first year. But that party was perfect: the food, the decorations, the drinks, everything. And our success was seen by a lot of people who used caterers regularly. In twenty-four hours we had three more jobs and a half-dozen inquiries about the future."

"You were on your way."

"Yes." Gwen nodded. "We drank the two bottles of champagne that hadn't been consumed, decided on our rather silly name, and we haven't stopped for a deep breath since."

Susan was just thinking that she didn't have to worry about her party Saturday night, when Gwen finished.

"Until Z disappeared."

FOUR

"Disappeared?"

"When did this happen?"

"How do you know?"

"Did he leave a note or anything?"

Susan and Kathleen could probably have gone on asking questions for an hour or so, but the door opened and a serious-looking woman, with a long braid falling from the chef's hat she wore, appeared in the doorway. "Gwen? I'm sorry to bother you, but I can't find the schedule that Z left last night."

Gwen excused herself to her guests and hurried out the door. Susan turned to Kathleen, who was helping herself to another tart.

"These are wonderful."

"Kathleen! How can you eat? Z is missing!"

"You're kidding." Kathleen finished chewing and picked out a shortbread this time. "Did you hear what that woman said? She said Z left some sort of schedule here last night. It's not even ten a.m.. How missing can he be?" She closed her eyes while she chewed. "You know, I thought your shortbread was the best there is, but this is fabulous. I think there are tiny slivers of nuts, almost crumbs. . . ."

"Kathleen, would you stop eating and pay attention? This could be serious."

"No, what's serious is that I have to buy new linens for the guest room before Jerry's parents arrive tomorrow. His mother is such a perfect housekeeper, and I want everything to be just right for their visit."

Susan frowned.

"Her tastes are very feminine. I've been thinking about those Martex sheets with all the ruffles, and maybe a paisley comforter. I really loved the Italian linen sheets that we saw at Bloomingdale's before Christmas, but they're so expensive, and I don't think she would like them. Although they would go awfully well in the guest room. I've made that the most tailored room in the house with all the mission oak furniture and . . . And you're not listening to me, are you?"

"Of course I am. Sheets for your mother-in-law. Italian linen versus ruffles. You like the shortbread here better than mine." She turned and gave Kathleen her complete attention. "We have to find Z."

Kathleen picked up a tart with a slightly scorched crust. "He's not missing," she said seriously.

"He's not missing," echoed from the doorway. Gwen had returned to her office. "I've been so silly. I guess I just need a vacation."

Susan stood up and looked at the other two women. "What do you mean?"

"I jumped to conclusions. Z left the day's instructions just like he was supposed to. And that means he was here early this morning," Gwen said, turning her back on the others to pour more coffee.

"That young woman said last night."

Gwen turned and frowned at Susan. "Last night?"

"The girl with the chef's hat and the long braid said that Z had left the directions last night. You just said he was here early this morning." Susan insisted on pursuing the subject.

"Yesterday was Christmas. We work on Christmas. We cater on Christmas. We don't do the usual paperwork. We try to get home in time for our own small celebrations. So Z dropped off the plans for today's work early this morning." Gwen was speaking slowly. "I just wasn't thinking.

He's probably out at the florist's right this minute. The flowers for the tea party today are going to be spectacular: hundreds of miniature bulbs have been forced in the hostess's own collection of celadon bowls and pots."

Kathleen, ever interested in gardening, asked a question about forcing fritillaria that lost Susan immediately. And she realized that they were being urged out of the office as gently as possible. "Ah, now you can see what this place usually looks like," Gwen said, as the trio achieved the top of the stairs. She waved down on the no-longer-deserted room.

A couple of dozen people, many wearing chef's hats and green aprons, were busy at various tasks. Previously empty countertops overflowed with fruits, jams, bowls of eggs, butter, and the like. Chocolate melted in copper double boilers. Strong young arms whisked egg whites in copper bowls. Mixers hummed, and food processors chopped. And the smells! Spices and herbs mixed with the scent of bread baking. As they started down the steps, there was a loud shattering of glass, and the rich aroma of bourbon filled the air.

"Do we have enough of that to saturate the bourbon cakes, Lulu?" Gwen called down the stairs. Her employee reassured her, and the women parted in the middle of the room. "I have to get back to work. There are two large dinner parties tonight as well as the tea. I have to call our fishmonger. The salmon should have arrived already." She started back up to her office. "I'll see you late Saturday afternoon," she said to Susan.

Susan just smiled. Kathleen was watching a bearded young man pipe green leaves on tiny sugar cubes. "They decorate the sugar?" she asked incredulously.

"With holly and ivy leaves," Susan answered absently. "You must have seen it at parties."

"I don't think so," Kathleen said, walking back down the center aisle of the room. "I'm really looking forward to Saturday night.

"Well, I hope sheets are on sale," she continued, following Susan back out into the cold. "January white sales usually begin right after Christmas, don't they?"

"Probably," Susan agreed, pulling her coat up around her ears. There were clouds on the horizon, and she wondered for the second time that morning if a storm was coming.

"Do you want to return the sweaters first, and then we can look for sheets or . . ." Kathleen realized that she didn't have an audience. "Susan?"

"Sorry, just thinking. You asked me about the shopping, didn't you? Why don't I return the sweaters, and then I'll help you pick out sheets?"

"Good idea," Kathleen said, starting her car.

They traveled to a large, nearby shopping center in silence. It was still early, but the lot was almost as full as it had been forty-eight hours before. That got Susan's attention. "I'll bet there are going to be long lines at the service desks," she said as Kathleen pulled into one of the few parking slots left.

"Maybe it would be better if we split up. I'll meet you for coffee in the bookstore in about an hour?" Kathleen suggested, locking her car after Susan had pulled her packages out.

"Coffee in the bookstore?" Susan called out to Kathleen's departing back. Sounded good to her. She slung her purse over her shoulder and marched off, determined to finish her errands as quickly as possible and with a minimum of fuss.

Two hours later she almost fell into an elegant, wire soda-fountain chair across a tiny marble table from Kathleen.

"Coffee? I'll get it," her friend offered.

"Please. Black." Susan tucked her packages under the table and leaned back, closing her eyes.

Kathleen was back almost immediately, two tiny cups slopping espresso onto their saucers in her hands. "They only have espresso and cappuccino, not plain American coffee."

"Goes with the Lilliputian theme here," Susan said, pouring in a packet of sugar and stirring her cup. "Maybe that's why they located the cafe next to the children's book department." She took a sip and sighed. "Wonderful. I was beginning to fade."

"Did you get everything exchanged?" Kathleen asked, watching a woman juggle twelve rolls of Christmas wrapping paper that had just escaped their bag.

"Not quite. I stood in three different lines for over an hour, and I got exactly what Chad wanted, almost what Chrissy wanted, and Jed is going to have to wait for a new ski sweater this year, unless I buy one someplace else. The ones they have left in his size are hideous." She took another sip of coffee and continued. "Do you think navy is preppier than charcoal gray?"

"I haven't the foggiest. Why?"

"They didn't have any black silk turtlenecks for Chrissy. There was a choice between dark gray and navy—and the pink that I bought before. I think she'd prefer the gray, don't you? Navy is pretty preppy."

"I suppose so. Does she have anything to wear with it?"

"Probably black leggings. That's what she wears with everything."

"Then the gray is much better," Kathleen agreed.

"Good point. How did your shopping go?"

"Not bad. There aren't a lot of people shopping for sheets the day after Christmas. I decided on a compromise. Tailored sheets on the bed and pillows, and four ruffled throw pillows for decoration on top. But I want to look for a comforter—the saleswoman said that new store at the other end of the mall has wonderful ones on sale. And you said something about a coat you'd seen at Saks?"

"Yes, but I was wondering if I should get home, or maybe . . ." She stopped talking.

"Maybe what?" Kathleen asked.

"Oh, I don't know. I was thinking that I might call The Holly and Ms. Ivy and ask to speak with Z."

"Not a bad idea," Kathleen said. "If you're worried about him, you may as well. I'm sure you can come up with an excuse to call."

Susan drained her cup and looked seriously at her friend. "You don't think I'm being silly?"

"I think you're worried, and if making one phone call will end that, you should do it. There's a phone by the rest rooms—right behind historical romances." She pointed.

"I'll be right back," Susan said, standing up. "I'll just ask for Z. I wanted to check about the bar for Saturday night. I think we should have something nonalcoholic, but more festive than Perrier to offer guests who don't drink. . . ." She was out of sight before she finished speaking.

Kathleen sat back and finished her coffee while looking around the room. She had given a lot of books for presents and had stood in line for almost forty-five minutes at this huge superstore only a week ago, waiting to get the autograph of one of Jed Henshaw's favorite thriller authors. There hadn't been a lot of holiday cheer in that line, and there didn't seem to be a whole lot around her now. Most of the customers were tired women, and many of them were accompanied by unhappy children. Kathleen would have been tempted to do a little bah humbugging if she hadn't remembered the look on her son's face yesterday morning when he discovered all the packages under the tree. It made the work before and the letdown afterward worthwhile.

"So what are you smiling about?" Susan had returned.

"Just thinking about how much I like Christmas now that I have my own family. Did you get through to Z?"

"No, but everything's okay. I spoke with one of the young women who works there, and she said she'd leave a message for him. So everything's okay."

"I thought you wanted to talk with Z about drinks . . . ?"

"I guess I really wanted to be sure that he hadn't disappeared," Susan admitted. "So, do you want to check out those quilts?" she asked in a perkier voice.

"Great."

"Where are your packages?" Susan asked, gathering hers together.

"I took them out to the car already. Sheets are heavier than you would think." She noticed Susan looking at a shelf of sale novels. "Do you want to look around first?"

"No. I have enough to read at home. I got some great books for Christmas this year. Tonight we're having leftovers for dinner, and I'm going to take an early shower and curl up on the couch next to the Christmas tree and start reading. I don't have to worry about my New Year's party this year, so I can really sit back and enjoy the holiday. . . . Maybe I will buy this one though," she added. "I'll have lots of time this week after all."

So they joined another line.

"They also serve who only stand and wait," Kathleen commented with a sigh.

"But who do they serve?" Susan asked, thumbing through another book from a nearby shelf.

By the time they had reached a cashier, Susan had four mysteries and a collection of Alice Adams short stories, and Kathleen was clutching a large missive on English cottage gardens.

"I can show this to my mother-in-law. She's always enjoyed gardening," she explained as she handed over her credit card.

Susan, having gained the attention of another cashier, just nodded. As soon as they were done making their purchases, she grabbed Kathleen's arm and pulled her from the store. "Shhh. Wait until I tell you who I saw over at the exchange desk."

Kathleen did as she asked, but no more. "Why were you rushing me?" she asked when they were standing in the middle of the mall again.

"Did you see the woman in line at the service counter? Well," Susan continued as Kathleen nodded, "that's Chad's music teacher. She was exchanging the book I bought for him to give her for Christmas. I thought she would be embarrassed if she saw me."

"And she should be!" Kathleen, an ever-loyal friend, exclaimed. "You spent hours getting that book. We even went into the Metropolitan Museum to buy it. . . . She won't be able to return it there."

"If she can, I sure wasted my time shopping in the city."

"No, you didn't. Remember the nice time we had visiting the angel tree at the museum . . . the decorations at Rockefeller Center . . . the lights on the trees on Park Avenue . . . and those wonderful caviar omelets at the Russian Tea Room. Are you hun—"

"Don't ask. We have some serious shopping left to do,"

Susan said. "You don't want Jerry's parents to freeze to death, do you?"

"Or are you thinking of that coat?" Kathleen kidded. "Saks is right here."

An hour later Susan was hungry also. Poor and hungry. But the coat really had been a bargain, she reminded herself, shifting from one foot to the other and resting her packages against a counter covered with piles of embroidered fabrics.

"Those are handmade in Madeira."

Susan, startled, looked around to see where the voice had come from. An elderly woman, who looked as if she also believed it was time America adopted Boxing Day, was frowning at her. "It is very difficult to find women who can do handwork like that. Most of our imports are from the Orient, and there just isn't the tradition there." Susan must have looked perplexed for she continued to explain. "I'm speaking about the linens upon which you just dropped your parcels."

The demonstration of exemplary grammar was as intimidating as the tone of voice, and Susan hurried to gather up her belongings, apologizing all the while. "They really are very nice," she agreed. "And very expensive," she added, noticing the discreet tag hanging from a dainty square of embroidery. "I guess I should go help my friend."

Kathleen was standing on the other side of the small store, examining two large, puffy comforters. She turned when Susan appeared. "Which do you prefer? I think the deep green satin twill will look nice with the room, but I'm afraid I've fallen in love with the pastel paisley."

"I'd get what I love—besides, one of these days Bananas will insist on getting a cute little puppy that will grow into a monster that will shed on everything. And that dark green will show every long hair."

"I think I'll take the green," Kathleen said to the saleswoman who was hovering nearby. "You're right, but Jerry grew up with black Labs, and I suspect that's what we'll end up with when we join the doggy set. The green will disguise dark fur better . . . Susan?"

"I'll be right back," Susan said, hurrying to the door. "There's someone I want to see."

Kathleen glanced out the door and saw a long, blond ponytail extending from a huge bunch of green-and-red Mylar balloons. Susan was chasing after it, only to return as Kathleen was completing her purchase.

"I thought it was Z," she explained, panting.

Kathleen nodded. "I assume it wasn't." She put her credit card back in her wallet and picked up the voluminous bundle. "I hope this fits in the car."

"We could have it sent . . ."

"I need it tomorrow night," Kathleen said. "But thanks. Want to go to the inn for lunch?"

"Wonderful. I'm starving." Susan started for the door.

"Madam!" The saleswoman sounded as if she were tired of this particular problem. "You forgot your packages!"

Susan looked around. "I'm so sorry . . . Where . . . ?"

"On the Madeira, madam. On the Madeira."

Susan grimaced. "I was thinking of someone . . . of something else."

FIVE

THE FRIENDS WERE GREETED ENTHUSIASTICALLY BY
Charles, owner of the Hancock Inn. Susan had helped solve
a murder there last spring, and he felt he was in her debt.
It got her the best seat in the house every time.

Not that there were any bad seats at the inn. One of the
original inns in this part of Connecticut, Charles had remodeled and modernized, maintaining charm while adding
comfort and convenience. Menus were created on a com-
puter, but guests saw a hand-lettered sheet of heavy parch-
ment. The restaurant was decorated for the holidays with
tiny yellow lights echoing the flames in the three fireplaces
and many armloads of pine and holly. Susan and Kathleen
were smiling as they were led to their favorite booth.

"Your decorations seem to be holding up better than
mine," Susan commented, thinking of her shedding wreath.

"They've been replaced more than once," Charles assured her. "We decorated three weeks before Christmas,
and we've been renewing the holly and candles ever since.
We keep all this until New Year's." Charles handed
Kathleen a menu. "If you're still hungry after the feast I
know Mrs. Henshaw fed you yesterday, I recommend the
wild partridge with red cabbage *confit* and fresh fig chut-
ney. It's light and delicious."

"I always take good advice," Kathleen said. "And a glass of Beaujolais, please."

Charles turned to Susan. "How are the sea scallops in pastry?" she asked.

He beamed. "Excellent. Would you like arugula salad? And I'd suggest a Chablis?"

"Wonderful." Susan prepared to let out her belt another notch.

Charles hurried off with their order, to be replaced by two fur-wrapped women, giggling like girls.

"Susan! Kathleen! Merry Christmas!" Well-coiffed heads and exotically made-up faces leaned on their table for support. "Guess what we've been doing?" the ash blonde asked, blinking under the weight of thick gray mascara.

"Returning the presents our husbands gave us!" the aggressively frosted brunette answered her companion's question.

"And getting complimentary makeups!" the blonde continued. "They wanted to do me in plum colors, but I insisted on cooler tones. Do you think I made a mistake?"

"You look lovely," Kathleen lied.

"What did your husbands give you?" Susan asked, hoping she could avoid a public declaration on the subject.

"You won't believe!"

"Negligees!"

"Hideous ones!"

"She got green, and I got plaid satin! Plaid! Who sleeps in plaid?"

Susan had a plaid flannel granny gown that she had worn since college. She was so fond of it that she saved its threadbare comfort for nights when she really needed it. She couldn't imagine plaid satin.

"They shop together the day before Christmas every year!"

"And we return everything the day after!"

A calm voice appeared behind them. "Your table is ready, ladies." Charles was back. "And the hot buttered rums that you requested."

"Rum!"

"Susan, did you hear about that good-looking hunk who runs the catering business? Z?"

"What about him?" Kathleen asked, wondering what had happened to the wine she had ordered.

"He's involved with JoAnn Kent. Her husband found them together in the bedroom! Unwrapped! Get it? Like Christmas presents! Merry Christmas! Ho, ho, ho, and a bottle of rum!"

Susan and Kathleen watched their departing backs. "This is probably how Fellini spends his Christmas holidays," Kathleen commented, smiling as she spied their wine arriving.

Susan didn't answer until after the waitress had left, then she took a sip of her Chablis and frowned. "Have you noticed how many rumors are going around about Z?"

"He seems to be the type of man that people are going to talk about."

"What does that mean?"

"He seems to be the type of man who gets involved in the lives of other people. I've never heard of Z alone, just Z and Gwen, and Z and this woman or that woman."

"He's not like that."

"So, you know him. Tell me about him," Kathleen suggested, picking up her glass.

Susan hesitated before answering. "It's hard to describe someone."

"Susan, you've been telling me about people for years and years. You can describe anyone. Start by telling me the basic things: his age, what he looks like—stuff like that."

"I don't know his age. I'd guess somewhere in his late thirties."

That didn't jive with what Gwen had said about him, unless he'd been much older than the average college student, but Kathleen didn't interrupt.

"He's very good-looking. Blond with a long ponytail—but not at all feminine."

Susan noticed Kathleen smiling. Their salads had arrived, and Susan continued with her description as she ate.

"He's very sweet. And very bright. You can talk to him about anything, not just food and decorations, you know?"

"Like what?"

"Well, you heard what Gwen said: he was an American studies major."

"You've talked about literature with him?"

"No. . . . Not really. But you feel like you can."

Kathleen concentrated on her chewing.

"He's fun, too. I mean, he has a really great sense of humor. And, of course, he has wonderful taste, and he's very creative."

"Creative? Intelligent? Good-looking? Masculine? Good sense of humor? And he can cook? Who do we know who is single? He sounds like quite a catch." Kathleen changed the subject abruptly when she noticed the scowl on Susan's face. "Tell me about your party Saturday night. We've been so busy discussing plans for Christmas that I haven't heard anything. Did I tell you that I bought a new dress?"

Susan didn't answer, and Kathleen babbled on about fashion, and then segued to makeup, diet, exercise classes, and the impossibility of finding good-looking, waterproof boots before Susan spoke.

"I can't imagine Z involved with JoAnn Kent. She's so tacky."

"Nothing's quite as tacky as bringing another man into your own bedroom," Kathleen agreed.

"That's exactly what I mean. He'd never be involved in something like that. . . . I sound like a kid with a serious crush, don't I?"

"Not really . . ."

"A good friend would tell me the truth," Susan insisted, smiling at Kathleen's tact.

"A good friend would assume that you don't have to be told how you feel."

"I am acting like an idiot, aren't I?"

"No." Kathleen shrugged. "You like Z. He's a lot like you. You're allowed to have male friends—this is the nineties, after all. And here's our food."

Susan wasn't sure if she was as grateful for the interruption as Kathleen seemed to be. Something in her wasn't sure exactly how she felt about Z. And talking about it might have helped. She slowly picked up her fork.

But, as usual, the meal was a delicious distraction, and Susan was feeling comfortably full before she and Kathleen broached the subject again.

"No matter what you think about him, it's interesting that Z is a topic on so many people's minds right now, isn't it?" Kathleen asked, picking up the dessert menu. "I think it would be nice to have something sweet with our coffee, don't you?"

"I've had something sweet with coffee, tea, and almost every breath of air I've breathed ever since Thanksgiving," Susan said. "So why stop now?

"But you're right," she continued. "Z does seem to be the hot topic these days, but maybe it's just because there's so much entertaining going on and The Holly and Ms. Ivy are in such demand."

"Gwen Ivy is an impressive woman," Kathleen commented, obviously more interested in the menu than anything else. She frowned. "Would it be piggish of me to have the dessert platter? I can't seem to make up my mind—everything sounds wonderful."

The dessert platter was a large plate that contained a taste of every dessert on the menu. Susan and Jed had shared one on those rare occasions when she felt thin and had forgotten that cholesterol existed. She knew Kathleen would graze her way through the entire thing with no apparent bad effects. "I'll have the zabaglione with raspberries," Susan told the waitress. "And espresso."

Kathleen placed her own order, sat back, and looked around the room. "Have you used the espresso machine that your kids gave you?"

"Late last night. They had even included a package of decaf beans with the machine. It was wonderful."

"Your kids are so thoughtful. I can't wait till Bananas is older. Right now his idea of an appropriate Christmas gift is a Matchbox car. That's what he wanted to get his father for Christmas."

Susan wondered how Kathleen could have watched Chrissy and Chad go through their teens and still be looking forward to her own son's future. She shrugged. It must be one of those things that people have to experience for themselves. "Well, the cappuccino was wonderful. I wonder if we could serve it Saturday night? There must be machines that make it more efficiently."

"I don't know. Even in coffee houses, it's produced a cup at a time, but they do it fairly quickly."

"Maybe the bartender could move over to an espresso machine late in the evening," Susan muttered. "I think I'll give Gwen a call and suggest it." She stood up. "I'll be right back."

"I'll be fine," Kathleen assured her. "Go ahead."

Susan trotted off to the phone booth, wondering if she would be able to speak with Z this time. She dialed quickly, having memorized the company's phone number the day after Thanksgiving.

The phone was answered on the first ring.

"Hi, this is Susan Henshaw," Susan began.

"Mrs. Henshaw? Please hang on. Gwen Ivy wants to speak with you immediately. I'll call her."

Susan heard the tension in the speaker's voice. She closed her eyes and leaned back against the wall, imagining all sorts of things: the invitations for her party were just discovered in a desk drawer; no one was going to come. There had been a mix-up: six parties were planned for New Year's Eve; The Holly and Ms. Ivy couldn't handle all that; her party had been canceled. The check she wrote to the caterers had bounced. Etcetera. Etcetera.

"Mrs. Henshaw? Did you hear what I said?" Susan's attention returned to the present. "Z is dead."

"Dead? Z Holly is dead?" Susan repeated into the mouthpiece.

A woman standing behind her screamed and ran off, wondering aloud what was going to happen to her party tomorrow. Susan wasn't so distracted. "Who is this?" Gwen?"

"Ms. Ivy is busy with the police. I'm Jamie Potter. I'm one of the pastry chefs. Ms. Ivy told me to tell you that Z is dead, and could you please come here as soon as possible. She needs your help."

"I'm at the Hancock Inn. I'll be there immediately." And Susan hung up without bothering to say good-bye. She leaned against the wall and took a few of the long, deep breaths she had been taught in natural childbirth classes. They didn't work well in this situation either, and she wiped a tear from her eye and hurried back to the table.

Kathleen was just dipping her spoon into a miniature crème caramel. "Hi, you look terrible. What's happened?" she began anxiously.

"Z is dead. The police are at The Holly and Ms. Ivy. Gwen says she needs to see me right away."

Kathleen may have loved her calories, but her priorities were in the right place. "Then let's get going," she insisted, standing immediately.

An attentive waitress hurried over to them, and Susan explained that there had been an emergency, and that they needed their bill immediately.

"We'll worry about that later." Charles had appeared with their coats over his arm. "I hope everything is okay with your families, and you will let me know if I can do anything."

Susan wasn't so upset that she didn't have time to stop and reassure him. "Our families are fine, thank you, Charles. We appreciate your concern."

"I'm glad to hear that," Charles said, rushing over to open the door for them.

Susan and Kathleen pulled on their coats and almost ran back to the Jaguar. They didn't speak again until they were squashed inside between the packages. "Where's the body?" Kathleen asked, putting the car in gear.

"I don't know."

"How did he die?"

"I don't know that either. I guess I don't know . . . What are you eating?"

"I just grabbed this little eclair off the tray as we left," Kathleen said. "Do you want half? Well then, what do you know?" she continued as Susan shook her head no.

"Nothing. I called and introduced myself, and before I could say anything else, the voice on the other end of the line said that Gwen wanted to speak to me and vanished to get her. But I didn't get to speak to Gwen. A woman named Jamie Potter told me that Z was dead and that the police were there and could I please come help immediately. She's a pastry chef."

"The woman on the phone is a pastry chef? How do you know that?"

"She told me so."

"Of course." Kathleen munched on the last of her own pastry. "So that's all we know."

Susan nodded. "That's all we know," she agreed quietly. There was a pause before she spoke again. "Do you think you could drive faster?"

Kathleen accelerated.

"I wonder where they found him," Susan muttered.

"Hmmm." Kathleen's response was noncommittal. She was concentrating on passing a dark green van. The task was complicated by the fact that the van itself was trying to pass two joggers.

"Looks like they're trying to work off your big meal yesterday," Kathleen said, when she had accomplished her mission.

"What?"

"Wasn't that Gillian and Alexis? The joggers we just passed?" Kathleen added when Susan didn't answer.

"I don't know. I wasn't paying attention." Susan leaned forward in her seat as though she might arrive a little more quickly if she did. "Don't miss the turn up here."

Kathleen turned where indicated (and where she was going to anyway), and they arrived in front of the carriage house. The lot was crowded: there were three police cars, an ambulance, a few dozen cars, and three vans identical to the one they had just passed. "I'll drop you off and park on the street," Kathleen offered, noticing that the driver of the van behind her was eyeing the last available parking spot.

Susan had opened the car door before the words were out of her friend's mouth. She ran up the sidewalk to the cheerful building. She pulled open the door, experienced enough in emergency situations to expect to find bedlam within. But the long room was empty.

Susan heard Kathleen run up behind her. "Wow!" she whispered, peering over her friend's shoulder. "What a mess!"

"I've never seen anything like it," Susan said.

Kathleen had: It looked a lot like Susan's kitchen the afternoon of a dinner party—times twelve. Every single surface was covered with evidence of food preparation. Kathleen noticed pots of pâté being glazed with some sort of clear brown liquid, beef fillets wrapped with bacon, tiny birds stuffed by the dozen into long pans ready for the oven, cakes, cookies, cheeses, tiny vegetables, so many different things that she didn't know where to look.

Susan sniffed.

"What's wrong?" Kathleen asked.

"Something's burning."

"Where?"

"One of the ovens . . . ," Susan muttered, heading into the middle of the mayhem.

"Susan, there are dozens of ovens here," Kathleen protested.

"Three per workspace," Susan agreed. "Don't open the ones that have soufflés or something that might fall. . . ." She peered into the closest appliance.

"We came here to help out Gwen, not help with the cooking."

"I can't let this food burn," Susan insisted, opening the door of a double wall oven that emitted fabulous spicy scents. "Not this one." She was heading for the next oven when a door at the back of the room was flung open, and the girl they had seen in Gwen's office dashed in. She had obviously been crying.

"Oh! You're here!" The young woman stopped, but only for a moment. "Something's burning!" Her freckled nose twitched. "Smells like . . . oh, shit!" She dashed to the middle of the room and jerked open the correct oven, pulling out a tray of scorched meringues in the same movement. "My meringues!" she wailed, smashing the tray down on a marble counter. "My goddamned, stupid meringues!" She took her fist and smashed each and every one of the pastries.

Kathleen's years on the police force had taught her how to deal with hysterical people, and she grasped the woman's hands. Bits of hot sugar stung her, but she continued to comfort, and in a few minutes, the young woman was calm.

"Z is dead."

"That's why we're here," Kathleen explained.

"Where is everybody?" Susan leaned across her friend's shoulder to ask.

"The garage. It's out back. His body . . . he was found out there."

"Maybe we should get out there," Susan suggested.

Tears rolled down the young woman's cheeks as she nodded her agreement. "I'll show you."

But when they arrived in the brick courtyard behind the carriage house, all they saw was a green, The Holly and Ms. Ivy van filled with helium balloons and surrounded by dozens of people.

SIX

GWEN IVY WAS STANDING CLOSE TO THE VAN, FLANKED BY Hancock's finest, but she glanced over as the women approached.

"Everything all right inside?" she called out to her employee.

"Just some scorched meringues."

"Perhaps my chefs could return to the kitchen, Chief Fortesque. There are at least twelve ovens full of food that is going to be ruined unless they do. And people are counting on us to cater their parties. . . . We wouldn't want to disappoint them—especially not the mayor's wife—would we?"

Brett Fortesque was not only the chief of police but arguably the best-looking single man in town. Now a scowl marred his rugged face. "You're catering a party for Mayor and Mrs. Logan? Tonight?"

"Dinner for twelve of their nearest and dearest. I don't know what Mrs. Logan will do if we don't show up. You know what she's like when she thinks something is wrong,". Gwen continued, seeing that she was winning her argument.

Susan found herself smiling. Brett had entertained her and Jed over dinner one evening with tales of Camilla Logan's demands on the police department. From Camilla's request for police protection the night her husband was elected to office (she feared the masses might try to invade her celebration party) onward; Camilla apparently felt the Hancock police department existed to function as a sort of palace guard for the mayor and his wife. Susan knew Brett's stories were a way of hiding his irritation with the situation. "You know, if she has a bunch of friends coming over and there's no food, she's really going to have something to complain about," Susan reminded him.

"And you know that murder investigations take precedence over social obligations—even the mayor's," Brett said, not returning her smile.

"Murder. You're sure?" The question came automatically; she knew Brett wouldn't say something like that unless he was sure.

Brett nodded, but didn't elaborate. "The body's in the van."

Gwen Ivy wasn't going to be ignored. "My staff needs to continue with their work," she reminded him. She raised her voice so that she could be heard by everyone in the yard. "Z wouldn't want his death to destroy the reputation of The Holly and Ms. Ivy—and we are known for our reliability. Besides the fact that we are accomplishing nothing by hanging around out here while the food is burnt to a crisp."

"If you'll just wait a moment," Brett suggested, walking over to three of his officers and speaking with them in low tones. They nodded and headed back to the main building. Brett returned to Gwen. "Your employees may go on with their work inside, but this is a murder scene and everything that leaves here is going to have to be inspected by my men. And no one is allowed to leave until they have been interviewed. That means some people are going to be around pretty late. . . ."

"Then the delivery people had better be interviewed first. They're going to have to start heading out in all directions. And—let me think—Penny. Yes, Penny, you're going to have to blow up more balloons and put them in another van to be delivered as soon as the police allow anyone to leave."

Gwen Ivy was back in business. Susan watched as the woman organized her staff, making decisions and issuing orders. If there were tears in the eyes of some of her employees, they could see from the expression on their employer's face that she was on the verge of tears herself. They followed her orders, moving back into the main building quickly. A young woman with blonde curls hanging down to her waist headed into a small building at the back of the property. A uniformed policeman hurried after her. They returned together; the policeman pulling a heavy canister marked HELIUM in block letters behind him, the woman carrying a large cardboard box. Together, they followed the crowd back into the kitchens, leaving Susan, Kathleen, Gwen, and the policemen alone. Everyone waited for Brett to speak.

And they waited awhile. Brett moved over to one corner and spoke into his two-way radio. Susan took the opportunity to examine the large wreath hanging on the fence that surrounded the courtyard. Apparently Gwen Ivy or one of her minions had discovered an excellent. method of attaching freeze-dried roses to balsam.

"The coroner's on his way," Brett announced. "He has trouble getting his car started in cold weather. That's what happens when there's no money in the budget to replace old equipment. Maybe you ladies should think about organizing a bake sale or something."

Susan just nodded at the suggestion. She had visions of posters all over town: BUY A BRIOCHE. HANCOCK NEEDS A HEARSE. She doubted if the cause had the appeal of new uniforms for the junior-high marching band. "The body's still in the van?" she asked, needing to say something. Where else would it be? She moved around to look in the rear windows of the van. "Where . . . ?" she began, continuing around the vehicle in a speeded-up gait.

"Don't bother. He's not in the front seat," Brett said, seeing what she was doing. "He's back there—under the balloons." He glanced over at Gwen Ivy, who was staring up at the second-floor windows of her building. "You can see later."

Kathleen, silent until now, suddenly moved across the

courtyard toward the garage door. "What's in here? Another
van?" she asked Gwen.

"Not these days. We outgrew our storage capacity in the
carriage house itself about two years ago. Since then the
vans stay outside, and the garage is full of supplies."

"Supplies? Like food?"

"No way. It wouldn't be sanitary, and the health department would have a fit. What's stored in there is nonperish-
able. Extra chairs, tables, tents, folding floors for dancing,
arbors to decorate, gilt candelabra, flower pots, vases, balloons like you saw . . . Millions of things. Z handles all that
stuff." And finally, Gwen let go and cried.

Susan rushed to comfort her as a long gray station
wagon pulled into the courtyard. Seeing that Gwen was
taken care of, Brett and his officers went over to greet the
coroner. Kathleen followed.

There isn't much you can say to someone who's just discovered their best friend murdered, especially when you're
feeling like crying yourself, so Susan just held Gwen's
hands and made what she hoped were soothing noises.

"Maybe we should go inside," Susan suggested when
Gwen's sobs seemed to cease. "You don't have a coat or
anything, and your hands are like ice."

"I have to talk with them . . . with the police."

"Of course, but they don't expect you to freeze to death.
Come on," Susan urged. She was getting cold herself.
"We'll talk to Brett and make sure it's okay if you're wor-
ried about it."

Gwen nodded and pulled her outer layers closer. "You're
right," she agreed, "Brett will know what to do."

It took a few seconds for Susan to realize what she had
just heard. "You know him? I mean, more than just as the
chief of police, don't you?"

"We've gone out a few times, yes."

Susan waited for the usual "but we're just good friends"
and continued a little too loudly when it wasn't forthcom-
ing. "Then why don't we tell Brett that you'll meet him in
your office? That way you won't freeze to death before he
speaks with you. If he doesn't feel comfortable with that,
he can always send along one of his men to guard you."

Brett, overhearing her, raised an eyebrow in their direction and nodded at a uniformed officer nearby. To Susan, their guard looked too young to be an eagle scout, but that didn't seem to prevent him from taking his job seriously.

"We can go inside, ma'am, but no one should speak to nobody—anybody," he corrected his own grammar and pointed the way.

"I need to—" Gwen began.

"Nobody."

"I just wanted to go to the bathroom."

The man looked confused. "You can't go alone." He glanced around and found an answer in Susan. "You'll have to accompany her, ma'am."

Susan reminded herself that she was a big girl. "Whatever you say . . . if Gwen doesn't mind."

"Not at all." Gwen shook her blonde helmet impatiently. "Let's hurry though."

There were a lot of curious stares as the unlikely threesome trotted through The Holly and Ms. Ivy workroom and up the stairs. One or two people who seemed to want to speak with their employer were put off by a surprisingly stern look from the young officer.

The bathroom was next to the office Susan had seen this morning. She didn't have time to build up expectations, but the shining white room still came as a complete surprise. As well as a toilet and sink, there was a large shower and a dressing area complete with table, chairs, and mirrors. It was large enough to afford Gwen some privacy, and Susan studiously examined the various brands of expensive makeup until she heard the toilet flush.

"I feel better." Gwen appeared in the reflection of the dressing table mirror.

"This is some setup," Susan commented. "Very luxurious." She touched the efficient light strip.

"It's a necessity, not a luxury. Z and I often work right up until time to start setting up an affair. We need to shower and dress. Our presence isn't actually necessary— our staff are all quite reliable—but usually our clients feel more comfortable if we put in an appearance."

"Both of you?" Susan inquired, watching as Gwen, having washed her hands thoroughly, touched up her eyes. The shadow blended into her lids in a manner that Susan had never mastered.

"Sometimes, Z is . . . was the most likely to go along with the setup crew. Then he could calm down nervous hostesses. Sometimes he opened a bottle of champagne, and they toasted the evening. Z was very, very good at that. Much better than I ever could be. Some of the women get very nervous—Z tells a lot of funny stories." But she seemed to remember that humor might not be appropriate at that moment. "I suppose we should get back to my office before that kiddie cop out there starts imagining that I've murdered you, too."

"Surely they don't think . . ."

"Surely they do. Z was an orphan, and when his aunt died a few months ago, he was left without a family. He wasn't married. So, with no spouse available, they're going to look at me. I'm closer to him than anyone else."

"I wouldn't worry about that now if I were you," Susan lied. "Let's just get back out there. Get all the routine questioning over with so you can get on with your work."

Brett was waiting in Gwen's office. Susan, who had been involved in many murder investigations, was astounded when Brett politely, but firmly, insisted that she was not expected to hang around for Gwen's interview. Not that she had even an unofficial capacity, of course, but in the past she had always been more welcome, she thought. She wondered exactly what sort of relationship Gwen and Brett had, and whether those few dates had made an impact on the lives of either one. She thought about this as she pretended to examine the glossy photographs hanging in the hallway. When she could do that no longer, she headed on to the stairs.

The room below was bustling. Whether from respect for their dead employer, fear of the one that was still alive, or just self-discipline and habit, the workers at The Holly and Ms. Ivy were doing what the English called carrying on— and Susan was impressed. She noticed that the concern about her New Year's Eve party that had been haunting her since getting news of Z's death vanished.

Kathleen had disappeared, but Susan spied the young woman who had been so concerned about her meringues and hurried to where she was bending over a tray of animal-shaped cookies. Susan watched as a beige, four-legged creature was turned into a tiger by an experienced hand. "That's amazing! What are you making it for?"

"There's going to be a Noah's ark on the children's table at a party we're doing tonight. It's one of our specialties—I've made dozens of them, but we're running late. Usually this type of thing is done two days before the event. But, with yesterday being Christmas, we're behind. It's always like this at this time of year. Z's always saying that we just have to hang in there, and we can collapse on January second."

"Not the first? Although I guess there are some people who give parties on New Year's Day. . . ."

"More than a few. But The Holly and Ms. Ivy won't accept jobs for events that run later than six P.M. on January first. So usually everything is cleaned up and put away by midnight around here. Then we can all rest."

"There's a separate cleaning crew?" Susan asked, admiring the chef's technique as she painted black stripes on white horses turning them into perky zebras with wreaths of holly hanging around their necks.

"No. Some places do, of course, but we're all assigned our own work space, and we're responsible for keeping it clean. It's better that way. Then each chef knows exactly where everything is." She painted orange feet on a pair of penguins.

"So you always work here?" Susan asked, examining the assortment of cake and pie pans hanging above the counter.

"Usually. I'm the chief pastry chef—but you can probably tell that. I also do most of the elaborate decorating of other dishes. Not that there aren't a lot of people around here trained to do it, but I'm faster. Lots of practice," she added, piping eyes on over a dozen animals and stepping back to view the results of her work.

"This must be very upsetting for everyone here," Susan suggested.

"It is. The room is awfully quiet. Most of the time, this

place is bedlam—everyone chattering and calling out to each other. Everyone liked Z and ..." She paused. "And murder is so unexpected, isn't it?"

"Yes, of course." But that wasn't the word Susan would have used to describe it. She looked at the girl curiously. "Are you Jennie Potter?"

"Jamie Potter. I'm the person you spoke with on the phone. Gwen seemed to think you could help." Her tone of voice implied that she couldn't imagine why.

"Gwen found him? Found his body?"

"I guess. She came into the building screaming for someone to call the police—that Z was dead."

"Just the police?"

"Yes. Then everyone ran outside to see what was going on, and as I happened to be closest to the phone, I called. Then, I went back outside. A little while later the phone rang again."

"That was me," Susan guessed.

"Yes. I answered, but Gwen had returned, and when she heard it was you, she asked that I tell you about Z's death and that the police were here—and ask if you would come over. Which, of course, I did."

"I've helped out in some murder investigations in the past," Susan explained, correctly interpreting the confused look on Jamie's face. "And I'll certainly help Gwen, if I can. But I need to call my family first. Is there a phone around that I could use?"

"Right under the steps—it's in the employees' locker room."

"Thanks. I'll be in there if anyone needs me ..." She turned and ran right into Kathleen.

"A phone," her friend cried, proving that great minds actually did think alike.

Susan pointed, and they were on their way. The door under the stairway was easily found. Not bothering to knock, they entered the small room dominated by a large oak library table surrounded by utilitarian metal lockers. Holiday decorations on the walls consisted of a large sign saying I LIVE FOR JANUARY 2ND! and EAT, DRINK AND BE MERRY, FOR TOMORROW WE ALL DIET! Susan raised her eyebrows over that one, as Kathleen had beaten her to the wall phone. All of the lockers were tagged with the names of their users, and many were decorated with notes and quotes. Susan was reminded of a high-school hallway. She wandered around, reading quotes from DeGustubus, Brillat-Savarin, Epicurus, and the Marquis de Sade. Some of the lockers had been left ajar, and she spied coats, purses, chef's hats, and aprons hanging inside.

Kathleen had finished explaining her absence to her son's hosts and was going into minute detail as to his requirements for meals, so Susan continued to poke around.

Kathleen had dialed again and seemed to be speaking to someone official down at the municipal building. "Brett's checking out Z's address with the tax office. He thinks that's the place to start."

"Start what?"

"The murder investigation."

Susan stared at the cheerful room with a sad look on her face. "How was he killed?"

Kathleen looked around, making sure they were alone before she answered. "He was strangled. Probably last night. When the back doors of the van were opened this morning, dozens of balloons flew out. . . ."

Susan had seen the Mylar balloons, shaped and colored like stars, Christmas trees, wreaths, bells, ornaments, even decorated gingerbread men. "Weren't they tied down in some way?"

"They are usually. But whoever put Z in the bottom of the van just stuffed him in. When the door was opened, the balloons took off into the sky, and there he was . . . colored ribbons tied around his neck . . ."

Susan cringed. "Oh God."

"Yes." Kathleen nodded, and both women were silent for a few moments.

"Where did Z live?" Susan asked, hoping the change of subject would erase the image in her mind.

"An apartment—second floor of a house near here— 142 Chestnut. Susan, you're not planning on investigating this murder, are you?"

"Why not? I've done it before," Susan replied indignantly.

"You weren't quite so connected with the victim before."

"Z and I weren't emotionally involved," Susan insisted. "We were just . . ." She stopped and thought for a moment. "We weren't even friends. He was working for me, that's all. He was just like someone that Jed might have hired to mow the lawn in the summer. That's all."

"I have to get back to Brett. But, Susan, I'm your friend, and I really think you should stay away from this investigation." Kathleen turned to leave the room. "Coming?"

"In a second. I'm going to leave a message on my answering machine in case anyone gets home early," Susan answered as the door closed behind her friend. She made the call quickly, looking all the while for paper and a pen. She just wanted to write down that address before she forgot it. There was a scrap of paper being used for a marker in this month's *Gourmet* on the table, and she pulled it out and wrote quickly, stuffing it in her purse when she was done. Then she, too, left, closing the door behind her.

"Damn!" She was back in the large workroom before she realized that she didn't have her own car.

"What's wrong?" Jamie Potter asked, busy scraping burned meringue from a dark metal cookie sheet.

"I don't have my car here. I came with my friend, but there's someplace I have to go. I don't think it's far from here. . . ."

"Where?"

"Chestnut Street."

"It isn't. Just about five blocks. It's an easy walk. I know. My aunt lives there."

Susan perked up. "Then you can point me in the right direction."

"Sure. I'll be going over in about half an hour myself if you want a ride."

"I think I'll get going," Susan insisted, thinking that she had been effectively cut out of the action here—and she felt she had to do something.

"Well, then. Turn left at the end of the driveway. Then

right at the first corner. Then ·just five blocks to Chestnut.
Maybe I'll see you there later."

Susan just smiled and pulled her coat closer around her
neck. "Thanks," she added, moving toward the door.

"Be sure to turn at the house decorated like a Christmas
present," Jamie called after her.

Susan had no trouble finding the home Jamie had de-
scribed. On the corner of Elm and Chestnut stood a white
Colonial house, square and imposing, wrapped in monster
red ribbons tied in a gargantuan bow above enameled double doors. A pseudotag was attached to the bow, wishing
the world a Merry Christmas and a Happy New Year from
the Albertson family.

The Albertsons lived at 438 Chestnut. Susan turned right
hoping to find 142. The blocks in this part of Hancock
were square and filled with gracious traditional homes with
large lawns and garages tucked out of sight around back.
Flakes of snow were beginning to fall as Susan arrived at
142, a yellow Victorian with electric candles in each of its
numerous windows. A sidewalk led straight from the street
to the porch. Susan hurried up the path and onto the porch,
where she was confronted by a pastel wreath that seemed to
have been fashioned from plaster worms.

She had just realized that they weren't worms, but dyed
pasta, when the front door opened and an elderly lady appeared. Susan took a step backward, almost tripping over a
cement Santa Claus that she hadn't noticed before. "I'm
afraid . . . I guess I've come to the wrong house . . . ," she
stammered.

"No. You're looking for Z, aren't you?"

"Well, sort of," Susan admitted.

"Did he tell you to meet him here?"

Susan had just noticed the poinsettia the other woman
wore on her pink sweater. Like the wreath it seemed to be
made of something strange. . . . She leaned slightly closer.

"Bread dough."

"Pardon?"

"You're admiring my pin, aren't you? It's made of bread
dough."

"Amazing," Susan said truthfully. "Where do you find something like that?"

"Oh, my goodness! Everywhere! This came from the Presbyterian's Holly Mart. And I bought the wreath at the Episcopal's Mt. Bethany Bazaar. There's also the Hancock library's Holiday Fun Fair. And the Seventh Day Adventist Oh Little Town of Bethlehem Craft and Garage Sale . . ." She was leading Susan into her home as she spoke, and Susan could tell her hostess was a serious supporter of the events she was listing. Not only were her rooms filled with crafts of extraordinary garishness, but in the bay window of the living room stood a fake balsam with an amazing collection of ornaments hanging from its synthetic boughs.

"You're admiring my tree, aren't you?"

"Who would have thought so many different things could be made from clothespins," Susan said honestly.

"It is remarkable, isn't it?" her hostess replied complacently.

"Z lives here? Z Holly?"

"Yes. Well, not here, of course. Upstairs. It's a completely self-contained apartment. Not exactly legal, perhaps, but who's to know?"

In a few hours Hancock's chief of police would, Susan thought. But she didn't say anything. Brett would have more important things to worry about.

"Would you like to go on up? Did he ask you to meet him there?"

"I'd like to go up," Susan answered slowly, wondering if strange women appeared frequently with the same request.

"Then follow me. It's not locked, and you can wait for him there."

"Thank you." Susan scurried up the stairway behind the surprisingly spry woman. Shopping in church halls must be excellent exercise.

SEVEN

THE DOOR OPENED AND SUSAN FOUND HERSELF IN AN APART-
ment remarkably unlike the rest of the house. This entire
floor had been gutted, and except for three freestanding
brick chimney flues, the area was open, decorated in shades
of beige, brown, and ecru¯ with a minimum of handcrafted
fruitwood furniture placed strategically on handwoven area
rugs. Only the electric Christmas candles peeking from behind rough cotton curtains betrayed any connection with the
scene downstairs.

Susan walked around slowly, glancing at mail left on a
small sideboard near the door and admiring the collection
of copper pans hanging over the counter that divided the
kitchen area from the rest of the room. An elegant daybed
stood near a window and Susan noticed it was unmade, an
Ed McBain paperback peeking out from the Ralph Lauren
sheets, a Christmas card marking the reader's place. Susan
picked it up and read the inscription. It promised eternal
gratefulness that the sender's daughter's wedding had been
so successful, with much love from a woman who lived on
Fifth Avenue in New York City.

The card wasn't the only symbol of the season in evidence. A Mexican tree of lights stood on the sleek marble
mantel, candles extinguished halfway down. Susan couldn't
help but contrast this with all the tinsel and glitter for

which The Holly and Ms. Ivy were known. But, she decided, the fact that Z's private life wasn't identical to his professional side wasn't all that unusual. And maybe there wasn't that much contrast after all. Z's parties were examples of great style, creative and unusual. The same could be said of his apartment.

Susan wandered around, picking up bowls and magazines, then putting them down, wondering what she was doing here. Brett had wanted Z's address. He must think this place had some sort of significance. Maybe Z had been murdered here, and the police crime unit would ... She stood still as the implications of the rest of the thought struck home. They would come here and collect fingerprints—hers among the rest.

And the casual manner of the landlady's greeting implied that she was accustomed to the presence of strange women ... women who were strangers, she amended, walking over to the nearest window and peering out. Neighborhood children, drawn by the snow, were gathering in the middle of a lawn a couple of doors down. One red-jacketed child optimistically pulled a wooden sled across the frozen grass. Another waved an elaborately embroidered mitten and called out a greeting to the baby blue Volkswagen Bug moving down the street ... and stopping at the curb in front of 142 Chestnut.

Susan's mouth fell open as Jamie Potter got out of the car and trotted up the sidewalk toward the Victorian. She looked around the apartment, realizing immediately that the urge to hide was absurd. After all, the woman downstairs knew that she was there. Had even let her in. There was no rational reason for the guilt she was feeling.

Which changed to embarrassment when the door opened and Jamie Potter walked into the room followed by the landlady.

"Hi!"

Susan opened her mouth and then closed it again without speaking as she realized what she was seeing. "You two look alike. . . ."

"I told you my aunt lived on Chestnut, didn't I?"

"You didn't tell me she was Z's landlady."

"You didn't tell me that you were coming to this particular address on Chestnut, did you?" Susan realized this was said in a friendly manner.

Everyone smiled.

"Why don't I go downstairs and get us all some tea?" Jamie's aunt offered, turning to leave.

"We don't really need very much," Jamie said quickly.

"I just had lunch," Susan agreed, thinking she would be saving the older woman some work.

"Nothing like a little something in the middle of the afternoon, I always say. You two come on down as soon as you're ready."

Jamie didn't speak until her aunt had disappeared. "Watch out for the jelly and jam. She buys it all at church sales. You wouldn't believe what people make conserve from these days."

"I gather you don't get ideas for your professional life from your aunt's purchases."

"I'd love to see the look on Gwen's face if I suggested parsnip-and-clove preserve for the English tea we're preparing." She walked to the middle of the room and looked around. "Different from downstairs, isn't it?"

"Did you find him this apartment?"

"Sort of. I came to The Holly and Ms. Ivy about four years ago. I'd just graduated from C.I.A.—the Culinary Institute of America—and I was lucky to find a job right away. And, while I grew up in New Jersey, I had always visited my aunt and uncle here, so I knew what a nice town this is.

"When I moved here, I stayed with my aunt, naturally. Uncle John had died years ago, and she was thrilled to have the company. Hancock is a pretty safe town, but she had gotten older, and worried about living alone, so she really enjoyed having me. So much that she wanted me to stay, offering to turn her second floor into a separate apartment."

"And you offered it to Z?"

Jamie crumpled up her nose. "Sort of. I love my aunt, but I really wanted to live on my own. And Z was moving out of Gwen's house so . . ."

"I didn't know he and Gwen used to live together."

"Yes. They rented a house near downtown and ran the business from their basement. But they'd just bought the carriage house, and Gwen was moving to a house down by the water, and someone said that Z was looking for a place of his own. So I told him about this place, and when he seemed interested, I introduced him to my aunt. Z looked around, charmed her, charmed an entire company of house renovators into working overtime and . . . And he's been living here ever since."

"Charmed your aunt so much that she preferred him as a tenant to her own niece?"

"It's not that she preferred him; it's just that he made sure she wouldn't mind me living my own life. He probably made her think that it was her own idea."

"Really? How did he do that?"

"How well did you know Z?"

"Just professionally," Susan said, as she heard a voice call them from downstairs.

"I think my aunt's ready for us. You don't mind, do you? She's going to be very lonely without Z. . . ." Jamie grabbed Susan's arm. "You didn't tell her that he was murdered, did you?"

"No."

"Good. Then I will, but let's go have some tea first. I called Auntie's minister from the carriage house. He said he'd be here in about an hour. I'll tell her before then."

Susan was thinking about how impressed she was by the young woman's consideration for her elderly relative as she followed her down the stairs.

"I'm back here in the kitchen, Jamie."

"If it's fluorescent, don't eat it," Jamie whispered, opening a white door on which hung a large stuffed angel with a malevolent grin embroidered on her face.

The kitchen could have served as a photo layout for a magazine offering an article entitled "50 Things to Make for the Holidays (Directions Inside)." Susan was drawn to a wall covered with swags, wreaths, and hangings fashioned from fragrant herbs and spices.

"This is fantastic," Susan enthused, gently touching a

wreath made entirely from cinnamon sticks, anise stars, and gilded nutmegs.

"Congregational Church over near Stamford. Sit down at the table and have something to eat. Jamie is so thin, and she works around all that food. I worry about her."

Susan sat down on the oak chair offered. She would have examined the cross-stitched tablecloth if it hadn't been covered with food: a pot of tea and three matching mugs, a plate of buttered toast, and over a dozen tiny bowls of jam. Jamie had been right; one or two of the choices were, shades popularized by Day-Glo paints.

A local radio station was playing Christmas carols, and Jamie's aunt reached across the counter to turn down the volume before she began pouring out the tea. "Did you find what you wanted?" she asked Susan.

"I . . ." Susan had no idea what she was going to say and was relieved rather than annoyed when Jamie interrupted.

"Mrs. Henshaw just wanted to look around Z's apartment, Aunt Flo." Jamie was piling sour-cherry jam on a slice of toast as she spoke. "This looks good," she added.

"Probably is. Methodist," her aunt replied.

"Do a lot of women want to see where Z . . . Z's apartment?" Susan asked, trying to phrase the question without using the past tense.

"Oh, yes. He frequently sends them here for some reason." The woman Susan had come to think of as Aunt Flo spooned a remarkable amount of golden honey into her tea as she spoke. "I always kid him about it." She took a sip of her tea and smiled. "Z and his women. We all love him, don't we?"

"I don't know him all that well . . . ," Susan began.

"Oh, that's what all his women always say. But we do love him, don't we?" Aunt Flo insisted.

"But why?" Susan asked, thinking she might as well get what information she could.

"Because he made himself so lovable, of course. Oh, there's the front door." The elderly woman again popped up with a display of energy that Susan envied.

Jamie grabbed her aunt's arm. "Aunt Flo, before you get that, there's something you should know."

"Why, dear, what could it be?"

"Oh, I didn't want to tell you like this." Jamie looked around as though hoping an answer might pop out of the air. Then she took a deep breath and continued. "Z is dead, Aunt Flo. He was . . . The police think he was killed."

"Killed? Who would kill Z? Everyone loves him." The doorbell rang again. "Maybe you could get that for me, dear. I think I need to sit down." And she did.

"Go ahead," Susan insisted, worried by the loss of color on the elderly woman's face. "I'll take care of your aunt. That's probably the police at the door." She moved her chair closer to the elderly woman as the door closed behind Jamie. "I know Jamie didn't want you to learn about Z's death this way."

"That's because she thinks old people are fragile," Aunt Flo surprised her by answering. "Of course, I'm upset at losing a friend, but I've gotten used to it over the years. I'll miss Z though." She smiled, but Susan noticed tears in her eyes. "He was such a charmer, always ready with a kind comment, always trying to please. And he did it all without seeming to be false or cloying. It was just the way he was. Do you know what I mean?"

Susan nodded. "I do, and you're right. It must have been nice to have a neighbor like that."

"Wonderful. Even better than having a relative. Because Z didn't really care all that much, so I didn't feel obligated to pretend that nothing was wrong all the time."

"I don't understand."

"Well, as much as I liked the idea of having Jamie living nearby, I would always have had to be making sure that she wasn't worried about me. So I couldn't tell her about my various aches and pains and little worries because she would take it all so seriously. Every twinge of arthritis would become a malignant tumor; every time I forgot something, Alzheimer's would be in the offing. So I would end up being quiet about things like that. But Z was super-ficial and uninvolved. If I told him about my aching hips, he'd just make a joke about my active sex life, or if I forgot something, he'd just say that lovely ladies like me should have people to take care of the small details for them. All of it was complete nonsense, of course, but it was nice."

When Susan didn't answer, she continued. "I'm not such a fool as I look. I was a home economics teacher until I retired three years ago. I listened to teenage girls chatter while they learned to hem their skirts or roast a chicken for over thirty-five years. It's not a vocation that's likely to leave a person naive, and I certainly have heard more tales of self-deception about the opposite sex than most people. I knew what Z was, and I knew how to enjoy it."

"What about other women? Do you think he deceived them?"

"Probably some were deceived, but they must have wanted to be." She poured herself another cup of tea. "We're not talking about a man who seduced young girls, you know. Z worked his charm on middle-aged and older women like you and me."

Susan got a small jolt of reality, but continued on. "Really? You're sure about that?"

"I certainly don't know everything about his private life, but that's what I observed. I was concerned at first about Jamie. Not that she doesn't have a good head on her shoulders, but she had just finished school and was living on her own for the first time. I didn't want her to get involved with the wrong man. But Z left her alone. He didn't even flirt with her the way he did with me. And then I noticed that the same thing was true with other young women that Jamie would bring over here. He was personable, but that's all."

"I . . ." Susan wanted to ask a lot more questions, but neither woman could ignore the commotion coming from the hallway.

Her hostess got up and started from the room. "I think I'd better go. That doesn't sound like the police department, unless you believe this nonsense about them all being thugs."

"I'll go with you."

The sight that greeted them in the hall had nothing whatsoever to do with any images of police brutality. Jamie Potter was standing on the bottom step, arms stretched from wall to banister, blocking the path to the second floor. Directly in front of her stood two arguing women, whom Susan identified as Gillian Davies and Alexis Cutler. They both were elaborately garbed in the finest cold-weather running clothes. But she thought that their red faces were the result of extreme emotion rather than serious physical exertion.

As Jamie loudly announced that she was not going to allow either of them to enter Z's apartment, Alexis Cutler, the taller of the two, pushed by the young woman and dashed up the stairs, closely followed by Gillian Davies.

"Let them go," her aunt insisted.

"But won't the police be very upset that we allowed . . ."

"What were we supposed to do? Attack them and tie them up?" her aunt answered logically. "We'll just be sure that the police know they were there."

. "And we can go up and see exactly what they're doing," Susan insisted, starting up the stairway. Fake evergreen roping had fallen off and was threatening to trip her. "Come with me, Jamie. We'll be able to confirm each other's story." Susan was aware that the police were probably going to be told of her own admission to Z's apartment, but she didn't want to think about that now. There wouldn't have been a problem if Brett had just asked for her help, she thought, entering Z's apartment for the second time that day.

Alexis Cutler was a tall shapely brunette, always dressed in predictable good taste. For exercise, she had chosen bright Lycra and microfiber outerware designed with the fashionable suburbanite in mind. Whether the designer had imagined that it would be worn while moving the contents of a man's closet to the floor of his living room is unknown. Her cropped hair (off the shoulders to lift the face, as her hairdresser insisted) was bouncing up and down while she worked.

Gillian Davies was English, with light brown hair and the type of pale skin that gave that country its reputation. She also wore running clothes, but with her own imprint. Susan had often envied Gillian, not only her taste, but her ability to wear fashions in which Susan would have felt silly. Today, Gillian wore running clothes with a Tyrolean air. Black leggings were topped with an embroidered red anorak that would look at home in the Alps over a white turtleneck. Her hair was twined into braids. Instead of scaling the Matterhorn, she was climbing on a very modern cherry stool and peering into the cabinet above the Sub-Zero.

"Maybe," Jamie began, arriving at Susan's side, "maybe they're taking part in some sort of unusual treasure hunt. I know games are being played at some of the parties The Holly and Ms. Ivy cater. They're becoming fashionable."

"They should find a better place to play than in a murdered man's apartment," Susan said.

Alexis backed out of the closet with a leather-brimmed hat falling off her head and a look of astonishment on her face. "What did you say?"

"Who said anything about murder?" Gillian asked, spinning around so fast that she almost tipped over the stool she was standing on.

Susan and Jamie exchanged a glance. "You didn't know he was dead?" Susan asked slowly.

"We heard he was dead," Alexis said, a sad look on her face.

"But we didn't hear anything about murder," Gillian added, then looked down on her friend. "At least, you didn't tell me anything about murder."

"I didn't know anything about murder. I just heard that he had been found dead at the carriage house," Alexis insisted.

"That must be where all the police cars were heading in such a hurry," Gillian said thoughtfully. "I just assumed there had been a bad traffic accident." She looked at Susan and Jamie. "Who murdered him?" she asked accusingly.

"I don't think anyone knows yet," Susan answered.

"Unless you want to confess?" Alexis said sarcastically to Gillian.

Susan thought the question was rather mean. There was something about all this that seemed a little . . . well, a little contrived. "How did you find out that he was dead?" she asked.

"Gillian and I were out jogging."

"We just started. This is our first morning. We're trying to get rid of some of the fat that the holidays always bring. All those cholesterol-filled foods . . ." Gillian stopped speaking, perhaps remembering that the cholesterol-filled foods most recently imbibed had been prepared and served by the woman she was speaking to. "Anyway, we passed The Holly and Ms. Ivy, and Alexis thought . . ."

"We both thought," Alexis corrected her.

"I guess so. We both thought that we should take the opportunity to check on the parties that we're giving. So Alexis ran into the building, and someone told her that Z had been murdered."

"Was dead," Alexis corrected quickly. "Just that he was dead, not how he died."

"And so you both decided to jog on over to his apartment to . . . To what?" Susan asked, looking around at the mess they had made in just a few minutes. Even the candles had been knocked out of the Mexican tree of lights.

"That's none of your business, Susan Henshaw," Alexis said, kicking a running shoe back in the direction of the closet.

"She's right," Gillian said. "You weren't with the police at the carriage house. You're not helping investigate this murder. We don't have to tell you anything."

"But I am. And I think someone had better tell me exactly what is going on here."

All four women in the room turned to find Brett Fortesque standing in the doorway. Directly behind him was Jamie's aunt, an embroidered tea cozy in her hand.

EIGHT

"THIS IS THE MOST RIDICULOUS THING EVER."

"You know—"

"I know that I've helped Brett in the past. I've even solved murders in other states. Why is he excluding me from this one? I even know the people involved in this. I knew the man who was killed, for heaven's sake!" Susan flung herself back in the seat of Kathleen's small car and smacked her head on the heavy cardboard box stowed away behind her. "I absolutely do not understand."

When Kathleen finally spoke, it was quietly. "You know, it just might be that your involvement with Z is the reason Brett thinks it might not be appropriate."

"I can't believe it!" Susan tried not to shriek. "You're on his side, aren't you? I can't believe it!"

"There aren't sides here."

"No, you're wrong. There are sides here. Or groups rather: an 'in group' and an 'out group.' And I'm in the out group!" Susan bit her lips. She was uncomfortable sounding like a petulant teenager and was glad that neither of her children was witnessing her tantrum.

Kathleen was quiet for a few moments before speaking again. "Susan—"

"Don't try to defend Brett."

"Susan, you haven't let me finish a sentence, how can I defend him?"

"I—"

"No, now listen to me. Brett is right. You're too involved in this case. Brett's protecting you by keeping you away from this. You have to believe me."

Susan was silent. If Kathleen thought she was buying that, then she was living proof that eggnog caused brain damage.

"You understand, don't you?" Kathleen asked again.

"Of course," Susan lied. There had been a murder and someone was trying to keep her out of the investigation. And she certainly wasn't going to let that happen. It might be a few days early for New Year's resolutions, but this was number one.

"Susan ..." Kathleen's voice rose in an unspoken question.

"I'll stay out of it," Susan lied. "Not because I was involved with Z in any way, but because ..." She thought quickly and came up with an answer. "Because Chrissy is home, and I haven't seen her in so long. It's best that I spend time with her."

"You know, you're right about that. I know when Bananas leaves for college, I'll be thrilled with his visits."

Kathleen babbled on, and Susan wondered where her friend's mind had been for the past few years. Teenagers didn't come home to see their parents; they came home so that someone would clean and cook for them while they visited their friends.

"And I really have to pick him up," Kathleen ended.

"I've got a lot to do at home. I still have some cleaning to do from yesterday. It wouldn't pay to get behind before the party on Saturday night."

"True." Kathleen agreed, turning her car into Susan's driveway.

"Well, I'd better get going," Susan said, hopping out of the car into a snow drift that was forming down the center of her sidewalk.

"Call you later."

Susan got the feeling that Kathleen was in as much of a

hurry to part as she was. Probably heading back to Brett, she decided, unlocking her front door and ignoring the two dried roses that fell to the ground as she pushed her packages ahead of her into the hallway.

"Anybody home?"

She didn't expect an answer, and she didn't get one. But she heard scratching sounds, indicating Clue was trying to escape from the kitchen. Susan tossed her packages on the hall chair and hurried to the back of the house, hoping to release the dog before it was necessary to replace the door. She opened the kitchen door and crunched across the quarry-tile floor.

"What the . . .?" Visions of broken glass ornaments filled her mind before she realized that Clue had gotten hold of a pinecone wreath that had been in the middle of her kitchen table, with a chunky beeswax candle at its center. "I should have learned my lesson when you stole that pound of butter last week," Susan said, frowning. She still got slightly nauseous thinking about the pound of butter, wrappers and all, that Clue had consumed when her back was turned—that reminded her. "Do you need to go outside?" she asked her dog, opening the back door. The animal flew out into the recently fenced backyard, and Susan turned to pick up the glass on the floor, flicking on her electric kettle along the way. She could use a cup of tea. The phone answering machine was flashing, and she pressed a button and listened to the tape.

As usual, most of the messages were for her children. After leaving notes for Chad to call six of his friends and for Chrissy to remember a party that evening, she sat back and considered her messages. Two friends had called with the news of Z's death; one had called to announce that she had heard from her cleaning woman that both Z Holly and Gwen Ivy had been murdered, and was Susan going to give her party Saturday night because, if she wasn't, they would have to go to her husband's mother's house, and she couldn't bear to start 1995 with her in-laws; and the mayor's wife had called and asked Susan to call her immediately. She had left her private, unlisted number. Susan raised her eyebrows and dialed.

"Camilla Logan here."

"Oh, hello. This is Susan Henshaw," Susan sputtered, slightly surprised by the abrupt announcement on the other end of the line.

"Mrs. Henshaw. How nice of you to call," Camilla Logan trilled.

Susan was even more stunned. Camilla always acted as though Susan was a dust mote in the air around her, something to be ignored or even brushed away. "Well, I got your message on my machine." Maybe it had been a mistake? Perhaps Camilla had dialed a wrong number?

"And you answered so promptly. I can't tell you how I appreciate that during this holiday season when some of us are so busy."

Susan wondered exactly why she got the impression that Camilla pictured her lying around and eating bonbons while the rest of the population baked, bought presents, wrapped, decorated the house . . .

"We just returned home from Aspen, and you know how exhausting unpacking can be," the mayor's wife continued.

"Ah, yes." Susan wondered if it would be rude to ask Camilla why she'd called.

"I was hoping, Susan, that you would be able to come to my dinner party tonight."

"I . . ."

"I know what late notice this is, and I'm so sorry that I can't ask Jed to accompany you, but maybe you'll just let me explain the situation. . . ."

"Of course."

"I have planned this dinner for months. In fact, it's going to be one of the social events of the season. And then, this morning, I arrived home to find out that one of my guests has the flu. Her husband is just fine, and he's going to come, but . . . Well, I hate to sit down to an uneven table. I know that's old-fashioned of me, but that's just how it is. And, when I was wondering who else to ask, your name just popped into my head."

"I . . ."

"It's a wonderful group of people. My very best friends are in town. I know you'd love everybody. You may actu-

ally know some of them. And The Holly and Ms. Ivy are
catering, so you know the food will be wonderful. I'd be so
delighted if you'd say that you'll come. Please do."

Susan got the impression that Camilla didn't expect to be
turned down. And, in fact, Susan was happy to accept. She
was more than a little curious about the Logans' friends as
well as whether or not The Holly and Ms. Ivy were going
to be able to continue as usual. And she knew that Jed
wouldn't mind staying home. He hated stuffy dinner parties. Besides, there were plenty of leftovers to feed the
troops at home, and she liked the idea of being a guest instead of a hostess for a while. "I'd love to come."

"Wonderful! Drinks at seven. We're a pretty casual
group. I'm wearing a long velvet skirt and a wonderful silk
shirt that I bought out west."

Susan thought of casual as jeans, but she was willing to
adapt to the customs of the upper crust. "I'll see you at
seven then," she said, getting ready to hang up.

"Yes, or perhaps a little later," Camilla suggested in what
Susan assumed she thought was a tactful manner.

Susan was aware of the fact that her social skills were
being questioned. "Of course, see you then." She would
have changed her mind if she hadn't been so curious about
this dinner. Hancock, like many towns, had its own social
strata: churches, schools, neighborhoods, even parents with
children who play hockey, soccer, or baseball had their own
groups. But the most politically involved people in all the
groups funneled into Camilla Logan's social circle.

Susan thought about the Logans on the way to her bedroom closet to find something casual as well as chic. She
didn't know either of them well. Their only child, a daughter, had graduated in Chrissy's class, so of course, she'd
seen them both over the years at school events. Camilla
was what she herself referred to as "old Hancock," having
been born and raised here. For most of the town's residents,
commuters to the city, that meant nothing. But enough people appeared to care to make Camilla queen of the town's
society (which consisted mainly of the Field Club, the Junior League, and the committee that ran Hancock's yearly
hospital benefit ball). A born committee woman, Camilla

ran all of these things efficiently. Her husband had been Hancock's mayor ever since Susan could remember.

Susan stood in front of her closet as though expecting to discover a smashing new outfit that she had forgotten about. The black skirt with the lamé vest needed to go to the cleaners; the green velvet slacks were too tight; she'd worn the chenille top yesterday; her new crushed velvet was for New Year's; and she couldn't even begin to imagine why she had allowed the saleswoman at Bergdorf's to talk her into buying red leggings. If only she had something new . . . What an idiot! Susan headed down to the living room and the goodies under the Christmas tree.

Her new cranberry cashmere cowling around her neck, a pair of winter white slacks miraculously disguising her hips, makeup perfect and hair combed, she was putting on her new emerald earrings before she started wondering if her acceptance of this invitation hadn't been a bit hasty.

She didn't particularly like the Logans, and the invitation had certainly been extended rather begrudgingly. She knew she wouldn't even have considered going if The Holly and Ms. Ivy weren't scheduled to cater. She checked in her mirror and, satisfied, headed toward the stairs. Maybe it wouldn't be such a bad evening.

She was going to avoid cooking and do a little investigating at the same time. As the song said, who could ask for anything more?

She was humming Christmas carols as she approached the door of the Logan's large Tudor home. The party seemed to be going strong. Maybe no one else had been ordered to wait until after seven to arrive, Susan thought, picking up the brass angel door knocker to announce her arrival.

Buck Logan answered so quickly that she wondered if he had been lurking behind the heavy plank door, waiting for her. "Susan Henshaw! How nice to see you!"

There were people who found artificial heartiness appealing. Susan wasn't one of them. "It was nice of you to ask me," she answered politely, walking into the spacious entryway. "I don't think I've been here before," she added.

"Surely not. We moved almost two years ago. You and Jock have been ignoring us! I'll have to show you around."

"I'd like that," Susan said honestly, ignoring the fact that Buck had gotten Jed's name wrong. She was admiring the hall table adorned with a half-dozen rose-bud topiaries about three feet tall.

"Like them?" Buck asked, handing her coat to a uniformed attendant waiting nearby.

"They're wonderful." She knew better than to ask if Camilla had made them. Camilla always made it absolutely clear that she didn't have time for crafts, usually while professing to admire someone else's work.

"My wife chose them." He made it sound as if she had grown and dried the roses, and then fashioned the ornaments by hand. "She has wonderful taste."

"Yes."

"Every year she selects a different decorating theme for the holidays. Then the entire house can be coordinated. I think it works particularly well, don't you?"

"Camilla is wonderfully organized," Susan admitted. It wasn't that Camilla was organized that bugged her, but that she made Susan feel so disorganized. The Henshaw Christmas decorations were coordinated, too—at least to begin with, but she hadn't the heart or the desire to leave out all the family mementos that had been cherished over the years. Camilla Logan wouldn't have a threadbare elf or bells fashioned from cardboard egg cartons hanging on her Christmas tree, Susan thought, following Buck into the living room.

"We moved to have more space to entertain," he was explaining.

"You certainly have it," Susan said, stopping in the doorway. The huge room was two stories high, with an elaborately carved wooden balcony running around it. Large brass chandeliers dangled from the beamed ceiling, and matching sconces hung on the walls. Pastel silk Bokhara rugs on the flagstone floor led to a massive fieldstone fireplace where a large log blazed. Huge velvet chairs and sofas were piled high with pillows made from satin ribbons. "It's fabulous," Susan said, knowing that the sight was just

waiting to be admired. Standing in the alcove of a semicir-
cular bay window, a large pine tree was decorated with
matching pastel balls, lacy bows, dried rosebuds, and pink
lights. Not a family memento in sight, but perhaps none
was necessary. The most prominent object in the room was
a larger-than-life photograph of the Logan's daughter. Susan, feeling politeness demanded a comment, struggled to
remember the girl's name. It was unusual, she knew. . . .
Fortunately, Buck unwittingly helped her out.

"You're looking at the photograph of Cameo, aren't you?
I know a father shouldn't say it, but she is a beautiful girl,
isn't she?"

"Yes," Susan said. It was an honest assessment. Cameo
looked like a blonde Breck girl. "She's home for the holidays?"

"Alas, no. Skiing with some friends in Switzerland. The
parents of popular children have to learn to live without
them, I'm afraid."

There was no response to that, and Susan was relieved to
see Camilla heading their way, her arms open in greeting.
"Susan, merry Christmas. It was so nice of you to rearrange
your schedule so you could be with us. I just know you
were expecting to spend the night in your kitchen cooking
up delicious snacks for that annual New Year's party that
we're always hearing so much about."

Since Camilla had refused an invitation to Susan's first
party in a manner that had certainly discouraged her from
ever asking them again, Susan just smiled. "Actually, I'm
not doing the cooking this year. I hired The Holly and Ms.
Ivy."

"You hired The Holly and Ms. Ivy for a New Year's Eve
party?"

Susan worked not to be offended by the surprise in
Camilla's voice. "Yes. I understand that they're catering
your dinner tonight."

"I was one of the first people in town to hire them—
back when they were just getting started. In fact, I used to
tell Z that he should give me a discount, that I'm responsible for some of his popularity. But I must get you some
of their famous grog or mulled apple wine to drink. They're

both delicious, and I don't think The Holly and Ms. Ivy will be serving them at just every party this season."

Susan followed her hostess to a bar set up before shelves filled with leather-bound books. She had heard the past tense and was anxious to get to the bottom of it, but didn't feel comfortable announcing a murder at the beginning of a holiday party. "Did they tell you about Z's death?" she asked quietly, nodding at the young bartender, easily identified as a Holly and Ms. Ivy employee by the tiny horticultural trademark woven into his black satin vest.

"They have been very professional, despite the tragedy," Camilla muttered. "I'd expect nothing less from The Holly and Ms. Ivy's employees—even if some of them will naturally be the main suspects. Now, what would you like to drink?" she asked, changing to her bright hostess voice.

"The mulled apple wine sounds good."

It was fabulous, spicy, warm, and mellow. She sipped appreciatively as she was led over to the rest of the party—and discovered that her tactful desire not to speak of Z's murder was entirely unnecessary. The news had spread, and she found herself in the middle of a discussion of murder.

To Susan, the other guests were familiar faces. To them, she was the local expert in murder—and they had a lot of questions to ask.

Susan spent most of the polite forty minutes before dinner sipping mulled apple wine and repeating that she didn't know anything about the murder. She wasn't sure whether or not she was glad that the other guests didn't believe her. After all, she told herself, reaching for another smoked salmon quiche, everyone likes to think of themselves as the possessors of inside information. No matter how many times she denied helping the police department in their investigation of Z's murder, there were still questions about what she knew regarding this particular crime.

Dinner was a bit different. Perhaps she should have been flattered to be seated next to Buck in the baronial dining room, and perhaps she was—through the first course of rosemary shrimp in potato baskets. But while the salad was tossed and served, she was being interrogated about her knowledge of Z's murder. And, during the beef fillet en brioche, she was lectured about her civic responsibility in the affair (which Buck seemed to feel was to be his own personal conduit to the police department). As the pineapple sorbet cleansed her palate, she was dismissed as disloyal and, apparently, a very poor guest and left to listen in on the conversations of those around her—which had mainly to do with wines of the Northwest versus those of France. Susan was about to die of boredom when she noticed Jamie Potter motioning to her from the shadows.

NINE

SUSAN LEANED ACROSS THE TABLE AND INTERRUPTED THE elegant lady insisting that the finer wines of northern Italy simply didn't travel and that you hadn't really tasted them until you had visited the vineyards. "Do you know where the bathroom's located?"

The woman raised her eyebrows and stared. Susan wondered if perhaps she didn't use bathrooms—or perhaps only those located in the tiny, as yet undiscovered, towns in France. Buck, ever a good host, offered directions, and Susan excused herself to no one in particular and left the room.

"This way!" The electric sconces were apparently on rheostats and had been turned down so far that Susan didn't actually see who was whispering to her down the long hallway. But that didn't stop her from following the sound through a doorway and into a kitchen so bright her eyes had trouble adjusting.

"Wow!"

"Fabulous, isn't it?" A young man leaning over and filling a large German dishwasher agreed with her unspoken appreciation of the long white room. Every appliance was the biggest and the best, and they were wedged between so many banks of cabinets that Susan was reminded of the carriage house's professional facilities. "The best of everything and in multiple dozens," he continued, motioning to cabinets, open to reveal tall stacks of dishes and rows of glasses.

"It's fine, unless you want to cook something," another man in a chef's hat said. "Not even a jar of stale paprika. Just pepper and this dreadful salt substitute stuff." He frowned and picked up the offending mixture. "Maybe I can borrow this—it might improve some of our more healthy recipes.

"I'm glad we brought along our own spices this time. Last year I had to send out a platter of seafood risotto that looked a little pale."

"But I'll bet the platter was hand painted," the cleaner said.

"Mrs. Henshaw doesn't care about all this," Jamie Potter insisted.

Actually, Susan was endlessly curious about the intimate details of her neighbor's lives, but she did have to hurry. "You're probably right. I'm supposed to be in the bathroom," she explained.

"You're going to investigate this murder, aren't you, Mrs. Henshaw?" Jamie asked, hopping up and perching on a counter.

"That's what we were hoping, but when I was serving, you were telling the mayor that you weren't involved in this," a young man said, reentering the room with a tray piled high with used silverware.

"But at my aunt's house, I got the impression that you were planning to help the police," Jamie insisted.

"We do hope you're going to look into all this," another young woman said, stirring a large steaming pot on the stove.

"It's important," the dishwasher said.

All the young people in the room nodded, and Susan suddenly saw the sadness in their eyes. "The police . . . ," she began.

"The police will think Gwen did it," Jamie said.

"The police already think Gwen did it," the other girl insisted.

"Why?" Susan asked the obvious question.

"Because they've been fighting," the dishwasher answered promptly.

"Because his death means that she owns the business," the other young man added.

"Because everyone heard her threaten to kill him on Christmas Eve," Jamie said.

"And everyone else loved him," the other woman said.

Susan thought for a moment. She intended to investigate, but that didn't mean she wanted to make promises she either couldn't or might not want to keep.

"Did you know that you were invited here because Z was killed?" the young chef asked, apparently not concerned that she might be hurt by this revelation.

"It wasn't difficult to guess," Susan said. "This isn't my social group, and no one has talked to me about anything else except for a comment about the Logan's daughter—I can't ever remember her name."

"Cameo," Jamie said.

"Yes, no one in this room can forget good old Cameo," the woman stopped stirring and switched off the flame on the gas burner.

"Why?" Susan asked.

"Well, about this time last year, right at the end of the Logan's annual Christmas celebration, good old Cameo drank just a little too much grog—"

"I think it was eggnog," someone else corrected her.

"Maybe. But whatever it was, she wasn't used to drinking, or she just didn't know how potent The Holly and Ms. Ivy makes their nog—"

"Unless the customer asks for less brandy," Jamie broke in.

"Anyway, Cameo came down to the kitchen right after we'd served the cappuccino."

"Because last year's meal had an Italian theme."

"And she took off most of her clothing and tried to seduce Z!"

"She only had on her underwear when her father came in," Jamie explained.

"She had on a black lace camisole, black bikini pants, and a red satin garter belt holding up black net stockings," the cleaner said, closing the dishwasher and pressing the buttons that would set it going. Then he turned and looked at Susan. "We're not talking white cotton here. Our esteemed mayor almost split his guts."

"Did he threaten to kill Z?" Susan asked hopefully. She'd love to pin this murder on that obnoxious man.

"I think he threatened to kill his daughter," Jamie said.

"Well, that will help us if she turns up dead," Susan said.

"But it means that other people might be suspects, doesn't it?"

"And you'll investigate?"

"Please. Gwen Ivy could sure use your help."

Susan looked around at the pleading faces. The Holly and Ms. Ivy sure hired nice young people, she decided. And she was going to investigate anyway. What harm would it do to let them know about it? It occurred to her that they might even be a big help. She made her decision.

"Listen, I'm going to look into this. I might not succeed. And you might be wrong, and Gwen might not even be a suspect." She heard footsteps in the hallway and hurried to finish. "I have to get back. Why don't we meet someplace later and talk?"

Before anyone could respond, the door behind her opened and Camilla Logan entered the room. "Susan? I thought you were going to the powder room."

"I—"

"Isn't it time for dessert?" Camilla continued angrily to the young people in the room, not bothering to wait for Susan's answer.

"Yes, ma'am," Jamie answered. "We were just putting the finishing touches on the sauces."

"Then maybe you'll go ahead and serve as soon as all our guests have returned to the table."

Susan resisted glaring at her hostess. She'd never been so badly treated as a guest in anyone's home. Furious, she left the kitchen and returned to the dining room. The conversation had made the giant leap from wine to vintage brandy. No one bothered to notice her entrance.

Her place had been cleared, and she leaned her elbows on the table and tried to look interested in the conversation while thinking over what she'd just learned. It was not difficult, sitting here with him, to imagine Buck Logan's face when he discovered his daughter trying to seduce the caterer in his own kitchen. After a few glasses of wine, Buck was already flushed. How red had he been last year? And, was this skiing trip for the popular child really a vacation, or was it important that she leave town before the holidays and this party? Susan looked down to the other end of the table where a large silver bowl had been set before Camilla Logan. Unlike her husband, she looked cool and relaxed.

The conversation around the table stopped as the lights in the room were turned off and whatever was in the bowl was lit with a match. Flames flew into the air as, with a wooden-handled ladle, Camilla poured the liquid back and forth. As the fire died out, coffee was poured into the hot bowl. Cups of the brew were distributed around the table.

"Camilla makes the most wonderful *café brulot*, doesn't she?" the man next to her murmured to everyone except Susan.

"Our family has been ending the Christmas party with *café brulot* for over twenty years. And with God's help we will continue to do so for twenty years more," Buck Logan said pompously.

There were appreciative murmurs around the table, and Susan wondered if she was about to participate in another Logan family tradition: long-winded speech making. She dug into her dessert. Fabulous. She was grateful that she had chosen a dress with an elastic waistband to wear on Saturday. Of course, it's possible that she should have picked out a caftan, she decided as a tray of chocolate truffles appeared over her right shoulder.

"Have a truffle, ma'am?"

Susan looked up into the serious face of Jamie Potter.

"There's a large one with an extra holly leaf," Jamie added, gently nudging Susan's shoulder.

"I'll take that one then," Susan said, picking up the delicate silver tongs and placing the confection on her plate. She'd seen the tiny pieces of white sticking out from the bottom of that particular truffle.

Jamie Potter moved on down the table, and Susan nudged the candy over with her fork. A small rectangle of egg wafer was revealed. Tiny letters spelled out a message: 12 Carr. Hse. Susan glanced at her watch. It was just after ten. She doubted if any of the guests would leave for over an hour. If she interpreted the note correctly, she wouldn't have any trouble being at the carriage house at midnight.

"Good, aren't they?" The man next to her had apparently decided to speak.

Susan popped the piece of meringue in her mouth. "Excellent," she agreed, nodding and swallowing.

"I understand it's very difficult to get these caterers to work on parties around here these days," he added indifferently. "At least, that's what Camilla was saying earlier—perhaps before you arrived."

"Yes. I was late," Susan admitted, resisting the urge to brag that The Holly and Ms. Ivy were going to be catering a party at her house next weekend.

"So you investigate murders—like that lady from Maine on television. My wife watches it sometimes."

"I've had a little experience investigating murders," Susan admitted.

"And you're looking into the murder of this caterer," he added.

"I . . ."

"Don't you get bored denying your involvement?" he continued.

"Then there's no reason for me to do so, is there?" Susan asked, picking up the truffle in her fingers and taking a bite.

"You don't look like a detective," he insisted, looking accusingly at her new sweater.

Susan, realizing her neighbor was very drunk, wondered if he expected her to wear a Sherlock Holmes hat. "I'm just an ordinary guest."

"Really? I don't seem to remember you as part of the group before."

Susan took a deep breath, but Camilla interrupted before she could think of a sufficiently insulting reply. "Why don't we go into the library? I'm feeling a little stuffy."

"Excellent idea, my dear. Hey, listen to that, I'm a poet, and I don't know it!" Buck chuckled at the age-old witticism. "I'll lead the way, shall I? If you will accompany me?" He stood and offered Susan his arm. She felt silly accepting, but she would have felt sillier to refuse.

The party trailed down the dim hall into a tiny book-lined room. Except for a few obligatory pink ribbons tied around andirons in the fireplace and a bowl of shiny silver balls on the mantel, this room seemed to have been spared the excesses of Camilla's theme decorating.

Buck got busy turning on the gas fire in the grate and switching Christmas carols on the stereo, and Susan was left to wander and look at the bookshelves as the rest of the guests seated themselves on the two large sofas and in the four window seats this corner room boasted. Accustomed to judging people by the books they owned, Susan had decided that she had been all wrong about the Logans, when Buck joined her and explained that the reading material had come with the house.

"Quite a collection, isn't it? And it sure looks better than the piles of Robert Ludlum paperbacks that we moved here with."

"Then you and Camilla don't read these?" Susan asked, aching to open the leather-bound Trollopes and early P. G. Wodehouses.

"Nah. Actually we're too busy to get much reading in. Just the odd chapter or two before we drop off at night. You know how it is."

Buck looked so self-satisfied that Susan didn't bother to answer. She returned to her examination of the shelves. The Holly and Ms. Ivy workers were scurrying around, doing their best to adapt to the sudden change in plans, passing cups of coffee, brandy, and candied peels as well as chocolate truffles. Susan made a mental note to speak to Gwen about adding the candied fruit peels to her menu Saturday night. If Gwen was still running The Holly and Ms. Ivy come Saturday night, she reminded herself.

The rest of the evening (about double the time she had estimated; the group didn't break up until almost midnight) continued to be boring. Apparently unaware that the wine they loved to discuss was alcoholic, the guests, depending on their personal reactions, became either more voluble or sleepy as the evening wore on and the vintage bottles were passed around repeatedly. Susan wasn't sure the party would have broken up when it did, if the wife of the editor in chief of the county's only newspaper hadn't started explaining in detail exactly how inadequate her husband's bedroom performance had become in the last few years. The guests practically flew into their furs and out the door to their cars.

Susan knew that she was going to be late for her assignation with Jamie and her friends. But, when she arrived at the carriage house, she wondered if she had misunderstood the tiny edible note. Old-fashioned gas lights lit the brick walkway, and tiny Christmas lights were wound around the variegated holly wreaths that hung up on the double doors, but other than that, the building seemed to be dark. Feeling a little nervous and trying not to slip on the fresh snow, Susan carefully made her way up the walk to the door. She didn't expect the building to be unlocked, but she was cold, so she tried the brass knob.

And, there she was, inside the building. Susan carefully closed the door behind her, wondering if she should turn on the lights, wondering if she could find the switches. She backed against the wall and thought, her eyes picking pools of dim light out of the darkness. The tiny red and green knobs on some of the appliances were visible, and, as her eyes adjusted, she was able to see around the room—at least enough to keep her from crashing into anything while she searched for the light switch.

She moved slowly, following the wall around the room. The switch must be by the door at the rear of the room, she decided. That's probably the way the employees entered the building. She was headed there when she heard noises coming from the employees' locker room under the stairs. She almost called out before realizing that it might not be the people she'd come to meet. Jamie would have turned on the lights, wouldn't she? Susan decided to remain quiet.

She edged toward the door and tried to figure out what she was hearing. Then she realized that someone was, one by one, opening and closing the employees' lockers. She wondered who it was and moved back into a shadow to wait and find out.

But the person was taking his or her time, and Susan was beginning to think that hiding was foolish. What if this was a common burglar? She should call the police. Or maybe it

was just an employee who had lost something. She was trying to make up her mind what to do when she heard a car
pull up in the courtyard behind the building.

The cheerful voice of Jamie Potter rang out, and reassured, Susan left the shadows and headed toward the back
door. "Jamie! It's me! Susan." Relieved to have company,
she ran out into the courtyard.

"Susan! I'm glad to see you." Jamie was heading toward
the carriage house, her arms loaded with foil-covered trays.
"That bitch kept us around forever. Her husband vanished
almost half an hour ago. I didn't think we were ever going
to get away. Is Gwen around?"

"No, I . . ."

"Really? She or Z are usually here until everything is put
away. . . ."

"That's when there were two owners," the young man
who had been cooking reminded her. "Running this company is going to be a lot more difficult for just one person."

"True."

"Well, let's get all this stuff back inside, and we can talk
while we put it away and check into tomorrow's setup,"
Jamie suggested. "Is that all right with you?"

"Of course," Susan said. "But someone's in there—in the
employees' locker room. It might be Gwen."

"Gwen wouldn't be in our room." Jamie hurried into the
building.

"And she wouldn't walk around with the lights off," one
of her fellow employees said, hurrying behind her.

But the building seemed deserted when they entered and
Jamie turned on the lights.

"Maybe in the locker room," Susan suggested.

"Or upstairs in the office," someone said, and headed up
the stairs to find out.

But Susan had noticed that the front door had been left
open and ran in that direction. She was in time to see a
white Range Rover speeding off.

"Is that the person who was here?" Jamie came up behind her.

"I don't know," Susan admitted. "I sure wish I did."

TEN

The lights on Susan's tree were still shining through the window when she arrived home. She had visions of a cup of hot tea and a nice chat with her husband. Instead, a note on the kitchen table suggested that Clue needed to go out because Jed was exhausted after a difficult day in the city. Susan wondered briefly what her daughter's and son's excuses were to stay inside, but the dog's wagging tail enchanted her.

"Okay, Clue. Just give me a few minutes to get into warm boots," Susan suggested, automatically heading for the cookie jar on the counter. After all, it was cold outside. Cold burned calories, didn't it?

The animal pranced around until they were walking down the sidewalk; at least they were walking on what Susan thought was the sidewalk. The snow had obliterated any sign of the cement. Clue, happiest when outside in cold weather or swimming in an icy ocean, pulled against her leash, and Susan realized that she was going to have a difficult time making the walk a short one.

It was very late, and hers were the only lights still on in the neighborhood, so Susan walked carefully, paying attention to every step. She had admired black-fur-lined red boots at Saks today, and she was wishing she had decided to treat herself when she realized that a white Range Rover was sitting at the curb about four houses down the block from hers. Of course, there were a lot more cars around than usual. She knew a few of her neighbors had houseguests this week. But this car was different.

This car wasn't covered with snow.

Susan had circled around for about half an hour after realizing that the car was empty. But she got so cold that even Clue was pulling toward home when she decided to go back inside. She would set the alarm to go off before daylight and maybe see who left in the Rover.

But in the morning, she was to learn once again that the best-laid plans do, in fact, go astray.

She woke up to the sounds of Jed's electric razor. A glance at the alarm clock told her she'd overslept. Leaping out of bed in a manner usually foreign to her in the morning, she hurried to the window. No Range Rover. "Damn."

"Merry Christmas to you, too," Jed said cheerfully, appearing in the doorway between bathroom and bedroom.

"Hi. Did you sleep well?" Susan asked politely. No reason to be mad at him when she'd made a mistake.

"I woke up once, and you should be glad. I checked the alarm, and it was set for five-thirty. I turned it off. You'd have hated to wake up that early after getting in so late last night."

Susan got back in bed and snuggled down under the quilt. "Will you make coffee before you leave?"

"Leave? I'm taking the day off, remember?"

Susan realized that Jed was wearing chinos and a plaid flannel shirt. "Of course, I'd forgotten." She yawned and then frowned. "We're going someplace, aren't we?"

"We promised Kathleen and Jerry that we'd spend the afternoon with them up in the country. You don't remember?" Jed squinted in her direction. "Are you feeling okay? Catching a cold?"

"I hope not," she answered, mentally knocking on wood. A cold was the last thing she needed now. "I don't remember what time we're due up there." Kathleen and Jerry had bought a vacation home, a few hours away, in late September. Susan had seen it the weekend of the purchase, and she and Kathleen had shopped together for antiques, but this was the first time she was going to see it furnished. Normally, she would be looking forward to the afternoon, but she had planned on trying to track down Gwen today. Maybe before they left this morning, she thought, sitting up in bed.

"Why don't you take a break this morning? I'll bring up something for you to eat," her husband offered. "I promised Chad and Chrissy I'd make them my famous eggnog French toast."

Susan decided this was no time to mention cholesterol. "No thanks. I know Kathleen will have lots of food." She paused for a second. "I have a few errands to do."

"We're supposed to be there between two and three, and I think it took us over an hour to drive up there. . . ."

"I'll be back by noon. Don't worry." Susan got out of bed while speaking. If she hurried, she'd be out of the house before Jed realized that someone had to walk the dog—and this morning that someone was going to be him.

Susan didn't see a lot of point in going back to the carriage house, but she didn't know where else to go. Jamie was right when she worried about Gwen being the primary suspect. As far as Susan knew, Gwen was the only suspect.

Once again, the carriage house was full of activity. As Susan entered, she saw Gwen leaning over a large roasting pan that had just been pulled from an oven. She was thinking that maybe Jamie had been worrying needlessly when she spotted a uniformed police officer standing near the stairway to the office floor. Gwen Ivy noticed her presence at that moment and came over, arms out.

"Susan, good to see you. We're in the middle of a mess here. We had a break-in last night, as you can see."

Susan realized that two more policemen were at the top of the stairs, sprinkling something around a light switch. She could have told them that they were wasting their time; no one had turned on any lights last night. But, remembering that she wasn't involved in this investigation, she kept her mouth shut.

Gwen was walking at her side, down the main aisle of the room. "I was going to call you . . . ," she began.

"You are going to be able to do my party Saturday night, aren't you?" Susan asked before realizing that she wasn't being terribly tactful. "I mean, I know that you catered a dinner for the Logans last night. It was good. I was there."

"The Holly and Ms. Ivy will continue to work. The police have assured me of that."

"Really?"

"Yes." Gwen shook her head so that her gold earrings swung against her shoulder. "Apparently they don't have enough evidence to arrest me."

"Oh, I don't think . . ."

"You're very kind," the other woman said dourly, "but I'm a realist. I'm the primary suspect in this murder. I'd be a fool not to know it." She glanced up at the men working at the top of the stairs. "One of them even implied that I staged last night's break-in to distract them from the main issue."

"Do you have any idea why someone was here?"

"Well, if they came for money, they made a big mistake. We don't do any transactions in cash. We're paid by check, and we pay our suppliers by check. There's nothing to steal."

"That probably means that the break-in had something to do with the murder," Susan suggested.

"Or some kids. There are thousands of reasons that people do these things. Maybe it was a competing company that wanted the secret of our fried chocolate truffles."

Susan's mouth began to water at the thought of the confections with the crisp outside and the meltingly soft centers. She herself had wondered how they were made. "How did the person get in?" she asked, reminding herself what she was supposed to be doing here.

"Through the back doorway—the one that goes out into the courtyard. Apparently it hadn't been dead bolted, and whoever it was just broke one of the tiny panes of glass, reached in, and turned the knob."

"You don't have an alarm system?"

"Oh, we do. In this day and age, there's no way to get insurance without it. But we don't bother to set it until our day's work is over. We catered three parties yesterday. People were working here from six A.M. until well after one A.M. today."

"But apparently there were times when no one was here—like when the break-in occurred."

"True. But people come and go. Catering a party involves lots and lots of hard work, but things go wrong—you can depend on it."

"What sort of things?" Susan asked, following Gwen up the stairs.

"Well, let's see. We once catered a wedding where, in the middle of the service, the bride decided that she preferred the best man to the groom."

"What happened?"

"Well, there was a lot of shouting and a lot more tears, but it turned out that the best man was in love with the bride. So the service was reconvened, and they plighted their troth. I suppose that would have been fine except that the groom's family had been paying for half of a very expensive reception, and they decided that was one burden they didn't have to bear. The new groom's family wasn't in a position to pick up such a large tab. It was a huge wedding—over three hundred of their nearest and dearest—and we weren't going to start serving until we got paid. We expect some losses in this business, but not willingly. Luckily a rich uncle of the bride announced that he'd chip in, and all was well." She opened the door to her office and peeked in. "Looks like they're through here. Come on in. I'll tell you more stories of our near disasters."

"Such as?" Susan asked, accepting a cup of coffee.

"Well, there was the time that seventeen pounds of spiced shrimp collided with twenty dozen freshly shucked oysters minutes before they were to be served with cocktails at the opening of an art gallery. All that was left was the raw vegetable platter with tofu dip that was to be offered to anyone with a shellfish allergy."

"What did you do?"

"Robbed Peter to pay Paul. Luckily the event was just down in Westchester County so we could dash back here and pick up the seafood pates that had been made for a party the next day. Someone headed for the best bakery in Connecticut and bought out their supply of French bread to serve with them. Our fish supplier had special ordered the oysters for us, but he had dozens of tiny clams on hand, so we served them raw with the horseradish sauce that was for the oysters. We gave the client a very large discount. . . ."

"And he didn't object?"

"As it was his black Lab who had dumped the food in the first place, he really couldn't."

"Then you didn't actually have to come up with a substitute, did you?"

"Oh yes, we did. We have a reputation to maintain. For some insane reason, everyone wants to own a catering business. There's a lot of competition out there. We're the best because we work the hardest, and we adapt to any crisis. Balloons fly off, flowers wilt, band members show up too high to even find their instruments, much less play them, but the party goes on. And it goes on in the style people have come to expect from us. We cater special occasions. They're important moments for our clients. We work hard to make them special—no matter what happens."

Susan wondered why she felt that she was hearing a sales pitch.

"But we have to be on our toes and ready to improvise at the last minute. And that means dashing in and out of here a thousand times a day. And that's why we don't set the alarms. They'd be going off all the time. Want a cookie?"

Susan chose from the tray offered and continued her questions. "Thanks. So you allow all your employees equal access to the carriage house?"

"Pretty much. We have to be very careful who we hire. Everyone who works for us is bonded. They have to be. They work in homes where there are many opportunities to steal valuables. If they're not honest, we'd have a serious problem. Actually, we did once. One of the girls we hired to serve was stealing. Just small things, so it wasn't picked up at first. You know, a silver teaspoon here and there. But then she stole a candlestick that had actually been made by Paul Revere. Naturally, it was noticed immediately, and we conducted a search. It was found in her locker. We apologized profusely to the person that employed us, of course. Our employer that night was a famous psychiatrist, and as the young woman agreed to go into treatment for whatever her problem was, the whole affair was dropped. Of course, we didn't charge for our services that evening. He hired us when his daughter was married two years later, in fact. That was in the city."

"New York?"

"Yes. We do a lot of work there as well as in Connecticut and some in Westchester County."

"But you've never had problems with things vanishing from the carriage house?"

"No. What is there to steal here? Food? Some expensive kitchenware? No, I think whoever broke in here just plain made a stupid mistake." The phone on her desk rang, and Gwen excused herself and picked up the receiver. "Hello. The Holly and Ms. Ivy."

As the frown on Gwen's face became a scowl, Susan got up and left the room. Curious though she was, it was obvious that Gwen needed some privacy. She strolled out into the hallway, once again looking at the photographs of previous parties. She recognized Henry Kissinger in one photo and the view of Central Park that only an East Side penthouse affords in another. It was fairly obvious that these were posed publicity photographs, and it occurred to Susan that there wasn't any name dropping at The Holly and Ms. Ivy. She must ask Gwen if the confidentiality of her clients was guaranteed as well as the safety of their belongings when The Holly and Ms. Ivy catered a party.

As it seemed the conversation was going to continue for a long while, Susan moved farther away from the small office. The end of the hallway opened onto the large space that Gwen had mentioned yesterday. Here a round table was encircled by six chairs, where discussions could be held and decisions made. To help make those decisions, the walls were lined with shelves displaying dozens of napkins, swatches of tablecloth fabric, and many vases. There were rows of books that Susan knew contained photographs of balloons, floral displays, and the like. She hadn't planned her party here. Gwen had come to her house bringing those books along with her.

Susan picked up a linen napkin with tiny flowers embroidered around the hem and thought about the murdered man. She'd known her share of charming men, but even she had to admit that Z was at the top of her list. He was the type of man who expected to be liked, the type of man who called her Sue immediately after meeting her (although, in fact, she was known as Susan). He was probably a man who had always been liked by women. Sensitive, charming, good-looking, he was almost too good to be true, like the hero in a bad novel. Susan had been a little surprised to find out that Jed liked him.

Initially, she knew, Jed had been put off by the fact that Z was only known by his first initial, but they had met one evening when Z was checking out Susan's kitchen equipment, and that had been the last criticism she'd ever heard. Jed had been pleased when Susan hired The Holly and Ms. Ivy, saying that she deserved a break. He was smart enough to quickly add that he would miss her wonderful food and . . . uh, everything else.

That's when Susan began planning the fun she was going to have the week after Christmas. No longer one long session in the kitchen, which, let's face it, was a lot of tiring work, no matter how much she enjoyed doing it. Free from that, she had accepted invitations to every party she was asked to attend, more than one on some nights. Thinking about all this reminded her of their engagement this afternoon. She walked back down the hall and, hearing Gwen's voice raised in anger this time, sped up as she passed that doorway and went back downstairs. Maybe she could find out something from Jamie—wherever she was.

Fortunately, the long red braid was easy to find in the sea of chef's jackets, and Susan hurried over to Jamie's counter, hoping she wasn't interrupting something important.

"Thank goodness you're here. I tried to call your house, but your husband said you'd already left," the woman muttered, not looking up from the basket she was fashioning from chou paste. "You didn't tell Gwen about last night, did you?"

"About last night?" Susan repeated, not understanding the concern.

They had been joined by the young man who'd served dinner at the Logans. "She didn't say anything, did she?" he hissed.

"About what?" Susan insisted on knowing.

"About last night. About being here," he said, apparently thinking that was an explanation.

"She must know you were here," Susan insisted.

"We don't want her to know *you* were here. We're not supposed to have people in the building outside of regular working hours," Jamie explained. "Of course, you didn't know that, so if you said anything . . ."

"I didn't," Susan reassured them, and the young man went back to his own work with a look of relief on his face. "But why doesn't she want people around?"

"Oh," Jamie began, "that's not true. This was designed to be seen. Believe me, most catering firms are nothing like this. Everything is clean, of course, but utilitarian. The stoves aren't colored; the pots and pans are hung up for convenience, not as an attractive display; the employees wear clean white clothing, but not with this fancy embroidery; and the rooms they work in are nowhere near as attractive as this one."

Susan looked around. "So this is . . . ?" She didn't know how to finish the question.

"This is part of the charm of The Holly and Ms. Ivy. Part of what makes this firm unique."

Susan nodded. "And part of what you're selling."

"Exactly. And no one is supposed to see behind the scenes. It ruins the illusion."

"And Gwen insists on all this?" Susan asked, becoming interested in the extraordinary skill Jamie was displaying in her work.

"Well, Gwen will now, but I think it was Z's idea to begin with. When I first came to work here, he was the one who explained to me that all this had been designed to be seen. That's why the customers who come to the carriage house have to walk through all this to go upstairs and talk with Z."

Susan wondered if Z had created illusions about other things as well—perhaps even himself. But she didn't have any time to think about it. There was a loud yell, and Gwen got the attention of everyone in the room at the same time.

"I want an exact list of who made what for the Logan's party last night," she called down in an angry voice. "Which one of you is trying to kill our clients?"

ELEVEN

"AND SO IT TURNED OUT THAT TWO PEOPLE WERE COMplaining about upset stomachs this morning? That's all?" Jed was driving carefully as the unpaved road leading to the Gordons' cabin followed a winding stream. One skid on the snow-covered surface could send them into the partially frozen water.

"It sounded more serious than that," Susan said, peering out the window at the road ahead. "Is it snowing harder?"

"I was just thinking that it was slowing down," Jed answered, gripping the wheel tightly. "But I don't recognize any of this, do you?"

"Places always look different without any leaves on the trees," his wife answered, then returned to the original subject. "I think it was more serious than that. One of the guests went to the hospital. Dan something or other . . ."

"You're not talking about Dan Irving, are you?"

"That's it! Dan Irving. He went to the emergency room in the middle of the night. He tho—"

"—thought he was having a heart attack." Jed surprised her by finishing the sentence. "Dan always thinks he's having a heart attack. He's a hypochondriac. I used to play golf with him, but listening to his many symptoms made me sick. Some of the doctors at the club kid about the emergency room having forms made up ahead of time with his name and insurance information. The symptoms are left out—but not the diagnosis. Indigestion. That man believes every gas pain is fatal.

"I think we're lost," Jed added, changing the subject.

"What? Where are we?"

"If I knew that, we wouldn't be lost, would we?" Jed said, so patiently that Susan wanted to scream at him. "I do know that I've seen that barn up there more than once today."

Susan peered out the window. "I don't remember it."

"You were looking at the directions," Jed reminded her.

"Jerry's handwriting is very artistic, but it's impossible to read. What's this word? Ridge? What does 'Right on the ridge' mean?"

Jed slowly applied his foot to the brake and glanced over at the sheet of paper his wife held. "That says 'Right at the bridge.' That's what we did wrong. We were supposed to turn back at that sign that says one-lane bridge ahead. You said left."

"There was a sign there that pointed to Ridge Way Farm. I thought it said ridge. I thought we were supposed to turn toward the farm. You work with Jerry. You know his handwriting. Why didn't you just let me drive? We might even be there by now."

"You said you didn't want to drive. You wanted to look at the pretty Christmas decorations in all the little New England towns, remember?"

"Not over and over. I didn't want to see the same towns more than once. I never said that."

"Maybe we should have stopped for lunch."

Susan scowled. Her irritation didn't necessarily have anything to do with low blood sugar. At least that was all he would accuse her of having. They'd been married well over twenty years; Jed knew that one more mention of PMS would be fatal. "I'm sure Kathleen will have lots of food," was all she said.

They were quiet for a while before Susan spoke again. "There was a lot of drinking going on, but I don't suppose anyone would confuse a hangover with poison."

"Maybe someone had a hangover, but didn't want to admit to drinking so much and decided to blame the food," Jed suggested. "Besides, I don't see why this is so much of a problem. Someone gives a dinner party, and one or two people are sick afterward. What's the big deal? It could be the flu. It could be that they were allergic to one of the ingredients in something. I always wonder what's in those odd-colored pâtés—not the ones you make," he added quickly. "Anyway, it could even have been something they ate for lunch."

"Gwen seemed to be worried about the reputation of The Holly and Ms. Ivy."

"That's the catering company you hired to do our party on Saturday night? Well," he continued at his wife's nod, "I don't think they have to worry about business. Even I've heard of them, and from what I've heard, we were damn lucky to get them. Someone at work wanted them to cater his daughter's wedding next summer, and the company was fully booked. I suppose we should start thinking about where Chrissy is going to get married. . . ."

"What? She's barely started college. What did she say to you?"

"Just kidding," Jed assured his shrieking wife. "She didn't say a word to me about getting married or anything else."

"Don't scare me like that."

"I suppose you and Kathleen are going to spend the afternoon trying to figure out who killed Z. Jerry and I will have to amuse ourselves—and take care of Ban."

"Kathleen and I aren't involved in this investigation."

"You're not trying to convince me that you weren't running all over town asking questions while I was in the city yesterday. I know you better than that, hon."

"I did a little checking around," she admitted, "but not with Kathleen. Kathleen is helping Brett. They don't want me involved—not this time."

"What's different about this time?"

Susan just realized what she'd gotten herself into. What was she going to do? Tell her husband that Kathleen and Brett thought she had a crush on Z? But wouldn't he hear sooner or later? "It's a question of attachment," she began slowly, and glanced over to see her husband's reaction.

He nodded. "Kathleen and Brett. Right?"

Susan was so stunned that she couldn't think of anything to say immediately.

"I suppose it's not a surprise," Jed continued. "She and Brett were involved when they first came to town. Jerry is a lot older than she is. Maybe it's just something that was bound to happen. I sure hope Jerry doesn't hear about it. It would kill him."

Susan had no idea what to say, but she knew she couldn't let her husband believe this. "Kathleen would never have an affair with anyone! She loves Jerry," she insisted.

"I know that, but sometimes people find someone else attractive and they . . . they flirt."

Susan glanced over at her husband, wondering exactly what he was talking about. Or who he was talking about.

But she didn't think about it for long. The small log cabin tucked in the grove of white pine miraculously appeared in front of them. Jerry and his son were busy building a snowman next to the pine-draped porch railing. Wood smoke curled from the stone chimney as Jed parked the car. Susan got out and waved hello. and, as her husband walked over to join the males, headed into the house.

As she expected, a large fire burned cheerfully in the fireplace, warming the room. A small pine tree had been cut and stood on an old bench across the rear wall of the room, its trunk wrapped in a red and green striped linen dish towel, tiny brass and pewter ornaments hanging on its boughs. Antique elves marched in a line across the heavy fir mantel toward bayberry candles standing in birch holders, Susan's gift to the house. But not all her expectations were met. She had certainly thought Kathleen would be at home.

The first floor was almost entirely a great room that served as both living and dining areas; behind that lay a long red-and-white kitchen; a tiny half bath was tucked under the stairs that led to four small bedrooms and two minuscule baths on the second floor. It didn't take long for

Susan to realize that she was alone—and that no one had been busy preparing their dinner. The kitchen was immaculate except for an open bottle of apple juice on the counter near the refrigerator and an empty glass in the sink. Susan decided Kathleen must be out buying or picking up dinner. And hopefully she'd get back soon. It looked like the snow was coming down more heavily.

Susan peered out the window. Jed's navy wool cap was now on top of the finished snowman, and an energetic snowball fight was taking place. She wondered if she should look around the kitchen for the ingredients of a hot drink or whether, as a guest, she could flop on the plaid couch near the fireplace and begin reading the paperback she'd stuck in her pocket before leaving home.

She had just chosen the book when she heard another car drive up. Kathleen! Thank goodness the men were still outside. They could carry in all the groceries, deli, or whatever Kathleen was planning to serve for dinner. She was just opening her book when the door opened, and Jerry's parents appeared. Bananas was being held high in the air by his grandfather, and Jerry's mother carried a large, white bakery box tied with red ribbons. Jed and Jerry tagged behind, their arms full of brown grocery bags.

"I hope," Mrs. Gordon said, after wishing Susan a merry Christmas, "that Kathleen told you what she planned for dinner. We bought everything on the list, but I have no idea what she was planning to concoct. . . ."

"Where is Kathleen?" Susan got up from the couch, feeling fairly certain that her lounging time had ended.

"Didn't she call? That good-looking young detective appeared at the door in Hancock, and she just asked if we would stop on the way up and buy the groceries. Then she took off. I suppose we'd better get everything put away and dinner started. It sure didn't look like she was planning to come up today."

Susan followed the other woman's gaze toward Jerry and watched as he turned his back on his mother. What was going on here? Was it possible that Jed was right—that Kathleen and Brett were involved? She stared into the fire, oblivious to the activity going on around her.

Kathleen had claimed that Susan couldn't be part of this investigation because of her feelings for Z. But Susan knew that her relationship with Z had been a professional one and that any other thoughts or fantasies on her part were just that—fantasies. And there hadn't been any reason for anyone to think anything else. In fact, now that she thought about it, there was no way Kathleen could have even imagined that Susan and Z meant anything personal to each other. So the only other reason for Susan to be excluded from the investigation was—she stopped, unwilling to accept the next thought. Kathleen and Brett?

She had met them together years and years ago, both members of the state police, on duty in Hancock to investigate a murder. Kathleen had appeared to disdain what she imagined were the lives of suburban women. And Susan might never have seen or heard from her again if Kathleen hadn't been so attractive. Because when a police department is looking for an officer to speak at an elementary-school career day, they look second for competence, third for speaking skills, fourth for charm, and first for good looks. Kathleen, a stunning blonde, had fulfilled all the requirements.

When Susan had run into Kathleen in the city, a week before the program was scheduled to occur, she'd suggested that they make plans to lunch together after Kathleen's visit. That hospitable gesture led to an introduction to Jed's coworker and good friend, a widower. Jerry and Kathleen had married within the year.

When Brett had returned to Hancock, Susan had allowed herself to wonder (very briefly) about what sort of relationship had existed between Kathleen and him. But they had been friendly, nothing else, and Susan, slightly embarrassed by her thoughts, had gone on to other things. And now, years later, Jed had raised a question she thought was dead.

She followed Jerry's mother to the kitchen where it immediately became apparent that Susan's thinking on this subject was not unique.

"They're spending an awful lot of time together these days."

Susan glanced over at Mrs. Gordon, busily emptying the

brown bags onto the tile counter. Only her silver bun was visible.

"Kathleen and Brett?" Susan asked quietly, dropping arugula and bib lettuce into a bright red, enameled colander.

"Yes."

"They're working together," Susan leapt in with excuses. "Kathleen is helping Brett investigate Z's murder."

"I thought you usually did that."

"Well, yes, but . . ." Susan didn't know how to continue.

"Is there something different about this particular murder? Some reason why you're not involved this time?"

"Every murder investigation is different. Each one involves different people, different relationships." Susan began when Jerry came into the room, snow melting on his shoulders and a worried expression on his face. "Are you two going to be able to figure out the menu? Or maybe this is just too much work, and we should find a restaurant nearby. There's a diner in town. It's not fancy or anything, but . . ."

"There's no reason to spend a lot of money in a restaurant; we'll be fine here," his mother insisted. "Kathleen is always very well organized, and I've been hearing about Susan's ability in the kitchen for years."

"Yes," Susan agreed. "You're going to ruin my reputation if you keep doubting me, Jerry Gordon. You men just go on doing your own thing, and we'll produce a fabulous meal."

"You're sure?"

"Definitely." Susan started to sort ingredients into piles, hoping to see some sort of order emerge. "You go on back to the living room and ask how many hot buttered rums I should concoct." She had spied a bottle of Myers sitting by the refrigerator. "And your mom and I will cook a meal that will make you feel guilty for ever considering a restaurant."

"You're sure?"

"We're sure. We're sure," his mother insisted, a smile suddenly appearing on her face. "Aren't you ever going to learn not to question your own mother?"

Susan pulled a saucepan from the drawer under the stove

and filled it with apple juice, sprinkling in dark brown sugar and a cinnamon stick or two. She didn't know about everyone else, but she could use a drink.

She was surprised when Mrs. Gordon walked over and put an arm around her shoulder and gave her a gentle hug saying, "Don't worry. I'll keep your little secret."

"I . . ."

"You're right not to tell Jed. Now that the man is dead, it would only hurt him."

Susan, correctly translating the pronouns into people, decided to shut up and be thankful for small misunderstandings. Her reputation wasn't all that important . . . at least not as important as Kathleen's marriage.

The drink mixture was beginning to boil, and Susan found bright red mugs and plopped a ball of butter and a generous slug of rum into the bottom of each.

"Any ideas what this dinner is supposed to be?" Mrs. Gordon asked brightly. "I bought a lot of odd-looking mushrooms, and I managed to find the fresh fettuccine that Kathleen seemed to think she needed."

"Did you also buy sun-dried tomatoes and pecorino cheese?"

"Yes, but I certainly cannot imagine—"

"I can," Susan interrupted. "It's a wonderful pasta dish."

"Pasta!" Mrs. Gordon condemned the entire food group with one word. "Old-fashioned spaghetti is good enough for Dad and me."

"Well, then I'll make the past—spaghetti," Susan offered. "The salad is easy, with greens and a champagne vinaigrette dressing."

"We prefer Kraft Lo Cal."

"Maybe garlic bread . . ." Susan pulled a long thin baguette from its package.

"Garlic really doesn't agree with Dad and me."

"There is a wonderful panettone for dessert."

"I picked up a pie at a bakery on the way here. It's cranberry cream."

"Wonderful!" Susan enthused loudly. "We'll just have that." She carefully pushed the panettone to the back of the counter. She recognized it as one of Kathleen's mom's creations—always something to look forward to. "Why don't you serve the hot buttered rum and rest? After all, you did all the shopping. I can fix the dinner."

"Well, okay." Mrs. Gordon picked up the tray Susan had prepared. "But I hope there's not too much rum in these things. Dad and I aren't really accustomed to drinking a lot of alcohol."

The door swung shut behind her, and Susan leaned against the counter with a sigh of relief. She was inexplicably excluded from the current murder investigation; her reputation was in shreds; she was going to prepare a meal that a third of the guests would hate; but (count your blessings, kid) she didn't have to spend the holidays with Kathleen's in-laws.

Dinner didn't quite live up to Susan's worst expectations. True, the food that Jerry's mother didn't absolutely reject, she sniffed and ate with obvious reluctance (making no effort to hide those feelings either, Susan thought). But Jerry's father (who had consumed two mugs of hot buttered rum) ate everything with obvious relish. Jed and Jerry, busy talking about cutbacks at the ad agency where they both worked, didn't pay much attention to what they were eating. And Bananas, left to his own devices, ate almost half a loaf of garlic bread, ignored his salad, sorted the different varieties of wild mushrooms into five distinct piles, gulped down his orange juice, and inquired politely about the availability of the dessert course—specifically, where were the Christmas cookies?

"We're having cranberry cream pie, sweetie," his grandmother stopped frowning at her husband long enough to tell the little boy. "You'll like that, won't you?"

"Yes, Grannie."

Susan was profoundly impressed; it was easy to see that Bananas was disappointed. There wasn't a chance in the world that her own children would ever have shown such manners and self-discipline at his young age.

"Grannie has a bag of Christmas candy in her purse for you, too, sweetie." Jerry's mother redeemed herself in Susan's eyes as Bananas ran off to collect his prize.

A few minutes later, she was wishing she could be sucking on a candy cane, too. The bakery that made the pie had apparently mixed huge amounts of sugar, Dream Whip, and cranberries, and then filled prepackaged pie dough with the resulting mess. Susan gagged her way through a large slice, trying not to remember the wonderful Italian sweet-bread rejected and waiting in the kitchen.

Kathleen failed to appear, and Susan was wondering if she was going to have to do the dishes as well as cook the dinner when what Mrs. Gordon was saying came into focus.

"... her dress was still at the cleaners, so I guess she's not going to be attending. I understand the attire is formal."

"What?" Susan was aware of the fact that her impolite squawk had startled everyone.

"Kathleen was planning on attending the Hancock hospital holiday ball. Didn't you know?"

Susan stared at Jerry's mother and didn't answer.

"It had something to do with the murder of this caterer," Jerry added. "Kathleen called while you were in the kitchen. She said she won't be out tonight after all." He looked down at his son. "So we're going to go back to Hancock and wait for her, aren't we, Ban?"

"You live a very irregular life," his mother said.

"We do," Jerry replied, putting his arm around his son and hugging him. "But we like it that way, don't we, sport?"

Bananas, his mouth full of marshmallow snowman, didn't speak, and Susan was once again impressed with the child's manners. "What's going on at this benefit?"

"The Holly and Ms. Ivy are catering it," Jerry answered. "Kathleen and Brett felt it was important to attend for some reason, but it looks like they changed their minds."

"Really?" Susan absentmindedly put a forkful of fatty crust in her mouth. "Any reason why?" she asked, working to keep from gagging.

"Those two sure spend a lot of time together," Jerry's father commented casually.

"The Hancock police department was certainly lucky when Kathleen moved to town," Jed leapt into the conversation.

"But you're the lucky one this time. Your wife isn't involved in this . . . this investigation. You have your family together for the holidays," Jerry's mother insisted.

Susan, realizing that Jed was trying to protect Jerry from the possibility that Kathleen was involved with Brett and that Mrs. Gordon was trying to protect Jed from thinking that she had had an affair with Z, would have smiled if she hadn't been working so hard to figure out how to get to that party and do a little investigating herself. She was so busy thinking that she almost didn't hear what Jerry's father was talking about.

". . . then we'd just mingle like we belonged there. Got some pretty good meals that way, as I recall," he said, chuckling.

"You did what?" Susan asked.

"Don't listen to him. He's always talking about the nefarious deeds of him and his college buddies."

"But you said that you used to sneak into big charity balls?" Susan asked.

"All the time. I'd come home for the holidays, and the *New York Times* would have lists of upcoming balls. I'd pick one or two, borrow my father's tux, and go."

"How did you get in? Don't you need an invitation or a ticket of some sort?" Susan was so intent on her question that she didn't realize the sleeve of her favorite white cotton sweater was soaking up cranberry juice from her plate.

"It's a piece of cake. Security wasn't such a big deal back then, of course, but I'd just attach myself to the edge of a friendly group and walk right in. A friend of mine used to pretend to be one of the waiters—at formal affairs it's difficult to tell the difference between the staff and the male guests in their tuxes."

"Men!" his mother sniffed.

"Women are actually better at gate-crashing than men," Jerry insisted. "No one bothers to check out the credentials of a good-looking woman if she walks in next to a man—someone whose wife is in the ladies room, perhaps. Kathleen could do it in a pinch."

"I'm sure Kathleen wouldn't have been forced to deceive

anyone to get into a party. After all, she's working with the police department."

"I didn't mean this thing tonight, Mother. I meant in general."

"Yes . . . Well, I guess it's time to clear the table."

Susan jumped to her feet. "Yes, definitely." She grabbed all the dessert plates and hurried to the kitchen. She wasn't the type of person who could go to a formal ball without hours of preparation—not if she was going to sneak in with neither an invitation nor a police escort.

TWELVE

THERE WAS A TINY RUN IN ONE LEG OF HER SHIMMERING pantyhose, a small wine stain on the left side of her satin skirt (she had forgotten to send it to the cleaners after the last black-tie affair she'd attended), her makeup was rather hastily applied, and she didn't want to think what her impromptu French twist looked like from behind, but her new emerald earrings were a hit.

In fact, the earrings had much to do with the fact that no one questioned her entrance into the ballroom. It certainly wasn't on account of her good looks, Susan admitted to herself, avoiding her own reflection in the gilt-framed mirrors that lined the room.

But, while checking her coat, the earrings caught the eye of a beautifully dressed elderly woman. She asked about them, Susan responded, and if the other woman was startled by the way Susan stuck by her side until they had entered the ballroom, her manners didn't allow her to comment.

Having reached her objective, Susan smiled at her companion, waved at an imagined friend on the other side of the room, and took off. She accepted a flute of champagne from a handsome young waiter and headed for a tiny table set up in a dark corner. Years of waiting for a chronically late husband had provided her with lots of practice fading into the background. She put what she hoped was a perky

113

look on her face, sipped her champagne, and wondered why she was here.

It was the question she'd been asking herself since leaving the cabin. She'd cleaned the kitchen, taken Jed aside and explained what she was planning to do, and ignoring her husband's disapproval, had driven home, leaving Jed to ride with Jerry.

And then she started wondering exactly why Kathleen and Brett had been planning to attend this party, what they had hoped or expected to find—and where they were now. Refusing numerous offers of elegant appetizers from trays passed by The Holly and Ms. Ivy's staff, she realized that she didn't have a single answer. She didn't even have any questions.

The perimeters of the room were banked with what looked like hundreds of white poinsettias, and tall balsams, hung with miles of silver tinsel, surrounded columns supporting the ceiling. Susan noticed couples she had known for years, and a few doctors who knew more intimate things about her than she liked to consider, talking and laughing together. They would move into the main room to dine and dance. A massive blue spruce stood near the doorway between the two rooms, and Susan got up for a closer look at it, taking her glass along with her.

The tree was decorated with dozens of boxes wrapped in pink-and-silver paper and tied to the branches with gold ribbons. Gillian Davies and Alexis Cutler were chatting nearby.

"I'm just like a kid about Christmas presents," Alexis was saying.

"This isn't a Christmas present. It's a party favor," Gillian contradicted her rather sternly. "I don't see why tiny bottles of perfume or Swiss Army knives are things to get all that excited about myself."

"I wonder if anyone would mind if I took a man's gift. I'm allergic to so many brands of perfume," Alexis said, fingering one of the silver boxes.

"Maybe you can trade with your date." Susan was surprised by how catty Gillian sounded.

"He's not effeminate! Just because I don't feel a need to sleep with every man I date—"

"Whatever you say," Gillian answered in a manner that let her companion know exactly what she thought about that subject.

"Just because he didn't make a pass at you, doesn't mean he's not interested in women. He may be simply more discerning than your usual companions!" Alexis hissed.

Susan was edging forward, wondering if she was in time to prevent bloodshed, when Alexis stomped off, leaving Gillian alone under the tree with a smile on her face. Susan was hoping to leave without being noticed when Gillian turned and spied her. "Susan! I didn't know you were there."

"I was just looking for . . . for the ladies' room," Susan improvised.

"It's easy to find, just look for a line of women. In fact, I'll go with you.

"I suppose you heard us," she said, as Susan followed her across the room.

Susan nodded.

"I shouldn't have said all that to her," Gillian said.

Susan agreed.

"She's so upset about Z's death."

"Well, of course it's upsetting when someone you know dies suddenly."

"It's even more upsetting when someone you love dies," Gillian insisted. With her English accent, it sounded like a line from *Masterpiece Theatre*. Only this was real, Susan reminded herself, hurrying to keep up with Gillian.

The ladies' room was, as Gillian had suggested, crowded, and they joined the line, making the standard humorous comments to each other and the women who had suddenly become their companions in waiting. They couldn't talk without being overheard, so Susan was forced to wait.

A booth was finally available, and Susan hurried in, wondering if it would be possible to accomplish her task without completely shredding her damaged stockings. She was pulling them up as carefully as possible when she overheard a conversation that caused her to forget sartorial considerations.

"I heard that Z used to make fresh *tekka maki* for the two of them afterward . . ." a voice announced from the booth to her left.

"Sex and sushi—sounds good to me." The appreciation came from the booth to her right.

"I don't know. I'd have a difficult time sleeping with a man that young . . . I find it impossible to keep my stomach sucked in for more than a few minutes at a time."

"That's why dark rooms were invented, my dear."

Susan bent down and peeked under the bottom of her booth. Black silk heels, black stockings, and the bottoms of long black dresses surrounded her. Since every other woman in the room was wearing black, Susan didn't see how this information was going to help her identify the speakers. And she was beginning to wonder if every other woman in the room had been involved with Z when she heard something that argued against this particular conclusion.

Left side spoke up again. "I don't believe it."

"You don't believe that they had an affair? Why would she lie about it?"

"Oh, you know Lauren. If it's the chic thing to do, she does it. Remember her roller-blade period. And when she believed that aromatherapy was going to bring world peace."

"And when she heard that Princess Di was bulimic, she started . . ."

"No way. You're kidding!"

"She bragged about it," the left side insisted.

"I love it. Did you hear . . ." But the toilet flushed, and the hinged doors slammed, and Susan didn't.

The run got just a little wider as she hurried to catch up with the speakers, but they blended into the crowd of black silk, velvet, and rhinestones gathered before well-lit mirrors. Susan looked around and discovered that she had been abandoned by Gillian. She suspected it was intentional and rejoined the party.

This time, one of the people guarding the doorway actually smiled at her, and Susan was beginning to think that this gate-crashing was as easy as Jerry had said, when she felt a hand press down on her shoulder.

"If you'll just come this way, ma'am."

Susan followed the black back of the tall man's tuxedo, wondering if she was going to be arrested. He was leading her down a long hallway with scuffed walls that spoke of heavy use. Was there a holding cell at the end of their path? "Maybe I could just buy a ticket . . ." she began.

"I don't think that will be necessary. We rarely charge admission to the kitchen."

Susan, startled, looked up into the eyes of the chef who had been working in the Logans' kitchen the previous night. "I thought you were a . . . well, a bouncer," she admitted.

"You're gate-crashing! A society matron like you! I don't believe it. I always thought that type of thing was confined to fraternity stunts."

"It's not something I usually do," Susan insisted, deciding not to bother to explain the difference between a middle-aged woman with an interest in civic affairs and a society matron to the young man.

"Hey, I believe you. . . ." He pushed open a swinging door and motioned for her to precede him into the bustling room.

Susan stopped so suddenly that the door smacked her from behind. "Wow."

"I gather you've never been in the kitchen while an event this size is being held," the young man said.

"No. I've never been in the kitchen of your average restaurant," Susan admitted.

"Well, of course, most of the actual cooking was done back at the carriage house—except for the fillets and the salmon with green peppercorns; that's the first course—very Christmassy it looks . . ."

"The main course is fillet of beef?"

"Or duck *confit*—that can be made ahead. And there are about a half dozen special meals—braised flounder cooked with mixed herbs—no salt and no fat."

Susan was wondering if that was the choice of the cardiologists or just their patients when she saw Jamie waving at her from the other side of the room. She glanced at her escort, and he nodded.

"That's right. She wanted to talk to you."

"Is Gwen Ivy around?"

"She just left," he said. "But she might be back, so . . ."

"I'll just go see what Jamie wants," Susan said, understanding his unspoken concern.

"I'd better get back to work. I think I heard something break behind the bar as I passed. Oh, don't worry," he added, seeing the expression on her face. "We expect that. We bring a lot of extra everything to events this size. Sometime, when this is all over, ask me to tell you about the time our van carrying glassware was in an accident two blocks from the Waldorf."

Susan smiled and hurried off, making her way through the room, past trays of food under warming lights, people bending over massive steamers full of barely born vegetables, yards of bacon-wrapped fillets, and dozens of crocks coated with rich yellow fat. She told herself that she couldn't possibly be hungry, but on this particular point, self-delusion wasn't her strong point.

Jamie Potter was working on the other side of the room. Susan walked around a line of six empty metal tables to get to what seemed to be the dessert area. "The appetizers were there—but they're all outside now. We try to keep desserts and the main course separate—no one wants cassis torte that tastes like beef broth."

Susan couldn't argue with that. "That's the torte?" she asked, looking at the large sponge cake that Jamie was brushing with imported crème de cassis.

"One of them." Jamie pointed. "We've made thirty in the last twenty-four hours. It's my favorite dessert, and I made a few extra. Let me get you a slice . . ."

"Oh, I don't . . ."

But apparently Jamie recognized that this was a half-hearted protest. She cut a slice off a cake with a dented side, put it on a plate, and doused it liberally with light English cream sauce. "Prepare yourself. It's wonderful."

It was. "But you didn't bring me down here as an official

dessert taster, did you?" Susan asked, eyeing large platters of petit fours and Godiva chocolates.

"No, we always have enough volunteers for that."

"Although if that bitchy mayor's wife keeps slandering us . . . ," a chef who was artistically arranging the trays began.

"The Holly and Ms. Ivy doesn't serve bad food," Jamie insisted rather loudly. "And if Gwen ever hears you talking about a client like that you're not going to have a job," she added.

"I'm a temp. I go back to school next week." The young woman shrugged and continued on down the table.

"Everyone's saying that, Mrs. Henshaw. That's why I wanted to talk with you."

"I did hear something about food poisoning, but Jed said that the man who complained is a hypochondriac and—"

"The mayor is a hypochondriac—"

"No, Dan Irving," Susan said. "You're telling me that Buck Logan got sick after the party last night?"

"I don't know. I heard what you heard about two guests being ill. And later, Mayor Logan's attorney called and threatened to sue. I was in the office when the call came in."

Susan wiped the plate with the last bite of her cake and put it in her mouth. "Why don't you tell me everything you know about it?"

"Do you think it has something to do with the murder?"

"I have no idea, but it might."

"Well, I was busy working. I had all these cakes to put together—the sponge layers have been frozen for a few weeks—and all the truffles to decorate after they were made, and Gwen was up in her office."

"That's unusual?"

"Not at all." Jamie picked up a fresh bottle and poured its purple contents into the bowl she was using. "Gwen or Z are very hands-on people. One of them was always around. And now Gwen is always around. We were talking about it today. She's going to need a new partner—it's too big a job for one person to do alone."

"The food poisoning." Susan insisted on returning to the

topic at hand, although not without noting that a potential future partner in a concern like this one might have a motive to murder the person he or she hoped to replace.

"Gwen was there when I got in. As well as four or five other people. But Gwen spent most of the day up in her office. The door was closed, but I guess she was talking on the phone. At least, I was busy slicing the cake layers—"

"You slice them frozen!"

"Yes, of course, it's much easier to get them thin without breaking them that way." Jamie frowned. "You're distracting me."

"Sorry. Go on."

"Well, I was slicing the cakes . . . Just let me strain the sauce anglaise. Sometimes lumps form as it cools."

"Can I help?" Susan offered. She hadn't known that strainers the size of the one Jamie pulled out from under the counter existed.

"No. I'm used to doing this alone," Jamie insisted, getting tall glass pitchers of custard from a nearby refrigerator and starting to work.

"Anyway, I went upstairs to check with Gwen about how many cakes we were going to need tonight, and she told me that she had been receiving calls from the mayor's wife all day long and that the Logans' lawyer had just called to announce that the Logans were planning to sue The Holly and Ms. Ivy for personal damages—or something like that. She was even more upset than she was over Z's death. It was horrible. I guess these last few days have just been too much for her."

The story was interrupted when two waiters ran into the room, slamming the metal swinging doors against the walls and yelling. "We need damp towels quickly! Cool damp towels! Come on, guys!"

Susan looked and realized that vomit was running down the tuxedos that the two men wore.

She didn't know what she was going to find when she joined the group running down the hallway to the room where cocktails were still being served, but she certainly didn't expect to almost trip over her own daughter, kneeling on the floor and holding the head of an elderly matron over what looked like a crystal vase full of vomit.

"Did you bring paper towels?" Chrissy asked, not taking the time to look up and recognize her mother.

"I'm terribly sorry to be such a bother." The woman gasped for enough breath to get the words out.

"No bother at all," Chrissy assured the sick woman, smoothing back her grey hair.

Susan, astounded by her daughter's competence, went to search for supplies.

The room was almost empty. Six or seven guests were suffering from upset stomachs, and one or two people were gathered around each one. Employees of The Holly and Ms. Ivy were rushing between the groups passing out large white dinner napkins. A tall man in a double-breasted tuxedo was walking between the groups, portable phone to his ear, medical bag in his hand. As Susan watched, four paramedics entered the room, equipment and stretchers smashing against the doors and snow falling from their clothing onto the shining parquet floor. Susan backed up and leaned against the wall. She didn't want to be in the way, but she sure did want to see what was going on.

The stench was pretty foul, and one or two of the guests left, gagging, as professional help continued to arrive. Every few minutes a door would open, and someone would pass in pitchers of water and heavy, white bath towels. As the doors opened and closed, Susan could hear the band playing show tunes, otherwise it was unnaturally quiet in the ballroom. Remembering the Logans' response to last night's problems, Susan wondered how many guests were calling lawyers on their cellular phones.

A second and third group of paramedics had arrived. The most serious cases had been stabilized and carried off on stretchers. There were more dirty towels being gathered up than clean ones given out when Gwen Ivy arrived.

She walked in through double doors left open by the last group to leave and stamped across the floor to the middle of the room, the layers of green and cream silk shantung she wore shimmering even after she stopped moving. Hands clenched, she revolved slowly and glared at all corners of the room, absolutely silent. And just as Susan was sure she was going to speak, a heavyset, middle-aged man with a remarkably red nose, his bow tie undone, his cummerbund falling around his hips, stumbled into the room, leaned against a stand of poinsettias, and groaned. "Someone has to help me. I think I'm having a heart attack."

Which is how Susan found out that Dan Irving was the man she'd always thought of as that drunk down at the club. She didn't know what everyone else thought of him, but she noticed that his statement was not regarded as compelling by at least half of the people present. As he slid to the floor, one of the medics strolled over, pulled Dan Irving's arm from his cuff and took his pulse with a bored look on her face—and then screamed. "Shit! This man's really sick. Where's that damn doctor?"

The man with the medical bag hurried to her side, calling over his shoulder as he went. "Go next door and find John Travers. Tell him we need a cardiologist in here right away. This man's in cardiac arrest."

THIRTEEN

SUSAN WOKE UP DETERMINED TO START GETTING SOME answers—right after she stocked her freezer with appetizers. If The Holly and Ms. Ivy shut down, she'd need something to feed her guests come Saturday night. The gourmet deli downtown carried tiny frozen brioche and croissants with a variety of fillings—not terribly original, but better than nothing if seventy hungry people show up at the door.

Maybe she should think of laying in a supply of champagne, she thought, taking the dog on her morning walk. If they didn't need it for the party, it could always be used to celebrate other occasions, she decided, having absolutely no idea just what such an occasion might be. Chrissy's engagement? She pulled Clue away from the pile of soiled cocktail napkins that someone had dropped in the street. Her daughter had been asleep when she left the house, but Susan knew they had to talk. When, she wondered, was she going to meet this new boyfriend? And why hadn't Chrissy introduced him to her family before this?

It was garbage collection day, and Clue was having a ball, jumping around on the Christmas trees left at the curb by neighbors lucky enough to fly off to someplace warm after Christmas. Susan sighed, wondering if she was feeling a normal post–holiday depression. And then decided that three days before her big party was no time to get like this.

123

Clue's head was stuck in the middle of a large tinsel-strewn balsam. "Come on, Clue," Susan insisted, pulling on the leash. The dog shook her entire body and, with a ripping sound, emerged, a branch bearing a candy cane held proudly between her teeth. Susan chuckled, her dour mood vanishing. "How would you like to do some visiting with me today?" she asked the happy animal.

Clue apparently approved of the idea, and they walked companionably back to Susan's car. "You wait here, and I'll go get my purse," Susan told the dog, as the animal climbed into her backseat. She hurried into the house, thinking that one of the nicest things about golden retrievers is their ability to look as though they are intensely interested in everything anyone was saying—without understanding a single word.

Susan entered her kitchen and wondered exactly what she was doing there, before the sight of her purse on the table reminded her of her goal. Putting any thoughts of Alzheimer's away in the back of her mind (where they would surely be lost), she wrote a quick note to anyone in her family who might be interested in her whereabouts, grabbed her purse, and headed back to the car. First the appetizers, then she was going to visit Alexis and Gillian. They were both giving big parties that night; she knew she'd find them at their homes.

The gourmet shop in Hancock had started out as a cheese shop. But the Brie had needed baguettes, the Camembert required crackers, and then pâtés, soups, salads, cakes, pies, rare fruits, and vegetables had appeared on shelves and counters, until it became an all-purpose grocery—if your purpose was to purchase the finest and most costly food available. She hurried past the elegant fare to the large freezers at the rear of the store. To her surprise, they were empty. She turned and found the rather snotty proprietor standing behind her.

"I was looking for frozen appetizers," she explained.

"Frozen canapés," the woman corrected her.

"Yes. Well, where are they?"

"We're out."

"Are you going to be getting more in before Saturday?"

Susan asked as politely as she could manage between gritted teeth.

"We hope so. Would you like me to reserve some for you?"

"Please."

"You can put your name down on the list by the cash register," the woman explained, obviously too important to do such menial tasks.

There were two young women chatting together behind the counter by the cash register as Susan moved there to accomplish her task.

"We're certainly making a lot of money because of his death. Our orders were way down this season because The Holly and Ms. Ivy were doing so many parties in Hancock. But now, we're raking it in. Everyone is stocking up at the last moment—"

"Did you hear that The Holly and Ms. Ivy are folding?" Susan interrupted to ask anxiously.

"Not yet. But the people whose parties they're catering this week are certainly getting prepared. We're doing record business," one saleswoman answered.

"But what can we do to help you?" the other saleswoman asked.

"I'd like to put my name down on the list to reserve some frozen canapés when they come in later this week."

"Of course."

That business complete, Susan returned to her car and started out on her next task.

Hancock was a pre-Revolution stage stop that had grown from a small hamlet into a small town, becoming a suburb of New York City back in the fifties and, like much of this part of Connecticut, enjoying a boom in the affluent eighties. During that decade, the few vacant lots had been bought up by smart investors who had built large expensive homes, selling them off at a huge profit. Gillian and Alexis lived next door to each other in two of these homes. Both houses had all the eighties requirements: roofs jutting out in all directions, three-car garages, and windows in every shape imaginable. Inside there were multiple bathrooms (each equipped with a whirlpool), spacious eat-in kitchens, so that the elaborate dining rooms need not be used, and massive family rooms to keep the living rooms impeccable. Each house also boasted a master bedroom suite as well as two other bedrooms. Alexis's son hadn't lived with her since her divorce. Susan wondered who was sleeping in the extra bedrooms as she walked up the sidewalk to Alexis's front door.

A pair of blue-spruce wreaths hung on the white double doors, and Susan inhaled their fragrance as she knocked. It was ten o'clock on the morning of Alexis's big Christmas party. Susan knew exactly how terrible she was going to look at this time Saturday, but Alexis, when she opened the door, looked wonderful.

As always, she was dressed beautifully. Black leather slacks, a bold red-and-black, geometric-patterned sweater, and two or three black silk barrettes in her hair completed her ensemble, and Susan, as always, wished she had dressed more carefully this morning. When was she going to learn? In suburbia, casual was not to be confused with sloppy. She tugged at the waistband of her too-tight jeans and smiled. "Do you have a minute?"

"Of course." Alexis opened the doorway wider to permit her to enter. "It's about Z's death, isn't it?"

"Yes. I'm looking into it," Susan said, not exactly lying, but perhaps implying police support of her activities.

Alexis looked as though she were thinking over Susan's words. Then she smiled and said, "Why don't we talk upstairs? The Holly and Ms. Ivy people are filling the kitchen with glasses and setting up the dining room and living room. It's quieter up there."

Susan readily agreed. She followed Alexis to the second floor.

They proceeded down a hallway to a large corner room with a fireplace on one wall. Another stairway led upward. Like the rest of the house, this place was decorated in the style known as country. Not that most country people had time to indulge in so many crafts. Every couch was covered with at least a half-dozen handmade pillows; the mantel supported dozens of wrought iron candleholders; wreaths hung on walls; and boughs of dried flowers were balanced above each doorway and window frame. Everything was lovely and very expensive. And maybe, Susan thought, just a bit overdone.

"Have a seat," Alexis offered, plopping down on a couch covered in fabric printed with green-and-gold duck decoys.

Susan followed the instructions.

"We should talk before the caterer's people start to spread out up here."

"This is going to be a big party then?"

"Very. Of course, it would have been bigger if Gillian hadn't decided to give a party the same night. Naturally, we invited many of the same people, and they can't possibly be at both parties simultaneously."

"Surely people will go to both," Susan suggested. That, at least, is what she and Jed were planning to do.

"Yes, I suppose so, but there will be fewer guests here at one time."

Susan had to agree.

"Do you have questions about Z? Or did you come here to talk about last night? I can't say I want to talk about that."

"It was pretty upsetting, wasn't it?" Susan agreed. "All those people getting sick, and someone even having a heart attack."

"True. And it's the first time I've ever had a date pass out on me—or on the decorations, to be more accurate," Alexis agreed in a bored tone.

"Dan Irving was your date! I had no idea!"

"Yeah, he's not much, is he?"

Susan was a little shocked by Alexis's attitude, but she didn't want to offend her before asking a lot of questions. "Have you two been dating long?" she asked politely.

"I date a lot of men," Alexis answered. "I get asked out a lot, and I accept if I don't find my date repulsive and if I want to go wherever he's taking me. There are a lot of couples-only events in suburbia—and the annual hospital ball is certainly one of them. Dan asked me, so I accepted." She shrugged. It was apparently as simple as that.

"Do you like him? Jed says he is a hypochondriac—although apparently Dan was truly sick last night."

"Jed's your husband? Well, he was right," Alexis continued after Susan had nodded her head yes. "That man is obsessed with every ache, every pain. Every cool wind is just waiting to give him a cold, and every bit of cholesterol is planning ways to escape his detection and end up on his arteries. I never accept a date with him unless someone else is choosing the food. Otherwise we would end up at one of those macrobiotic places near a university. I know that food is fashionable in some groups, but I don't like it at all. And last night, he only ate from the platters that were guaranteed to be health food. Ugh! Even The Holly and Ms. Ivy can't make that stuff taste good."

"But he drinks."

"He's a drunk," Alexis corrected her. "But only red wine to keep that nasty cholesterol level down. Apparently no one ever told him what a couple liters of red wine a day are doing to his liver. Not that, in my experience, drunks ever listen to reason."

Susan was wondering if this woman dated a lot of men she would describe as drunks when Alexis continued, explaining.

"There aren't a lot of single men in the suburbs. You'd never move here if you were single, and most men get the hell back to the city as soon as their divorce is final—unless they're remarrying immediately. That's usually the case. A lot of men just don't seem to be able to survive without wives."

Susan wasn't terribly surprised by that. She knew how much schlepping and caretaking was done by the wives of the most liberal of men. Every man needs a wife, she had heard. And so, of course, does every woman. "Why do you stay here then?" Susan asked. "I mean, you could move to the city and—"

"And lose my divorce settlement?" Alexis interrupted her. "No way. I got this house. My ex has to keep up payments, taxes, even pay for repairs. Believe me, I don't make enough money to live like this anywhere else. So I stay." She shrugged. "Who knows, maybe I'll catch one of those men who are divorcing before they make it back down the Merrit Parkway to the city."

Susan had always assumed that those men were actually marrying the women they were involved with when they were previously married, but she didn't know how to ask a woman she hardly knew whether or not she dated married men. But she did know one question she had to ask. "You dated Z, didn't you?"

"Well, sort of. We only met recently. And we spent a lot of time together planning my party, of course. He was wonderful. He spent so much time on all the details, from the decorations to the food. He even helped me pick out invitations. And everything was done with such style. This is going to be my first party since my divorce, and Z understood that I wanted everything to be perfect. And it would have been, if Gwen Ivy hadn't screwed up the date of Gillian's party!" She frowned. "I'm going to miss him terribly. You might not call it dating, but we spent a lot of time together recently. And I felt very close to him. You're wondering what Gillian and I were doing in his apartment that day, aren't you?"

"It did seem strange," Susan admitted. "You were both obviously looking for something."

"That's easy to explain. Embarrassing but easy. You see, Gillian and I are a little competitive." She shrugged her shoulders. "Well, a lot competitive. And these parties we're giving are bringing out the worst in our relationship. We've both been trying for weeks to discover the plans for each other's party. I know for a fact that Gillian went to Gwen Ivy about it. Gwen told me so herself. But Gwen couldn't tell her anything. Z was doing the planning for both events. That's what we were looking for in Z's apartment. We didn't know he was murdered then, you see." She looked earnestly at Susan.

Susan smiled back. This was going to make her job easier. Alexis was a dreadful liar. "So you were looking for plans for Gillian's party."

"No. I was looking for the plans for my party. I didn't want Gillian to see them. Z kept a lot of his work at home. He met with . . . with clients there."

"With you, you mean."

"Yes."

"And with Gillian?"

"Well, she did seem to know where he lived, didn't she?" Alexis smiled slightly.

Susan resisted rolling her eyes. Alexis must think she was stupid.

"You see, we were jogging along, and we saw all the police cars at the carriage house. So I went in and overheard someone talking about Z's death. And I went back outside and told Gillian. And then she said something about Z living nearby. And I said yes, I knew. And she said they had planned her party at his apartment. And I said Z and I had done the same. And one thing led to another and . . . well, you saw what happened."

"You really demolished that apartment," Susan said.

"We would have cleaned it up if the police hadn't come when they did."

"What did Chief Fortesque say?"

"Brett?" Alexis asked airily. "I know him, too. Not that I have any intention of getting serious about a policeman, but he's really a lot of fun and so good-looking. Well, he started to get angry, but I explained what had happened, and he sort of laughed and didn't say anything else about it."

Susan wondered if that could possibly be true. "He wasn't mad at you and Gillian for possibly destroying evidence?"

"Not that he mentioned. Of course, I understand that he and Gillian were once very close. If you can believe what she says about her personal life. Maybe you should ask her about him."

The sound of glass breaking traveled up the stairway and Alexis leapt up. "I think I'd better check out what's going on in the kitchen. I'll be right back."

Susan took advantage of being left alone to stretch her legs—and look around. She walked to the doorway and peered out into the hall. There were three other rooms on this side of the house. One was a blue-and-white tiled bathroom. The other two were bedrooms: in one, yellow and white daisies predominated; in the other, slate gray and maroon formed a more masculine color scheme. They looked more like rooms in magazines than places where anyone lived. And, considering the size of Alexis's family, no one probably ever did live in them.

She walked back to the room she had been in and was looking up the stairway when Alexis returned.

"Just a small problem with some martini glasses—theirs not mine," she explained, joining Susan. "Want to go up?"

"Where does it lead to?"

"The poop deck," Alexis said mysteriously. "Come on up, I'll show you."

Susan followed the other woman up the stairs and found herself in a long hallway. Because of the slanting roof, it was only possible to stand in the middle, and the women walked straight down the hall to a door, which Alexis opened. Two steps down and they were standing on a small deck set into the roof. A redwood lounge, a table, and two chairs filled the space. And, right now, everything was covered with snow.

"I can't believe it," Susan exclaimed. "Who would ever have known this was here?"

"It's how I maintain my all-over suntan," Alexis bragged. "No one can see over the sides when I'm lying down—and the sun feels so sexy."

Susan was busy looking next door. "Is Gillian's house exactly like yours?"

"They're identical. She has a deck just like this one. Although I think she only uses it at night. She seems to like that deathly pale skin." She shivered. "It's cold out here. Let's go back down."

They returned to the room they'd been in before, and Alexis flipped a wall switch and the gas jets in the fireplace burst into flame. "It doesn't actually warm the room, but it does make you think it's warmer." She sat back down on the couch.

Susan, who was dying to ask Alexis some really personal questions, began to worry about her own party. "How are The Holly and Ms. Ivy doing? Do you get the feeling that Z's death is going to affect your party?"

"I know what you mean. I panicked and bought every frozen canapé down at the cheese shop last night. But they arrived on time this morning and began setting up just like we planned."

"You and Z."

"Yes."

"Gwen really didn't do any of the planning?" In Susan's case, Gwen had done almost everything, with Z appearing at her home once or twice to talk about logistics.

"No, none. I'd only seen her a few times in the background until today. She arrived at dawn and stayed around for a few hours until she was sure everything was going the way she wanted it. Then she headed over to Gillian's. There were already vans there . . ." Alexis paused. "Gillian seems to be having hundreds of balloons delivered. I think balloons are tacky, don't you? I prefer more natural decorations. Z and I decided to go with the house, and everything has a country accent—the food is real Americana, and all the decorations are green and alive. Nothing synthetic."

"That will certainly go with the rest of your house," Susan agreed. "And did Z help you pick out everything?"

"Yes. He was wonderful. You know, I was thrilled to get The Holly and Ms. Ivy to do this party. I know Gillian's been trying to hire them for two years, and they were always busy. In my case, it seemed that they couldn't fit me into their schedule until after my divorce."

Susan wondered if she had just heard something significant.

FOURTEEN

SUSAN DECIDED THAT SHE NEEDED TO FIND OUT WHAT HAD happened to Dan Irving. But she had no idea where she was going to get that information. She had worked with the police so much that she had come to automatically assume that she had access to inside information. Even when Brett had been out of town last spring, she'd had a source inside the department. Susan smiled.

"I'm brilliant, Clue," she announced to the dog who was waiting for her in the car. "I just thought of someone who might be able to tell me exactly what I need. And you," she added, turning the key in the ignition, "could probably use a nice walk on that wide lawn down at the municipal center."

The streets had been plowed and sanded, and Susan quickly arrived at her destination. She was able to park nearby, walking around her car and letting Clue leap out into a nearby snowdrift. They were alone, so Susan allowed her dog to romp in the snow. The animal streaked after a large black crow, and then, failing to achieve flight, ran in circles for the pure joy of it. Susan pulled up her collar, tucked her hands in her pockets, and watched, hoping that Clue would trade all this for a dog biscuit in a few minutes.

She heard the jingle of bells before hearing the voice.

"Your dog is sure having a wonderful time."

Susan turned and found herself with Emily Benson, the police dispatcher. "I was just thinking about you!" she exclaimed happily. Emily's niece had helped her on her last case, and Susan was hoping the family tradition might continue. "Merry Christmas!"

"Merry Christmas to you, too." The woman wore her fluffy gray hair in a topknot tied with red-and-green ribbons and dozens of tiny gold bells. She shook her head. "Like it? My niece gave it to me. You know, she's still dating that nice young man she met last spring at the hospital. They're going to get married as soon as he finishes up at the seminary. I like to think of Betsy as a minister's wife. She'll sure perk up that congregation!"

Clue, ever sociable, had dashed back to greet the woman, and Susan attached the leash while they were speaking. "You know," she began slowly, "I came here to see you."

"I've been wondering where you were. Kathleen Gordon has been around ever since the day after Christmas. I just assumed you were out of town. Maybe lying on a beach somewhere warm."

Susan glanced at the steely sky. "Sounds good, but I'm here for the entire week. I'm even giving a party on Saturday night. Would you and your niece like to come? And maybe her fiancé, too? I'd love to see them again."

"Sure. I'll ask. Why don't we go inside and get warm? There are some wonderful Christmas cookies that someone brought in this morning."

Susan hesitated. "I really wanted to speak to you without being overheard."

"So we'll whisper. Don't worry. You don't even have to tell me why you're not involved in this investigation. But let's get warm."

"Let me put the dog back in the car. She'll be happy there, and we won't have to worry about her tracking snow all over." Or chewing on anything she shouldn't, Susan added to herself.

"I'll meet you inside."

The office was toasty warm, and Susan was happy to accept a cup of coffee and three sugar-coated crescents.

"So what do you want to know?"

Susan wasn't startled by Emily's characteristic directness. "I was wondering what made Dan Irving so ill. Whether it was his heart or food poisoning—"

"He's not ill," Emily interrupted her. "He's dead."

"Dead? Are you sure?" Susan was astounded.

"Definitely. Everyone's been talking about it all morning."

"Then it must have been his heart," Susan muttered. "Although I don't know if a person can die from food poisoning."

"You can if you get dehydrated, that's for sure."

"But could he become dehydrated so quickly?" Susan asked, trying to put the pieces together.

"I wouldn't think so. There's bound to be an autopsy, and that will probably cross my desk sometime, but you don't want to wait around for sometime, do you?"

"It would be helpful to know now," Susan admitted. "But if there's no way to find out . . ."

"There may be. Just let me make a few calls. I know some people down at the hospital. I might be able to find out something. Why don't you wait in the coffee room? There are more cookies on the table there and things to read."

Susan wasn't actually here for a break, but she didn't know what else she could do. She went into the small room off the lobby and sat down at the Formica table underneath a HAPPY HOLIDAYS sign falling from the ceiling. She was reaching out for another cookie when she realized what was under her hand—a pile of notes about food poisoning, notes written in what she realized was Kathleen's handwriting. Kathleen doodled when she was thinking, writing down phrases, ideas, whole thoughts. Susan examined the sheets before her. These pages looked like the result of the medical examiner's interview. Susan stopped snacking and concentrated on the words.

When she was finished, she decided to go on a diet. She'd eat only bread—no, that wasn't right, she reminded herself, skimming through the papers. She could still get mycotoxicosis from grain if it had been stored in a damp environment. She scanned the pages again. The only an-

swer was to live on vitamin pills. The repeated references
to salmonella bacteria reminded her of a conversation she'd
had with Gwen Ivy during the initial phases of planning for
New Year's Eve. Susan was looking for a festive drink that
would replace the punch that Jed had become famous for
concocting during the holidays, and Gwen had suggested
eggnog made with Grand Marnier instead of the traditional
brandy or bourbon. And then she'd mentioned salmonella.

"Everyone thinks of eggnog at Christmas, but for the last
few years no one drinks it. Raw eggs are completely out of
favor, and we have to cook chicken to death before anyone
will touch it," Susan remembered Gwen saying. She looked
down at the notes in front of her and wondered what else
caterers worried about serving. She'd noticed that Caesar
salad wasn't served for the same reasons as eggnog, but she
and Gwen had considered sushi for Saturday night and
nothing had been said about parahaemolyticus, cholera, or
hepatitis—according to Kathleen's notes all could be con-
tracted from eating raw shellfish. And there was a bacteria
called Clostridium perfringens, which was found in food
that had been cooked in quantity and then left out in a
warm place—in restaurants, cafeterias, and the like. Maybe
she'd just serve water Saturday night. No, they'd have
champagne, she decided, remembering the tragic deaths resulting from drinking polluted water in Wisconsin a few
years ago.

But where did this all get her? she wondered, picking up
another cookie. (The hell with Yersina enterocolitica,
Campylobacter jejuni, and Shigella bacteria! These were
great cookies!) Any one of these things could be making
the people sick, but none of them could have killed Dan
Irving instantly. And putting that aside, why would some
people get food poisoning and others feel just fine?

Emily joined her, and Susan asked the question aloud.

"I don't know much about that. I don't go to a lot of
fancy dos, but at the PBA party, there are lots of different
trays passed around. I don't suppose everyone samples everything."

"One tray of bad food," Susan muttered. "That makes
sense. Even at the mayor's house, there was a large selec-

tion of canapés. Maybe the people who got sick ate mushroom tarts and not miniature, sun-dried-tomato quiches . . . or something."

"Whatever happened to California dip and potato chips?" the dispatcher muttered, taking a cookie. "Find anything to help you here?"; she continued.

"Not really. Just a lot more questions. Did you get hold of your friend at the hospital?"

"Left a message. Don't worry, she'll call me back."

Susan stood up. "I suppose I should be going."

"Where?"

"I don't actually know." She peered out a window. "Looks cold out there."

"Well, there's no one else to talk to here—unless you need to see the mayor. I think he's the only person besides those of us in this department who are working regular hours this week."

"That's an excellent idea," Susan said, inspired. "I think I will see him. I have a few questions—that I don't know how to ask."

"Ask him anything. Remember his platform was open government for Hancock."

"But I don't think that included being open about his teenage daughter's morals," Susan said, starting off down the hallway to the rest of the municipal offices.

"I was thinking more of things like why there aren't annual raises for the municipality's clerical workers," Emily chuckled, bells on her head ringing. "Or maybe large holiday bonuses."

Susan chuckled and continued on down the hallway lined with pictures of Hancock's past mayors. Someone had draped balsam boughs over the top of each one. The effect was cheerful, despite the fact that drying needles had made the floor slippery.

Buck Logan was ensconced behind the large, antique, mahogany desk that dominated his spacious office. Sun streamed in velvet-curtained windows and fell on the carpet. Bookshelves lined one wall. Hancock chairs were provided for guests. Flags of the United States, Connecticut,

and Hancock unfurled protectively behind the snoring man.
Mayor Logan was taking a nap.

Susan knocked gently on the door jamb—and then more
firmly. Then she cleared her throat and knocked again. She
was beginning to wonder how she was going to wake Buck
up without actually touching him when the phone rang.

Buck, without opening his eyes, felt around on his desk
for the noisy object. When he found it, he was forced to
punch more than one button before he connected with his
caller.

"Hello!" The voice was strong and alert. The person on
the other end of the line would never guess that he or she
had just interrupted a sleeping man.

"Yes, of course I know it's you. Do you think I don't
recognize your voice after twenty-one years of marriage?"

He still hadn't opened his eyes, and Susan backed up a
step, wondering if she could make a fresh entrance.

"I'm not angry, but you know I asked you not to call me
here. My elected position is not a hobby, and people will
only respect the office if they respect me. So what's the
emergency?" He listened a while, still not opening his eyes,
but turning redder with every word that his wife spoke.

"So what the hell do we have lawyers for, if they won't
sue people who are trying to kill our guests?" he finally exploded.

Susan used his loud anger as an opportunity to make her
escape. She backed away, just out of view, but where she
could eavesdrop on this half of the conversation.

"You just tell that man . . . all right, then tell his secre-
tary that I expect immediate action . . . Yes, action, not just
threatening calls. Does he think Gwen Ivy is a simpering
woman who will quake at the first word from some unknown law firm in the suburbs? The woman has been deal-
ing with New York lawyers for years. It's going to take
action, not words, to scare her. You tell him that . . . Well,
then call him again . . . Yes, again . . . I keep telling you
that I'm here working. I can't be making a lot of personal
calls. You'll just have to do it. Okay. Good. Call me back
when you're done. I have to go now. There's someone here
to see me."

Susan was in time to turn his lie into truth.

"Hello? Buck?" she asked, turning the corner as though she didn't know he was in his office. "It's Susan Henshaw."

By the time she was through the door, he had hung up, and was coming around the side of his desk, hand outstretched, all signs of his afternoon siesta vanished. "Susan, my dear, good to see you."

They shook hands, and Susan accepted the seat she was offered.

"I just thought I'd stop in to thank you for inviting me to your party," she said politely.

"It was wonderful to see you," he answered in the same vein. "Camilla and I are always saying that we don't see enough of you and Josh."

Susan didn't correct him for a second time. She just smiled and leaned back in her chair. "We're always talking about you two, too." In fact the other night, Jed was blaming the mayor for the fact that their street was always one of the last ones plowed after a snowstorm, and she winced, remembering something catty she had said about Camilla's new hair color. But she mentioned none of that.

He didn't bring up the food poisoning, apparently not caring whether or not Susan had felt any ill effects after his dinner party. He didn't offer her refreshments now either, glancing at his watch as though hoping she would leave quickly. "Is there anything else I can do for you?" he asked pointedly.

"I was wondering about your daughter," Susan said.

"Cameo?"

Thank goodness he'd said her name; Susan was wondering how she was going to get around this continuing amnesia. "Yes. You said she was skiing," Susan began.

"I believe I did. She is. Skiing. In Switzerland."

"Where?"

"In Switzerland," he repeated a little more loudly, evidently assuming she was hard of hearing.

"But where in Switzerland? You see, Jed and I are planning on taking a family holiday sometime in February, and I was thinking of skiing in Switzerland, and I didn't remember the place you . . . well, you or your wife mentioned the other night. And someone said that it was a wonderful place. So I wanted to know the name," she ended feebly.

"How do I know? Camilla keeps track of all that type of thing! And how would you feel if I came into your home and started asking silly questions about your daughter? You wouldn't be thrilled by that, would you?"

"I . . . I don't see why not," Susan answered, startled and confused. Here she had tried to pick a neutral topic so she could start asking questions about The Holly and Ms. Ivy, and apparently she had stumbled on a very sensitive subject. Just as Susan was wondering what was going on here, the phone rang, and Buck Logan was distracted.

"Hello." The mayor glanced angrily at her, and Susan wondered if she should take this opportunity to leave. But his next words captured her interest. "I don't believe it. Why would anyone murder Dan Irving? He could be irritating, but not lethally so. Okay, I'll come on over to the hospital." He was standing before he hung up the phone. "I have to head over to the hospital. That stupid man got himself killed last night apparently."

"Was it food poisoning?" Susan asked, hoping to get a question in before he vanished.

"Food poisoning? Food poisoning doesn't kill perfectly healthy middle-aged men. He was murdered like I said. Someone suffocated him overnight in ICU at the hospital."

"Wait!" Susan grabbed his arm. "Some people thought he died last night at the ball."

"No. He went into cardiac arrest, but he was revived on the way to the hospital. He was killed sometime last night. At least, he was found dead this morning at five A.M. That's what that call was about. Why they think the mayor can do anything about this . . ." His phone rang again. "I'll bet that's the press. I'm leaving."

"But it could be your wife," Susan suggested as he left the room. "Maybe," she continued softly to herself, "maybe I should go talk to her myself."

Susan hurried back toward the police department's offices. Emily Benson was on the phone and waved wildly at

Susan's appearance. "I know something," she whispered loudly, putting her hand over the mouthpiece.

"About Dan Irving?" Susan asked. "I heard. Murder. Buck Logan just told me. I have to get going. Can I call you later?"

The other woman nodded yes, and her bells rang, and Susan hurried back out into the cold air.

She had forgotten that Clue was waiting in the car, and she screamed when the large square head popped up as she put her key in the lock.

"Susan! Susan, are you okay?"

She turned around and saw Brett running across the parking lot in her direction. "Are you okay?" he repeated.

"Yes. I'm fine. My dog just scared me," she admitted, feeling a little foolish.

"That dog scared you?" Brett asked, chuckling at the goofy-looking, drooling animal. "Isn't that the dog with the strange name?"

"Clue," Susan admitted, not, however, admitting that her family had registered the dog as "Susan hasn't got a clue." Today that was too true to joke about.

"Named him after the game, did you?" he asked, and Susan didn't argue. "What are you doing here?"

There was a serious note to his voice, and Susan decided it was time to go. "I just stopped in to ask Emily to my New Year's Eve party. Her niece and her boyfriend may show up, too. You're coming, aren't you?"

"I don't think . . . ," Brett answered, probably confused because Susan hadn't extended him an invitation until now.

"I sure hope Kathleen asked you," Susan continued, opening the car door and getting inside. "She was supposed to," she added and started her car. "Got to go. Lots to do."

She waved and drove off, feeling more than a little foolish.

But she didn't have time to worry about that. It was time to find Camilla Logan and hear more about this lawsuit—and maybe what her daughter really was doing over the Christmas holidays.

FIFTEEN

CAMILLA WAS IN HER ENTRYWAY, PICKING TINY ROSEBUDS from the topiaries on the side table. She looked furious—so furious that she didn't notice Susan peering in the storm door.

Like husband, like wife, Susan thought, knocking gently. But Camilla wasn't asleep. She spun around and frowned at Susan.

Susan smiled.

Camilla bent the ends of her lips upward very slightly.

"Hi," Susan tried.

"Hello. I'm a little busy," Camilla said, and then looked down at her hands, still shredding the flowers. "Actually, I'm waiting for someone."

"Oh? I just saw Buck," Susan said, hoping she could convince Camilla to invite her in. Surely it was extraordinarily rude to leave her standing here on the doorstep, yelling through the closed door like this.

"I hope you told him he could drop dead," Camilla surprised her by saying. "The gall of that man, leaving me here to cope with all this while he pretends he has something to do as mayor of this little town. Men are idiots."

It was a sentiment she occasionally agreed with, so Susan just nodded and entered the hallway when the door was opened for her. "What did he leave you to deal with?" she

142

asked, knowing that angry people frequently said more than they would when calm.

"Lawyers. Lawsuits. What do I know about that type of thing?"

"Surely no one is suing you or Buck?" Susan said, deliberately misunderstanding.

"No. We're the ones suing . . . the plaintiffs, I think."

"Who?"

"The Holly and Ms. Ivy. We're suing The Holly and Ms. Ivy for making our guests sick. They had food poisoning after coming to our party the night before last. Didn't you hear about it?"

"I heard something," Susan admitted. "Were you and Buck sick, too?" She thought it only polite to be concerned about them. Someone had to display some manners around here.

"No, just Dan Irving and that woman he brought as his date. He met her at his acupuncturist. The strange woman wearing orange velvet slacks—the vegetarian. I can't understand why people would go to dinner parties and refuse to eat almost everything there. Why don't they just stay home and graze on greens?"

Susan tried to remember the notes she had read down at the police station just a few minutes ago. "I'm not sure you can get food poisoning from salad," she started and then remembered the grain stored in moist places. "Although . . ."

"It's amazing that anyone ate anything with Dan talking about cholesterol, HDL, sugar, and heaven knows what else. You were at the other end of the room, but near the fireplace, everyone was forced to listen to a list of ingredients that could kill you. What a pest that man is. We always have to provide special foods for him when he's our guest."

"So he and his date ate a special meal?"

"Yes. And they were the only ones sick. I'm not even sure they ate the bad food at my house. They may have had a snack before they arrived."

"But I thought you were suing The Holly and Ms. Ivy. . . ."

"Only because Buck is worried that Dan might sue us. . . ."

"Dan Irving is dead," Susan said. "He died last night in the hospital."

"I thought he was revived. In the ambulance . . . that's what we heard this morning," Camilla insisted, looking confused.

"That's true. But he was murdered in the hospital."

Camilla looked at her and opened and closed her mouth a few times before deciding on her words. "Do you think it's too early for a drink?" she asked, turning and heading for the large oak dresser that served as a bar without waiting for an answer.

Susan followed her, wanting conversation not alcohol. The large picture over the fireplace reminded her of Cameo's now mysterious vacation. "Where's your daughter skiing?" she asked.

"In Switzerland." Camilla poured herself a large glass of red wine before remembering to offer Susan one.

"No thanks." Susan refused the wine. "But where in Switzerland? Your husband didn't seem to know."

"That doesn't surprise me—you know men. I'm surprised he remembered which country she's in. She's there with friends from school. They're traveling from place to place. Or from slope to slope." Camilla laughed nervously. "She'll be coming home late next week."

Camilla was rearranging ornaments on the large tree in the window, so Susan sat down and made herself at home. She had an hour or so before she had to be home to fix dinner for her children and get herself ready for the party—parties—tonight, and watching the way Camilla was polishing off her glass of wine and heading for another, she expected that she might learn something here.

But Camilla was more interested in asking questions than in answering them. "Who told you about Dan Irving?" she asked, sipping her second glass more slowly than the first.

"I heard about it down at the municipal center," Susan answered truthfully.

"Funny that he'd be murdered," Camilla said slowly. "He was always so sure that he was going to die from a heart attack."

"That's what my husband says about him. Did he have a bad heart? A history of heart attacks?"

"I always assumed so. He was so concerned about his health—what he ate and all."

"And all?"

Camilla chuckled. "Well, maybe only what he ate. I know he didn't get enough exercise, and he drank too much. . . ." She glanced down at the glass in her hand, shrugged, and polished it off in one large gulp. "But he did worry about what he ate. I hate health-food freaks, don't you? Cameo was dating this long-haired boy before her freshman year of college, and he was what they call a vegan. He ate almost nothing. Brown rice, beans, greens, squash. There was almost no way to have him to dinner. I understand it's very popular on college campuses right now. Has your daughter run into it?"

"Chrissy is dating a young man who's a gourmet," Susan announced proudly, ignoring the fact that her daughter had as yet failed to produce this paragon of the food world.

"The good-looking young man she was with at the ball last night?"

"Uh, yes." Well, she thought so.

"How did she meet him?" Camilla asked.

"I'm not sure. It happened at college."

"Oh. I thought maybe it had something to do with The Holly and Ms. Ivy."

"Not that I know of." Did this woman think they were a dating service as well as a caterer?

Camilla seemed to lose interest in the conversation and returned to her wine and her Christmas tree.

"It's a beautiful tree," Susan commented, although she wasn't terribly fond of "decorator" trees herself. "Buck said that you planned all this yourself."

"Not this year. This year I had a lot of help from The Holly and Ms. Ivy. When they agreed to cater my annual Christmas dinner party, they also agreed to take over the theme decorating."

"Really? Did you ask them to decorate for the holiday as well as your party?" This was something that Susan hadn't even considered. Everything that The Holly and Ms. Ivy were doing for her party Saturday was going on top of the decorations she already had up. There had never been any mention of anything else. Just some pots of fresh flowers on the bar and at the back of the serving tables in the dining room, napkins and tablecloths to match, confetti on the table, colored streamers hanging from chandeliers already decked with pine roping. That was it, and she couldn't remember anyone suggesting anything else.

"Of course I did. They're the best. I knew they would come up with something unusual. After all, they've done some of the best parties for years. I'd be crazy not to take advantage of their expertise."

"But you're suing them," Susan reminded her.

"I told you. That's just because Buck was so concerned about being sued. But I guess we don't have to worry about that now."

"Your lawyer already called The Holly and Ms. Ivy," Susan reminded her.

Camilla shrugged and downed her third glass of wine. "We were extraordinarily lucky that they would cater for us this year; it would never have happened again anyway. Besides, there may not be a The Holly and Ms. Ivy by this time next year. Z was the brains behind that company. Gwen Ivy is nothing without him.

"Are you leaving?" Camilla interrupted herself to ask.

"Yes. I have a few things to do, and we're going out tonight. . . ." Susan didn't think anyone was listening, so she didn't bother to explain as she left the house, crunching through dried rosebuds on the floor as she went.

The dog greeted her return enthusiastically, and Susan patted her head and promised to take her for a walk as soon as she got to her next stop.

Minutes later, Clue was prancing happily around the carriage house of The Holly and Ms. Ivy. The aromas escaping from large stainless-steel fans near the roof thrilled both pet and pet owner, and Susan realized that the cookies hadn't been very filling.

Clue pulled her around to the back of the building, and Susan noticed that there weren't any vans parked there.

Footprints in the snow indicated that there had been feverish activity earlier, but for now, everything was calm.

A pair of squirrels attracted Clue's attention, and Susan spent a few minutes untangling the leash where it had become wound around some tiny evergreens that had been planted near the driveway. Just as she was finished, a car drove up, and Jamie Potter leapt out.

"Hi! Can I ask you a few questions?" Susan called out.

"Sure. But I have stuff to do inside. Could you come in—but maybe not the dog."

Definitely not the dog. An animal with an appetite like this one would be completely out of control in a room full of food. Susan yanked Clue back to the car, promising rewards of dog biscuits as soon as they arrived home. Then she rushed back to the carriage house.

Jamie was at the rear of the room, pulling large ceramic bowls from the big refrigerator and slipping aside the plastic wrap that covered them to stick in a finger and taste the contents. "Garlic butter for the goat-cheese ravioli at the Davies party," she explained, evidently finding what she was looking for. "And I need a truffle slicer. . . . Here it is!" She pulled a paddle-shaped piece of equipment from a drawer. "It's going to be used for the risotto at the Davies', and then I'm going to steal it back for the Cutler do—nothing works better for shaving chocolate. Nothing."

"Must be very convenient giving two parties next door to each other," Susan commented, following Jamie on her path down the aisle, collecting tools and food on a cart in front of her as she went.

"I suppose so. It's the first time it's happened that I know of." Jamie had stopped at her workstation and was pulling out drawers and sorting through pastry bags. "It would certainly be easier if those two women had just planned the parties that they wanted to give instead of competing with each other. You wouldn't believe it. One wants three appetizers. So the other has four, followed by a choice of two main courses. And, naturally, next door must have three and six side dishes. And when it came to dessert they both just went hog wild. Alexis Cutler stuck to her country theme, and I made her twenty-three pies, four different cookies, two candies, and there are going to be two men on hand to turn old-time, cedar ice-cream makers that are supposed to produce both peach and apricot ice cream. I hate to think what the salt and ice solution is going to do to the hard-wood floors in her dining room. I warned her, but that's what she and Z decided, so that's what she's getting."

"And what's Gillian Davies serving?" Susan had to ask; her mouth was watering.

"Fabulous stuff. In fact, I think this could be my favorite of all the meals we've ever done in a private home. That woman has great taste. And she took Z's suggestions and ran with them. The goat-cheese ravioli is for her party as well as the risotto with white truffles. She's also having a boned turkey stuffed with sausage and chestnuts and Madeira gravy—very light. And a Parma ham, of course. But the dessert is the best."

"I can't wait. What is it?"

Jamie broke into a big smile. "You'll have to. It's a surprise. Just prepare yourself for a treat—one of my masterpieces."

Susan was thinking that Jamie had just solved one small problem for her: she would go to Alexis's party first and Gillian's second. "Did Z plan both parties?" she asked.

"Probably. He usually does most of the preliminary planning. Meeting with the client, going to the home or the place where the event is to be held, and getting some idea of the basics."

"The basics?" Susan watched as Jamie fashioned stars, comets, and moons from icing and laid them on wax paper to dry.

"What type of party it is to be—dinner, cocktails, what-ever, how many people are going to be invited and how many are expected to accept, if there's a theme, and things like decorations and food."

"What about cost?" Susan had been a little appalled to hear how much Saturday night was going to run.

"Gwen handles most of that type of thing. In fact, she usually picks out the exact menu."

"Z took care of the broad outline, and she managed all

the little details?" Susan asked, thinking that this sounded slightly sexist.

"That's the way it's been since I've been working here. Some of the older workers say that things were more equal in the beginning—but that's not right," Jamie corrected herself, turning a star into a blob, sweeping it off her work space with one hand and miraculously forming a perfect five pointer almost instantly. She concentrated on miniature suns and comet tails while she finished her explanation. "It's not a question of equality. At least, I've never gotten the feeling that Z or Gwen were anything but equal partners. It's just that they're good at different things, and after a few years in the business, they automatically started to take over the parts of the job that they did best and left the rest to the other."

"So you never got the impression that Gwen was uncomfortable with Z's more public position."

"Are you kidding? If anything, I think it was a relief to her." Jamie looked around to make sure they were alone before continuing. "In fact, I overheard them together once when he was going off to talk to someone about a party. He said something about taking care of his ladies, and she said better you than me, that she'd go crazy if she had to spend as much time as he did schmoozing their clients."

"Gwen planned almost all my party," Susan commented, taking a finger of the frosting that Jamie offered. "Z just came over to look at the house and make sure I approved of the final menu plans."

"That's somewhat unusual," Jamie said, "but not unheard of. They were pretty flexible."

"And I'm not giving a huge party. Seventy guests for New Year's Eve in my house. Not much in the way of decorations, mostly food."

"You're Saturday night!" Jamie exclaimed. "I'm glad you told me. Wait till you see what I'll dream up for your dessert table," she continued at Susan's nod.

"I thought cakes, cookies . . ."

"Something special," Jamie insisted. "You'll be pleased. I promise."

Susan looked at the work the young woman was finishing and agreed. "I haven't seen or tasted anything of yours yet that wasn't special."

"I'll use you as a recommendation when I open my bakery," Jamie assured her.

"I thought you liked working here."

"I love it. But most of us want to run our own businesses eventually. That's what we train for. But it's hard to succeed in the food business, and with the economy the way it is, I'm staying put for the time being."

Susan was silent for a few minutes before she posed the question she had come here to ask. "What was the argument about between Gwen and Z?"

"Argument?"

"It was mentioned right after Z's death. You mentioned it," Susan reminded her.

"I'm not sure."

"But you think . . . ," Susan guided her.

"I think Z had gotten involved with too many of the women that The Holly and Ms. Ivy cater for."

Susan thought about that for a second. "Is this a change in his behavior? I mean, was he suddenly sexually involved with more than one woman? Or had he broken off a relationship that he'd had with Gwen recently?"

"Oh, I don't think he and Gwen were ever involved romantically," Jamie insisted.

"Really?" Susan was perfectly ready to believe that men and women were capable of being coworkers and companions without romantic involvement, but she wanted to make absolutely sure on this point.

"I can't believe it," Jamie said. "You know how rumors spread in a place like this. And there's never been a hint of anything between the two of them—ever. Z has been rather, well, rather promiscuous, everyone knows that, but Gwen . . . Well, if Gwen has been involved with anyone in the business, she's kept it completely quiet. And if they were ever a couple, it was a pretty open relationship."

"Because Z was always involved with other women."

"Exactly."

"So what happened recently that was causing arguments?" Susan asked.

"I have no idea. And I've thought about it—and listened to what everyone has been saying."

"What has everyone been saying?"

"Well, there's been a certain amount of conflict in Z's romantic life recently because we're doing so many affairs in Hancock, and he's been . . . dating more than one woman in town."

"Alexis Cutler and Gillian Davies."

"And, of course, the mayor's daughter last year. And one or two others."

"There's no reason to be discreet in the middle of a murder investigation," Susan insisted. "You're talking about JoAnn Kent, aren't you?"

"I shouldn't be talking about this."

"Don't give me names, just tell me one thing."

"What?"

"Was Z frequently involved with the women The Holly and Ms. Ivy worked for?"

"No, of course not."

Susan thought Jamie had answered with a strange emphasis.

SIXTEEN

ALEXIS'S PARTY HAD BEEN GOING STRONG WHEN SUSAN EX-
plained to her husband that she was moving to the gathering next door. It was freezing cold, and she rushed through
the snow, congratulating herself on the self-control she had
shown this evening. She'd tasted only a small selection of
appetizers at Alexis's home: a few Johnson oysters from
California, steak tartare on homemade sweet-potato chips,
Cajun alligator sausages on sourdough, smoked salmon
from the Northwest on blue corn chips from the Southwest,
just the tiniest bit of Smithfield ham on beaten biscuits—
well, it was a party, after all, she reminded herself, knocking on Gillian's door. An arch of Mylar stars flew from the
awning above her head.

"Merry Christmas." Gillian, dressed in white with silver
accents, matched her home. "Come on in. That young man
over there will take your coat. Drinks in the living room
down those steps to your right. And food in the library to
the left."

Susan greeted her hostess, relieved herself of her coat, and
went to find a drink. The living room was beautiful. Modern
furniture was upholstered in white leather. Sea green rugs lay
on bleached oak floors, and pale silk cushions and chrome
lights reflected in glass coffee tables. Massed in corners and
flowing from crystal vases, silver-and-white glass balls and

grayish-green blue spruce discreetly proclaimed the joyous season. Three large evergreens were set up at one end of the room. Their only ornaments were white seashells tied to the boughs with silver threads. Susan accepted a glass of white wine and went in search of food.

In the kitchen, where next door Alexis had expressed her country theme with stencils of bucolic cows circling open shelves of canned produce from New England farm markets, Gillian had opted for rows of enameled white cabinets above deep green tile floors. Susan noticed Jamie Potter pulling cartons of triple cream from the refrigerator and waved before going on to the library.

Appetizers had been laid out on a glass (or, surely, heavy plastic) Parsons table. In keeping with the rest of the decorations, mirrored mats and trays gleamed with smoked salmon mousse, caviar dotted with Maui onions, hundreds of tiny canapés of exquisite design and the finest ingredients. But no one was eating.

Unable to resist, Susan filled a pearly white plate with food and picked up a silver-shot linen napkin.   .

"You're not going to eat that, are you? She's not going to eat that, is she?"

Susan looked up at the two women she had met at the inn the day after Christmas. They were wearing their usual makeup. "I know my skirt is a little tight, but it's Christmas and—"

"That's not what we mean. It's from The Holly and Ms. Ivy."

"I know—" Susan began, about to give the company an impromptu tribute.

"It might be poisoned."

"You're kid— You're not kidding, are you?" Susan asked.

"Of course not. You know that Dan Irving died after eating food from The Holly and Ms. Ivy, don't you?"

"I know that he died, but I understood it had nothing to do with what he ate," Susan said.

"Susan, how can you be so naive? First the mayor's dinner, then the hospital ball . . . sane people aren't eating anything that The Holly and Ms. Ivy have anything to do with."

"We had full dinners before we came, and we're sticking to wine—we watched the bartender uncork the bottle."

Susan looked down at the plate of food in her hands and up at the two women. They had a point, but before she had time to say anything she saw Jerry Gordon on the other side of the room. And, unless she was mistaken, he was accompanied by his wife. Susan made a weak excuse and hurried toward her friends.

Kathleen was wearing a red silk jumpsuit and, as always, looked fantastic—except that one of the accessories was a little inconsistent with Kathleen's usual style. "What is that thing on your shoulder?" is how Susan greeted her friend.

"Isn't it cute?" Kathleen said a little stiffly. "Jerry's mother made it for me." She glanced at her husband, but he was busy waving to a neighbor on the other side of the room. Taking advantage of his distraction, she made a face at Susan, who, now that she had gotten closer, realized that she was looking at a snowman crocheted from heavy silver-and-white yarn. It would have raised a feeling of envy in Jamie Potter's aunt, but it clashed with the pearls Kathleen's husband had given her for Christmas.

"Is she here?" Susan asked.

"No. She's at home with her favorite grandson. Ban is having a wonderful time with his extended family."

"It doesn't sound like you agree," Susan said.

Kathleen sipped the cup of eggnog she held before answering. "She's acting a little strange."

"In what way?"

"She seems to disapprove of everything I do."

It was a familiar feeling; Susan's mother-in-law was wonderful, but that's not necessarily the easiest thing either.

"It's particularly unusual in that she's always encouraged my work. You know, she worked all the time Jerry was growing up, and she wasn't thrilled when I gave up my police work to move to Hancock, or sold the security company after Bananas was born."

"But she doesn't approve now?" Susan asked, confused.

Why start to object to a mother working after her only child had begun nursery school?

"No. She's been very disapproving, in fact. I can't understand it."

Susan could. She assumed that Jerry's mother was still trying to discourage any possible relationship between her daughter-in-law and Brett.

"And she's making Jerry crazy."

Susan leaned closer, and Kathleen continued. "You know how investigations go. I'm out at all hours, and it's difficult to plan anything—and Jerry's used to it. But now, every time the phone rings or Brett comes over and I have to leave, Jerry's mom says something about how they will miss me at home and how lonely Jerry has been looking lately—or how she's always believed that families should be together as much as possible during the holiday season. I don't understand it."

Susan opened her mouth to make a tactful comment, but Kathleen was frowning down into her drink and twisting her wedding ring over and over around her finger. Susan saw that she was upset and hurried to change the subject. "How is the investigation going?" she asked quickly.

"Fairly well."

Susan was disappointed by the answer—and determined to elicit another one. "I know that Dan Irving died of something other than food poisoning."

"You should be careful what you say. You know how rumors start in this town—in any town when there's been a murder."

Susan reminded herself that there was nothing to be gained by anger; it was just possible that Kathleen didn't intend to be patronizing. She sat down on one of the leather couches and was pleased when Kathleen joined her, draining the cup of the last of her eggnog.

And then Susan realized exactly what she had just seen. "The food poisoning wasn't an accident, was it?"

Kathleen glanced down at the empty cup. "Let's just say there's no reason for anyone to worry about The Holly and Ms. Ivy's food."

"The people who were sick were faking it!"

"Not necessarily. We think they were really ill, but not from an accidental exposure to toxic bacteria."

"Which means intentional poisoning . . . ," Susan began.

"Which means I shouldn't be talking like this."

"Kathleen, why not?" Susan said, hoping that last question didn't sound like a whine.

"Susan, there are very good reasons that you shouldn't be mixed up in this investigation."

"Then tell me what they are," Susan insisted. "Kathleen, you know I'm discreet. And I'm not judgmental at all—well, not about people I care about," she amended. "I'm really very understanding."

Kathleen looked seriously at her friend. "This is no place to talk about it. Why don't we meet tomorrow morning . . . early?"

Finally. "Sure. Why not the inn for breakfast."

"I have a few errands to do downtown. Why don't we meet at the diner?" Kathleen suggested.

Susan switched from images of a nice light waffle to fried potatoes and eggs sunny-side up with rye toast. "Sounds good to me. What time?"

"This is going to run late, and I should take care of Jerry's mother and father before I leave the house. Is nine too late for you?"

"Not at all," Susan assured her as Kathleen stood up. "Where are you going?"

"I'm going to get more of that eggnog—it's delicious. There's a hint of something citrus. . . ."

Susan decided to keep The Holly and Ms. Ivy's recipe a secret. "Well, now that I know it's safe, I think I'll have some, too," she said, getting up and following her friend to the dining room.

The main courses had been laid out in here, and Susan recognized the risotto and the ravioli, the promised ham and turkey. Suddenly eggnog seemed rather trivial. She picked up a large plate and started serving herself. Kathleen followed suit.

"Well, I guess if the police are eating the food, it must be safe," came a voice from behind them.

"Maybe," she heard someone say, "maybe we should go back to Alexis's house and eat there."

"No," the unknown person's companion suggested. "Let's show up there for brunch tomorrow. The leftovers are going to be terrific."

"This is wonderful. Really wonderful!"

Susan agreed completely with the unknown speaker. She moved out of the way as more and more people crowded into the room behind her. She hoped there was enough food. It sounded like Gillian was going to be feeding both parties. Turning the corner, she ran into her hostess.

Gillian interrupted a conversation she was having· with one of the waiters. "Susan. Thank you for coming. Thank you· for eating! Everyone from The Holly and Ms. Ivy is talking about it."

"I didn't—"

"You did. Everyone knows your connection with the police department. Once they saw you eating, they knew the food was safe."

Susan looked down at the almost empty plate in her hand. She hoped everyone was right. "I noticed that people weren't eating at Alexis's party, but . . ."

"That bitch. Can you imagine anyone doing this to their friend?"

"Doing what?"

"Planning a party for the same day. I don't know what she told you, but I was planning on having this party for weeks before she decided on a date. And then, the day before my invitations were to be mailed, her invitation arrived! She blamed Gwen Ivy, but that woman doesn't make mistakes."

"It was lucky that you were both giving open houses so people could go to both. I know that's what lots of guests do at my New Year's Eve party," Susan added quickly, not wanting to offend.

"Yes, but they're always comparing. Not that I think her party could possibly be better than mine. I know American food is all the rage now, but I think Alexis took that a little too seriously. Who serves pies for dessert except on

Thanksgiving? And homemade ice cream? Does she think it's summer?"

Susan wondered if Z had been less than discreet when talking about Alexis's party. But, even if he had been, it wouldn't be a motive for murder.

Or would it? she asked herself, seeing the anger on Gillian's face.

"Do you know that some people actually thought that Alexis and I should give a joint party? Cocktails and dessert at her house, and the main course at mine? Or maybe we should have invited a third person to join us and had some sort of progressive dinner. Really."

The English have such expressive voices, Susan thought. Especially good at expressing disdain. "This is certainly a wonderful party," was all she said. "Your home is beautiful."

"All except for the kids' rooms upstairs. Their psychiatrist said we should allow them to express their individuality in their personal space. I keep the doors closed when they're off at school."

Susan had forgotten that Gillian was the mother of a boy and girl, twins of around nineteen or twenty, she'd guess. She couldn't recall very much about them, in fact. They'd always seemed to be away at boarding school or camp when they were young, and she was fairly sure that they were both attending college somewhere on the West Coast. "They're not home for vacation this year?" she asked politely.

"They're with their father and his new wife at some posh resort down in Costa Rica. They were going to kayak around the swamps and look at bird life. Sounded dreadful to me, but they chose to go." She shrugged. "You know how children are. Selfish."

Susan considered her own children and the thought they'd put into buying her Christmas gift. They weren't perfect, but there were days when they came close. And then there were other days . . .

"You must miss them. Is this the first holiday you've spent alone?"

"Yes. A completely adult life at last."

"Then you're enjoying it," Susan said since she got the feeling that it was what she was supposed to believe.

"Definitely. It's so difficult to have a real social life with children around."

Susan realized that Gillian was talking about sex. She smiled, embarrassed as well as curious. She remembered the comments that Alexis had made, implying that Gillian was promiscuous. "Are you dating someone seriously right now?" she asked.

"We're a little old for girlish confidences, don't you think?"

Susan couldn't miss the put-down. She was thinking hard for an appropriate reply when Gillian continued. "It's not like being a teenager, is it?"

Susan started thinking of Gillian's daughter. Maybe there was more than one reason for her to be away for the holiday. That thought would have led her to Cameo Logan even if her mother hadn't appeared by their side.

"Gillian, wonderful party," Camilla Logan trilled. "And people are eating the food. Amazing."

"Camilla! How nice of you to come." The two women exchanged air kisses.

Susan would have felt left out if she had particularly liked either of them. She took one step backward and absently ate the last ravioli on her plate.

"Where's your host this evening?" Camilla continued. "I thought you were dating that nice young lawyer who just graduated from Yale a couple of years ago."

"He's not that young," Gillian protested. "And he's not here tonight. He's spending the holidays in Akron with his mother—and not because he's young, but because she's old. She fell down the stairs and had surgery. He didn't think she should be in the hospital over Christmas without a close relative around."

"How thoughtful. So you're giving this party without help?"

"Well, I have The Holly and Ms. Ivy—and there are two or three men around here somewhere. . . ." Gillian glanced around as though expecting to find Paul Newman lurking behind a ficus tree. "I'm lucky to have so many friends here in town."

"I didn't know there were that many unmarried men in Hancock."

"Who said anything about unmarried?" Gillian ended her sentence with a smirk.

Camilla scowled, and her next words were spoken with strained sweetness. "I heard that you and Z Holly were involved. And you know what I thought when I heard that?"

Gillian shrugged as though the answer was of no interest to her, but Susan noticed that she didn't leave.

"I thought that the two of you deserved each other. You're not very nice people." Camilla Logan spun around and stalked off.

"I guess she's going to leave," Susan said to fill the silence.

"Not a chance. There are about a half-dozen people here that the mayor has to schmooze. She'll stand by her man until her feet drop off."

Susan decided to change the subject. "Do you know Camilla is the first person who has said anything negative about Z Holly since he was murdered?"

"Really? I would have thought that any woman whose daughter was seduced by him would feel the same way. You'll excuse me, won't you? I should check on my other guests."

Susan was on her way back to the dining room when Buck Logan grabbed her arm.

"Susan. You look angry. Come with me."

He had a tight grip on her arm, and Susan had no choice but to follow his directions. She preceded him up the stairs to the second floor, regretting that they were moving too quickly for her to examine the decorating scheme. Buck sat her down on the couch in the family room and grasped both her hands in his. "I'm so sorry about anything Gillian might have said to you. The woman's a bitch."

He continued. "She's a very attractive woman, but getting a bit long in the tooth; she's probably just jealous of the effect these young girls had on Z." He chuckled.

Susan was stunned by the way he was speaking about his own daughter. "Cameo is so lovely . . ." she began.

"Cameo? Who's talking about Cameo?" Buck's smile faded, and he began to frown. "There is positively no proof that there was ever anything between my daughter and that . . . that caterer. And repeating any stories could make a person liable to a lawsuit. And I'll thank you to remember that, Susan Henshaw!"

And she was left alone. Susan stood up and looked around the room. It was as beautifully decorated as the first floor, still modern and pastel. But there were dark, muddy-looking footprints across the light carpet. Susan remembered Alexis's house next door and realized that someone must have been up on the deck at the top of the house. She walked over and peered up the stairs.

A sharp wind was coming from above, and a muffled bang convinced her something was wrong. She looked around, embarrassed at the possibility of being caught going through private areas, but unwilling to leave without checking to see if the door up there had blown open. She hurried toward the stairway.

It got colder as she climbed, and the noise was getting louder and louder. She hurried through the narrow, dark hallway to the door. It was, as she had suspected, ajar. She reached out to pull it closed, but there was something blocking the way. She almost had a heart attack when she saw five fingers lying on the ground.

Her second thought was to wonder who was missing one tan pigskin glove. It wasn't very practical in this cold weather, but it was a beautiful piece of clothing. She pulled it gently from the door jamb and continued on up to the roof deck, vaguely thinking of searching for its mate. The full moon was reflecting off the snow, and she could see a couple of modern chairs and a table with a glass mug of eggnog freezing in it. The snow had blown to one side of the deck, and she could cross without getting her feet wet. It was cold, and Susan would have gone back into the house if she hadn't heard a commotion on the ground below.

Leaning over the balcony, Susan watched as a delicate

bunch of red-and-green balloons rose into the air above her head. She was admiring how elegant they looked sailing between the bare branches crackling in the breeze when she became aware of voices below. Angry voices.

"I thought you said he'd ignore us."

"I said me, not us! I never said us!"

"If he doesn't investigate you, he can't investigate me. You know that as well as I do...."

"You're getting hysterical. None of this matters. As long as we stick to our story, no one can prove anything. Besides, there are lots of other suspects."

"Name three."

"More than a few husbands, fathers, and mothers in this town. No one's paying any attention to us, and no one's going to unless you panic and forget the story."

"You and your stupid story. Do you think you're some kind of literary genius or something just because you're English?"

"I think my story was better than anything you could dream up on the spur of the moment."

"Okay. It served the purpose. I'll give you that. Even Susan Henshaw believed it."

"There's no reason to worry about Susan Henshaw. She's not involved in the investigation. I heard Kathleen and Brett talking about it the day Z was found. But I think I'd better get back to my party."

"I should, too. A good hostess sets the mood of the party, as Z used to say."

"I remember Z's pearls of wisdom as well as you do. But I think I should get inside. Brett may have arrived ..."

"You wish!" Susan heard a door slam.

"Bitch!" Apparently the houses were identical down to the smallest detail: Gillian's door sounded just like that of her next-door neighbor.

Susan, now that the scene was over, realized she was getting cold. She would have loved to go back inside. And she would have, too, if only the door hadn't locked when it blew shut.

SEVENTEEN

SUSAN WAS TRYING TO DECIDE WHETHER TOASTED STOLLEN was a better breakfast than gingerbread cookies when her husband asked another question.

"So how did you get back in?" Jed was sticking to his nonholiday breakfast of Grape Nuts and coffee.

"There was a lot of traffic between both parties all night long. I just waited until I heard someone outside, and then I screamed my head off. Whoever heard me told Gillian about it, and she came up and rescued me."

"Weren't you embarrassed?"

"Of course. An invitation to an open house doesn't generally offer unlimited access to every nook and cranny. Aren't you going to be late for work?"

"No one will notice. Nothing much is happening this week. I wouldn't even bother to go in if I hadn't scheduled lunch with a client." True to his word, he poured himself another cup of coffee.

"I haven't been into the city since the second week in December," Susan said, sighing. She loved New York City during the holidays.

"Why don't you come in with me? I can drive, and I don't even work this afternoon. Maybe we could have an early dinner."

It was tempting. "But I should do some investigating."

"Well, if you're busy . . ."

Actually, she wasn't. In fact, she had no idea where to go or what questions to ask. After last night, Gillian and Alexis probably weren't too anxious to see her. The mayor and his wife were fed up with her. Everyone at The Holly and Ms. Ivy was busy, and she didn't seem to be finding any answers there either. And, painful as it was to admit, Kathleen had broken their date for breakfast and was probably out with Brett solving the murder at this very minute. Maybe a break was exactly what she needed. "Can you wait about half an hour so I can get dressed and put on some makeup?"

"Don't rush. The roads have been cleared. We won't have trouble getting in."

Susan ignored his advice and hurried upstairs. She stopped in her son's room. He was still asleep, which might be why he agreed to make sure the dog got outside as much as was necessary. Her daughter was dozing in the next room, but she woke up enough to announce that she wasn't going to be in for dinner, but that she wouldn't be home too late.

Susan was so excited planning her day that she didn't stop to think about any of this. She hurried to get ready, mentally comparing the merits of uptown and downtown. By the time she was back downstairs, she'd decided to spend the day in Greenwich Village and Soho. She grabbed an elaborately embroidered ethnic scarf to hang around her neck, knowing such an accessory was almost required in that part of the city, and returned to her husband.

"I'm ready."

"Great!" Jed grinned. "You look super. Just let me get my coat."

Susan smiled back, wondering exactly why a compliment from someone she'd been living with for twenty-three years would still mean so much. She paused to say good-bye to Clue before following her husband to the garage.

After a surprisingly relaxing trip into the city, Susan and Jed parted at the parking garage. He continued on to his office; Susan found a cab to take her to a favorite shop on Waverly Place. She spent the next few hours poking around stores that were old favorites and exploring exciting new ones. She bought a dozen handwoven napkins, large green bars of soap purporting to smell like rainwater (probably not acid rain, Susan thought), a turquoise silk shirt, a new calendar, and a bright orange felt hat that she hoped wasn't too young-looking for her. She was glancing into windows as she passed, trying to find an answer to the last question, when she realized she was staring at gleaming white cloths on tiny tables in a wood-paneled restaurant. A wonderful scent of beef was in the air. Lunchtime.

A handsome waiter led her to a table near a window where she could watch the people passing as she sipped the mulled wine that he recommended while waiting for her shepherd's pie to arrive. She tucked her packages around her chair, feeling a little like a drooping Christmas tree. She was going to head south after lunch to forage in Soho, and she had to admit that she hadn't thought about Z's death all morning long. She leaned back in her chair and sighed. She was having a wonderful time.

And so, apparently, was Chrissy who had just entered the restaurant with a young man who reminded Susan of Robert Redford—about fifteen years ago. Her daughter was looking up at him and laughing. The laughter stopped when she spied her mother.

"Mother! What in the world are you doing here?"

Susan had been a mother for almost twenty years; she had become very good at recognizing when she was embarrassing one of her children. The look on Chrissy's face told her that she had surpassed herself this time.

But Chrissy's young man apparently wasn't of the same opinion. He hurried forward, a smile on his face. "This is your mother, Chrissy? You know how I've been wanting to meet your family." He took the hand Susan held out in both of his. "Mrs. Henshaw. I am Klaus Hoffmann. It is so nice to meet the mother of the woman I love. Wait, let me get us a larger table so we can all sit together." He turned and directed waiters and busboys until they had achieved the results that he desired. Susan was impressed with his self-assurance, and she could tell that her daughter was also proud of Klaus.

In a few minutes, they had all settled down. Klaus had ordered for himself and Chrissy, and Susan was digging through cheese-topped mashed potatoes to the delicious stew underneath. It was turning out to be a wonderful day. She was finally meeting Chrissy's new boyfriend, and he was everything that she wanted for her daughter.

Klaus Hoffmann wasn't just extraordinarily good-looking, charming, and competent. He was intelligent, articulate, and obviously smitten with her daughter. He and Chrissy ate steaming bowls of onion soup and crispy *croque monsieur*, and drank dark beer while he chatted with Susan, talking about his studies (Brown, prelaw), his family (as Chad had reported, owners of one of the most prestigious food emporiums in the city with branches in the more affluent areas on the East Coast), his travels (worldwide apparently), his politics (suitably liberal), and his future plans (possibly politics). Susan tried to avoid gushing. Chrissy was noticeably silent.

So silent, in fact, that Susan decided it was time for her to continue on her way. "I'd better get going," she said, nodding to a hovering waiter for the check.

"My treat," Klaus insisted.

"I can't let you do that...."

"Mother, let Klaus pay if he wants to," Chrissy spoke up for the first time.

"But ...," Susan began her protest.

"Please Mrs. Henshaw. My treat. I've enjoyed our lunch and meeting you so much, and this is a special day for Chrissy and me."

"Klaus ..." There was a warning implied in the way Chrissy said his name.

"We're going to go pick out my Christmas present for Chrissy," Klaus continued. "We waited until today to do it since we met one year ago today."

"Really? Where did you meet?" Susan asked, knowing that her daughter would think she was intruding, but unable to help herself.

"Here. In the Village," he answered.

"We met at a party I went to last year," Chrissy added with a sigh. "You probably don't remember. You weren't home. You and Dad went skiing with Chad for the three days right after Christmas."

Susan nodded. She remembered. Jed had felt it was okay to leave Chrissy, a high-school senior at the time, alone while the rest of the family got in a couple of days of cross-country skiing. She had worried about her daughter for almost every minute of the time they were gone.

"Of course, we didn't start dating right away," Klaus continued. "But then I ran into Chrissy at a party in Boston last fall, and well, we've been seeing each other ever since then." He had taken the bill from the waiter while speaking and, adding it to his own, had paid both.

"Well, I thank you for lunch, and I hope we meet again soon. Perhaps you'd like to come to our New Year's Eve party," Susan suggested.

"We have plans that night, Mother."

"But we'll be sure to stop in for a moment or two," Klaus said, standing as Susan got up.

It took more than a few minutes to gather all of Susan's packages and say some parting words. By the time she was back on the street, she could almost feel her daughter's annoyance, but she was still thrilled. What a nice young man Klaus had turned out to be. She had just decided that there was absolutely nothing to be gained by wondering just how serious their relationship had become since fall, when it occurred to her that the only type of present that couples usually choose together was jewelry—specifically a ring. She stopped dead in the middle of Houston Street, endangering herself and causing a taxi driver to show off the remarkable tone of his car's horn.

Was it possible that her daughter was getting engaged and keeping it a secret from her family? Had Jed been closer to the mark than he thought when he kidded about reserving The Holly and Ms. Ivy for their daughter's wedding reception? Were they already too late to get them? Would there even be The Holly and Ms. Ivy by the time Chrissy got married—even if it was soon?

Now wait, she ordered herself, having attained the other side of the street. This was her day off. She wasn't going to worry about Z's murder. She wasn't going to obsess about her daughter's future. She was going to have a nice day and meet Jed for dinner. She proceeded with a determined step down Greene Street.

Susan didn't have enough self-discipline to make it through the afternoon without mental distress, but she did manage to enjoy herself before returning uptown.

She got to the restaurant a little late, and Jed was waiting for her at their table. The Sign of the Dove was an old favorite, pretty in any season, beautiful during the holidays. Jed was interested in hearing about Klaus Hoffmann, completely unwilling to believe that their daughter would become engaged without introducing her parents to the young man, and he liked her hat. They had a very nice dinner.

"You're not going out tonight?" Jed asked, stirring his espresso while they waited for dessert.

"No. Of course not."

"You've been out every night since Christmas."

"I guess so. But it hasn't been very much fun."

"Susan, don't you think Brett and Kathleen can handle this one without you? There's the entire police force, too, you know. I hate to see you ruining your holiday this year."

"I'm not," she assured him. "I've had a nice Christmas. And not cooking for a party has really freed up my time this week."

"But?"

"But I miss doing it, I guess."

"If that's the only problem, we could give a Valentine's Day party."

"That's a good idea. But that's not all that's bothering me."

"I didn't think so. What else?"

"I don't feel comfortable being left out of the investigation of Z's death."

"Well, of course . . ."

"No, not of course. Why of course? There's no reason for me to be left out."

"You seemed to think Brett and Kathleen . . ."

"I did, but it doesn't make any sense. I know Kathleen. She's crazy about Jerry. She wouldn't get romantically involved with Brett. It's simply not like her."

Jed nodded. "I can't tell you how happy I am to hear that. I've been trying to convince myself that it isn't true."

"Did you ever see any signs that they were having any trouble in their marriage?" Susan asked seriously.

"None. In fact, Jerry said something recently that led me to believe that they were thinking about a brother or sister for Bananas."

"Really? Kathleen didn't say anything to me," Susan said, wondering if she knew her friend as well as she thought.

"Jerry just mentioned how nice it was that we had two children and how nice it would be for Bananas if he had a sibling to play with."

Susan once again wondered how the Gordons had stayed so naive about children after so many years of watching Chad and Chrissy. Not that they weren't good kids, but they'd had their problems like anyone else. She pursed her lips.

"Are you thinking about this young man of Chrissy's?"

"No, about the investigation. I'm not at all worried about Klaus. He's almost too good to be true."

"Then maybe he is," Jed said quietly.

"Is what?"

"Too good to be true."

"Jed, you haven't even met him, and you don't like him! That's not fair!"

"I didn't say I didn't like him. I just said that maybe he wasn't exactly what he seems. There must be some reason that Chrissy didn't introduce him to us."

"I've been thinking about that, and I'm not sure it's necessarily a bad reason. She finally has a life separate from her family; that might be very valuable to her, and she might not want to share it with us right away. Or . . ."

"Or what?"

"Or maybe she's involved in something she knows we wouldn't approve of."

"Like what?" Jed asked.

"I don't know. But I know if I let myself, I can imagine about twenty things that will make me crazy. And we still won't be nearer to the truth."

Jed dipped his spoon into the crème caramel that the waiter had just set in front of him and tasted it. "You know, Klaus and Z seem to be similar men."

Susan's mouth dropped open. "You know, you're right. I'd never thought of it like that. Do you think Z was a phony, too?"

"I don't necessarily think Klaus is a phony, but . . ."

"But it is something to think about," his wife agreed readily. "It's actually what everyone says about Z—that he was everything they wanted. And Jamie told me that Gwen left all the schmoozing of hostesses to him because he was so good at it. And Jamie's aunt said pretty much the same thing when she was talking about how he was such a good tenant because he always said the right thing, but she didn't have to worry about him because he wasn't really involved with her—he didn't actually care, he just acted like it."

"And you think someone killed him because of that?"

"I think that I don't actually know anything about him because of that."

"How can you find out?"

"Gwen Ivy could tell me. She knew him when he was in college. She probably knows him better than anyone else."

"She's also the major suspect in his murder," her husband reminded her.

"I know. Maybe it's time she thought about that and started telling the truth." Susan drained her coffee cup and put it down less than gently on the saucer.

"Does that mean you want to go home right away?"

"Actually, I think it means I'm going to be going to another party or two tonight."

"Ah, the life of a society dame," Jed kidded her. "Lunch in a small bistro in Greenwich Village, dinner at the Sign of the Dove, and then an appearance at a party or two later in the evening . . . Where are you going?"

"To find a phone. I think I'd better put in a call to Jamie Potter. She'll probably be able to tell me where Gwen is tonight."

"Then I guess I'll pay the check and get our coats."

They were back out on the highway, heading for Connecticut, in less than half an hour. Susan's call to Jamie had been a success, and she was, once again, deciding what to wear. "There are probably women who have whole wardrobes of party clothes," she commented to her husband.

"Makes a nice Armani tux sound like a simple solution to your problem."

"That's an idea. I'll wear my tux," Susan said, hoping that the pants would fasten comfortably—or at all.

Jed wasn't very interested in clothing. "What do you think you're going to accomplish talking with Gwen Ivy at this point? Hasn't she told you all that she is going to?"

"Things change. There aren't a lot of other serious suspects in this case. She's going to have to tell me more unless she wants to be arrested. Besides, just because I ask the same questions doesn't mean that I'll get the same answers."

"Good point." Jed nodded.

"I read it in a mystery novel last week. The detective said it while standing over the decapitated body of the latest victim of a serial killer."

"Doesn't sound like your usual reading."

"It isn't. I gave up midway through and started to reread a Barbara Pym."

Jed chuckled. "So you're going to wear your tux, but where are you going?"

"Jamie says there are three places that Gwen Ivy will be."

"Three parties that The Holly and Ms. Ivy are catering? Is that usual?"

"They work more than one party a lot of nights. But not, I think, when there are *big* parties—like the hospital ball the other night."

"So what's tonight?"

Susan checked out the list she had written down while talking on the phone with Jamie. "The biggest affair today is a huge holiday open house that the Fairfaxes are giving."

"He's that corporate lawyer who sued IBM last year."

"I guess. I know he lives up on the hill in one of the original mansions in Hancock. Anyway, Jamie said it's a major party. It started at two this afternoon and is expected to run till late tonight—possibly as late as midnight. But

most of the guests were to be there between four and eight.
So she thought that's probably when Gwen would have
been present."

"So you're not going to bother to check that one out,"
Jed said, glancing at his watch. It was almost eight-thirty.

"Well, I may just drop in at the kitchen—to see how the
party is going."

"And peek at the house?"

Susan smacked her husband gently with her purse. "You
know me too well. But really, Jed, there might be something going on. After all, think how many people have gotten sick at parties this week. And I never would have found
out about Cameo and Z if I hadn't gone to the Logans'
house."

"Okay. So where else are The Holly and Ms. Ivy working?"

"They have two evening parties tonight. The first is at
the Bennigans. They used to invite us to their annual
Christmas party—but I don't think we got an invitation this
year."

"Have we ever accepted one of their invitations?"

"Not the last few ones—we were skiing last year, and
the year before there was some sort of conflict. . . . And
there was something else the year before that."

"No wonder they stopped inviting us."

"True. Well, the other party is being given by the local
historical society down at the old mill. It's a buffet supper
for the thirty largest contributors to the society in the past
year. It's going to be entirely lit by candles."

"Nice and dark for hiding any evidence."

"Good point," Susan agreed, nodding seriously.

"Well, we're almost there. Are you looking for a date tonight?"

"You want to come with me?"

"If you need me."

Susan appreciated the reluctance in his voice and his
willingness to help her out despite his own desires. She decided to let him off the hook. "I don't think I'll need you
tonight. I'm not invited to any of these places. I'm going in
through the back door, so to speak."

EIGHTEEN

ENTERING THROUGH THE BACK DOOR HAS ITS ADVANTAGES. For one thing, you don't havé to wait for anyone to pass the food, Susan thought, swiping a tiny, filled cream puff from a large pile waiting to be served. "Ugh. What is this?" she asked when it didn't live up to her sweet expectations.

"They're appetizers. Crab and shrimp," a young man explained, a smile on his face. "Desserts are over there." He nodded toward a long counter where two people were busily cutting cakes and arranging trays of meringues, marzipan fruits, and chocolate-dipped strawberries.

"I'm Susan Henshaw."

"Welcome. Jamie said you might be dropping in tonight—that you're looking for Gwen Ivy."

"Is she here?" Susan looked around the busy room.

"I don't think so. She was earlier, while we were setting up, and she might be back. . . ."

"Do you have a few minutes when I could ask you some questions?"

"Jamie said you might want to talk with other people. I'd be happy to answer if you don't mind if I keep working."

"Great." She leaned back against the counter and tried to gather her thoughts. "You don't usually have visitors in the kitchen, do you?" she asked, noticing that she wasn't getting much attention.

"Never. Well, maybe that's a little strong. There was an article on The Holly and Ms. Ivy in an issue of *Vogue* last fall, and a reporter and a photographer hung around for about a week. And once in a while we get a mention in the *Times* or a local paper, and a reporter or two come out on jobs with us. But it's rare. Usually all of that type of thing is done back at the carriage house."

Susan wasn't surprised. This was a private party in a private home. The Holly and Ms. Ivy had obligations to keep it that way for those that employed them. "But doesn't anyone ever bring friends along—just to look around and see what a caterer actually does?"

"Well, it's a rule that gets stretched now and then. There have been boyfriends and girlfriends smuggled in once or twice. We work for some very famous people. It's impressive if you can let your date peer through an open doorway at Richard Gere or Neil Simon. I've never done it—but that might be because my wife is the fish chef. She's right over there opening oysters." He nodded at the pretty Oriental woman who was indeed up to her elbows in one of Susan's favorite foods.

"She's lovely," Susan said honestly, and continued her questions. "Does anyone ever get caught bringing a date along on a job?"

"Once in a while."

"What happens?"

"It depends. Mainly on the circumstances. For instance, my friend Oscar over there"—he exchanged grins with a young man who was arranging steamed baby vegetables on a large platter—"brought his date on a job down in Westport a few months ago—it was a Halloween party as I recall—and Z came in unexpectedly and caught her. He was pretty cool about the whole thing."

"He told me not to do it again, and that was it. Oh, and not to let Gwen know about it," Oscar called out, grinning.

"So Gwen Ivy is more likely to get angry about that type of thing?" Susan asked.

"Yes."

"No."

"Not necessarily," came a voice from the dessert display. "Remember what happened to Jeffrey."

"That's true," someone from behind Susan agreed.

"What," Susan asked the room at large, "happened to Jeffrey?"

"Someone else better tell her. I have to get these trays on the tables in the dining room."

"Don't forget desserts in the library next to the samovar," someone else reminded the man who had mentioned Jeffrey's story.

"I'll do it. You tell the story," someone else suggested, taking the dessert platters and leaving the room.

"About Jeffrey and his date . . ." Susan prodded.

"It wasn't a date. Well, he thought she was a date, but it turned out that she had other motivations."

"You are going to explain, aren't you?" Susan asked as patiently as possible. She did want to find Gwen Ivy before midnight.

"Well, Jeffrey was a pastry chef. A good one and a very nice man. But he was sort of gullible. He was dating a woman who kept begging him to bring her along on a job. She was just dying to see him work is what she claimed—or something like that. So he finally brought her along to a job we were doing at the River House in New York City. I don't remember who gave that party, but pretty much everyone who lives there is famous. Anyway, Jeffrey snuck this girl into the kitchen."

"But she didn't stay in the kitchen," a voice called out from the other side of the room.

"No, she claimed to have to use the bathroom, and instead of using the one attached to the maid's quarters, she wandered right out into the party itself. And, if that wasn't bad enough, she started taking pictures of the party. One of the people waiting on tables saw it and came back and told Jeffrey. He almost died."

"And she got caught?"

"No. In fact, no one would have known anything about it if she hadn't published an article about the party and some of the guests in *New York* magazine. Turns out she was just a reporter after a good story—not after Jeffrey. He was pretty hurt."

"But he did the honorable thing."

"He did. He went straight to Gwen and Z and explained that the pictures were all his fault, that he had invited the girl to the party."

"And how did they react?"

"They fired him. But they also found him a better job, so it didn't matter at all."

"What?"

"Well, they really couldn't keep Jeffrey on staff after that happened. We guarantee privacy for our guests. Someone had to pay for the fact that a client's privacy had been violated. But they saw that Jeffrey had been guilty of bad judgment and that he wouldn't do it again. So they fired him and found him an excellent job with another company out on the West Coast. Jeffrey grew up in San Jose and had been wanting to get back to California, so it worked out for him as well."

"And this was both Z and Gwen? A joint decision by them both?"

The question seemed to stump the group. "I don't think anyone ever knew," Jamie's friend finally concluded.

"They didn't disagree?"

"At least not publicly," someone amended.

"At least not until recently," someone else added, and Susan noticed many nods of agreement.

"Things were different recently?" she asked.

"Z was a little out of control the weeks before he died . . . ," a woman leaning over an open oven door said almost to herself.

"You know, I don't think that's true. I think people started talking like that after he was murdered."

Susan would have loved to get to the bottom of this, but a dignified-looking man with an English accent that would have done P. G. Wodehouse proud appeared in the doorway. It was Mr. Fairfax, and he was not happy.

"May I ask exactly what is happening here?" he began angrily. "The tables are beginning to appear ravaged, ashtrays are getting fuller, and I believe someone is supposed to be serving cappuccino in the library."

In the ensuing organized confusion, Susan discovered herself scooping hard sauce into the center of a ring of plum pudding, her back to the room. When things returned to normal, she quietly thanked everyone and left by the back door, scurrying to her car.

More questions, more questions, she thought, backing slowly down the Mercedes-filled driveway to the street. Was Z acting differently in the weeks before he died, or was that just a bit of revisionist history resulting from the shock of his murder? She bit her lip and turned her car in the direction of the Bennigan's house. That party should be in full swing. Perhaps Gwen Ivy would be there.

The Bennigans lived in a lovely old Victorian near Jamie Potter's aunt. The house was decorated with thousands of tiny lights wound around the half-dozen posts holding up the roof over the porch and hanging from evergreen swags draped from above. Wreaths, also wrapped with lights, hung at all the windows, and on the lawn, a flock of white wooden deer grazed, similarly lit wreaths encircling their necks. Susan, thinking of next Christmas at her own home, made mental notes as she parked her car and started around to the back of the house.

"Susan Henshaw! Good to see you! Where's Jed?"

Susan stopped. Ben Bennigan was walking down the sidewalk toward her.

"I wouldn't even have seen you if I hadn't been helping Harvey to his car. Merry Christmas late! Happy New Year early! Come on in and try some of the wassail this expensive caterer that Beth hired has made. Got to warn you—it's sweet, but it's got a real kick!"

Susan didn't think she had any choice but to follow the man into his house. It was apparent that the Bennigans' marriage was similar to her own in at least one respect: the wife organized their social life. Beth Bennigan would probably know that Susan hadn't been invited to the party. And Beth Bennigan was standing right inside the front door.

But Beth had beautiful manners. (Or a poor memory? Perhaps she wasn't sure to whom she had sent an invitation?) "Susan, so nice of you to come. Let me take your coat and get you something to drink."

Susan had no choice but to become the perfect guest. She handed over her coat, accepted a steaming cup of wassail (which was yummy), and chatted politely with friends and neighbors as she worked her way toward the food. Jamie had told her that she was scheduled to work this party as well as the one at the mill, and Susan hoped to find her in or near the kitchen.

But first, she ran into Jamie's aunt. "I remember you. You're that friend of Z's," the elderly lady insisted, grabbing Susan's arm.

Susan resisted the urge to claim that she had never met Z and, instead, complimented the woman on her unusual jewelry. She tried to continue on her journey until she ran into Jerry's mother.

"Mrs. Gordon! How nice to see you!" she lied. It wasn't that she didn't like the woman; it was just that she was beginning to think she'd never find Gwen Ivy. And Beth Bennigan was bearing down from behind, a typewritten list in her hand. Susan could only pray that it wasn't a copy of this evening's guest list. It was one thing to crash the hospital charity ball, but a friend's party. . . . "Where did you get that interesting necklace?" she continued to Jerry's mother. She could use the information to avoid that place in the future.

"Do you like it? I made it. I take classes in bead making at an art center near where I live. I gave Kathleen one just like it. Maybe . . ."

Too late Susan recognized the gleam of a true craftsman with closets full of product that she didn't know how to dispose of.

"This would look lovely on you. Just what you need to brighten up that drab pants suit. I don't know why designers have us all wearing black, do you?"

Susan was too busy trying to express her appreciation for a gift she definitely did not want, to answer that question. "Thank you for the necklace," she said as enthusiastically as possible. "You know, I've been trying to find Jamie Potter all evening. I saw her aunt, but I . . ."

"Don't you just love the pin that woman is wearing? You'd never guess it was made from empty toilet paper rolls, would you?"

That, in fact, was one of the last things Susan would have guessed. "Do you know where her niece is?" Susan asked.

"In the kitchen maybe?"

"Then I'll just try to find her there, if you'll excuse me," Susan said, and left without waiting for an answer.

The kitchen was usually behind the dining room in homes like this, and Susan hurried there as quickly as possible. Much to her relief, she discovered Jamie Potter, busy arranging stars of aspic around a cold, boned poached salmon. "Jamie! Have you seen Gwen recently?"

"About a dozen times, but the last I heard she was on her way over to the mill," the young woman answered without stopping her work.

"Damn!"

"Why is it so urgent that you find her?"

"Because she's the person who knew Z the best and can answer my questions about him."

Jamie paused in her task and looked up. "There might be someone else . . . someone else who knew Z very well."

"Your aunt?"

"No, Aunt Flo is a sweetheart, but she knows as much about people as she knows about art."

"Oh, no."

Jamie nodded. "Exactly."

"So who else?"

"Look, if I tell you, it's betraying a confidence."

"But in a murder investigation—" Susan began.

"I know what you're going to say, but I wouldn't feel comfortable telling you any more until I check with . . . with this person."

Susan frowned. "I can't argue. When can you see her?"

"Him. And I should be able to talk with him sometime tonight—if you can just hang around."

"Here?"

"For a while, and then I have to go over to the mill—I'm making currant fool."

"He works for The Holly and Ms. Ivy?" Susan asked, mentally running through all the male chefs as potential . . . potential what? she wondered.

Jamie nodded. "Yes. But not many people know about his relationship with Z, so I don't think you're going to be able to guess his identity."

"Okay. I'll wait. Maybe I'll run into Gwen in the meantime."

"It's more than possible. She's always around somewhere." Jamie began to pipe tiny red-and-green ivy around the platters she had just decorated.

"Everything looks beautiful," Susan said honestly.

"Thanks. It's what we're known for."

There was something in the way she said it that made Susan wonder what Jamie Potter thought about the product of The Holly and Ms. Ivy's efforts. "Is something wrong?"

"I'm just worried. We're all worried," she added, putting the salmon to one side and beginning to slice a many-layered pâté. "No one knows what's going to happen to The Holly and Ms. Ivy—and whether or not we're going to have jobs after the holidays."

"I thought you—or someone—said that Gwen would hire an assistant, and then things would go on as usual."

"Maybe." The pâté sliced, Jamie began to arrange the slices on a small tray, placing marinated mushrooms around the edges. "But maybe not. There's no information about our jobs next week."

"And there would be usually?"

"Well, we do take a few days off after New Year's, but The Holly and Ms. Ivy is always fully booked—even during the worst years of the recession, we were fully booked. And supplies can't be ordered at the last minute."

"And they haven't been?"

"Well, usually by now Gwen or Z would be talking to the chefs about anything unusual that might be necessary."

"And that hasn't happened?"

"No." Jamie finished the tray and went over to the sink to wash her hands. "I'm probably just making something out of nothing. Things just aren't the same as usual—which is to be expected. Z was such a . . . such a presence. You always felt that he was around to help out."

"But he was one of the owners—didn't anyone ever feel like he was looking over their shoulders just a bit too much?" That's what Susan had thought when she saw that the carriage house was arranged so the employers could always look down on the employees. "Didn't anyone ever resent how much Gwen and Z were around?"

"Oh, no. Neither of them is like that! They're both great to work for. And that's probably the problem. Everything has been so great. I just hate for things to change."

Susan didn't offer the common platitudes. She picked up a piece of pâté that had fallen on the counter, popped it in her mouth, and waited for Jamie to continue.

"Susan, what are you doing here?" The hostess had arrived to check out activities in the kitchen.

Susan couldn't think of an answer. She knew where the bathroom was in this house.

"Mrs. Henshaw was a little nervous about the menu for her party the night after next. I could answer her questions without stopping work," Jamie said, having no idea that the Bennigans weren't invited to that particular event—or that Susan had crashed this party, for that matter.

Susan just smiled awkwardly.

NINETEEN

Susan had always enjoyed Hancock's historic sites. She had chaperoned class trips to the town's picturesque Colonial cemetery and had visited re-creations of the Revolutionary War army encampment last fall. She had not only been to the old mill many times, she used the stone-ground flour produced and sold there. But she had never tried to sneak into the back door after dark.

The parking lot had been plowed and salted, and the paths in and out of the building were outlined with candles set in tin lanterns. Big fat candles were lit in the few windows that the building possessed, and their light spilled out onto the snow. But Susan didn't know how to find the place where The Holly and Ms. Ivy had set up. The mill was built on three levels, and through the nearest window, she could see people milling around with glasses in their hands. She scrambled down the slope toward the water, trying to find a window with a view of the middle floor. A rock slipped out from under her foot, and she grabbed the side of the building for balance as she made her way down.

As she had guessed, tables were set up on the second floor. From where she stood, she could see a few tables covered in heavy, unbleached damask. Hurricane lights stood in the center of each, freshly lit candles shining down on gleaming place settings. They had to be preparing the food on the first floor, where the sales counter was usually set up. That door was just off the wooden pathway built over the stream that ran the gigantic wooden wheel. Footprints in the snow confirmed Susan's guess that The Holly and Ms. Ivy were using this entrance.

A cracked window emitted the scent of charred beef fat. Susan entered without knocking. She had been in a lot of kitchens, but she'd never seen anything like this. Three ovens, a half-dozen double burners, and four microwaves (which explained the portable generator humming outside) were set up around a large fireplace in which a gigantic piece of meat sputtered and spit. A woman was busy basting the joint, a piece of aluminum foil tied across her chest. A long pine table stretched across the room (it was made from one continuous piece of wood, aged by hundreds of years of use, and Susan had always adored it), and a half-dozen chefs were gathered around it stirring, mixing, and preparing frantically.

Susan, unwilling to get in the way, leaned back against the cool stone wall and waited for a break in the action to ask if Jamie's friend had time to speak with her. But Jamie, who had left the Bennigans' an hour before Susan and was working busily, noticed her before she had time to cool down.

"I don't suppose you could give us a hand, Mrs. Henshaw?" Jamie cried out, seeing Susan for the first time. "We're having a few problems here."

"What do you—?"

Jamie rightly regarded the beginning of the question as an offer of help. "The beef. If you could take over basting that damn meat, then Meredith could get back to the Yorkshire puddings before they burn."

"I ..." Susan looked nervously at the flaming inferno that, admittedly, smelled wonderful.

"Don't worry. We'll wrap you up well in aluminum, and the oven mitts are old ones—lined with asbestos before it became illegal. You won't get burned."

Susan didn't want to refuse. She allowed herself to be aproned, tied up with two layers of foil, and placed on an unsteady three-legged stool.

"If you're going to fall, don't fall toward the fire," the young man who had arranged all this suggested lightly.

"I'll work on it," she assured him. She noticed that, with the current arrangement of the room, either the microwave or a large bowl of red berries sitting on the end of the table she admired were the alternative landing spots. She placed her feet as firmly as possible on the uneven floorboards and dipped the stainless-steel ladle in the cast-iron pot of broth that sat on the floor, then emptied it gently over the sizzling meat. She was rewarded with sputtering fat and a delectable smell.

She listened to the chatter of the chefs and concentrated on her task.

"This is insane," Meredith said, returning to pans piled high with fluffy dough. "Why did they hire The Holly and Ms. Ivy if they didn't want us to cook the food that we're known for?"

"Think how insane it would have been if they had insisted that we cook everything in the Colonial manner," came the answer.

Susan looked around the room. She seemed to be the only person who was doing anything historically accurate. Jamie Potter recognized her confusion.

"The historical society gives this dinner each year and usually all the food is historically correct—actually baked over the fire. But this year they hired us, and Gwen—"

"Or probably Z," someone called out.

"Right. Probably Z convinced whoever is in charge of this that they should alter the menu this year. We used old recipes—"

"And some of them are pretty good—lots of herbs." Susan recognized the voice of the person who suggested that Z was responsible for this year's change.

"But we're doing the cooking in a modern manner. Except for the beef that you're taking care of. The only way to get the flavor of an open fire is to cook over an open fire. So everyone is getting a slice of that meat over their baron of beef, and the gravy is going to be made from the broth that's falling into the pan by your feet."

Susan had noticed this particular pan. The drippings from

it were ruining her new Ralph Lauren velvet pumps. "When do you think this person you wanted me to talk to will arrive?" was all she asked.

Jamie didn't answer, but nodded toward the good-looking man pulling large roasts from the portable ovens. He reminded Susan of someone, but the air in the room was smoky, and it was getting more and more difficult to see. She continued to work and wait.

But just when Susan had decided that she needed to see her, Gwen Ivy walked into the room. Susan couldn't lean any closer to the fire without burning herself, so she just turned away and hoped that she wasn't too conspicuous.

However, Gwen Ivy didn't run a great catering company by forgetting to pay attention to every detail. "Mrs. Henshaw? Susan? What are you doing down here?"

Susan immediately realized that Gwen assumed she was a guest at this event. "Low woman on the totem pole in the historical society," she kidded. "You know how it is; I got the crummy job."

"I thought . . . ," Gwen said, and then stopped. "Well, whatever," she continued, apparently deciding that free kitchen help was nothing to be sniffed at. "Jamie, who's preparing the currant fool?"

"I am. I'll get started as soon as the main dish goes upstairs," Jamie answered.

"And the cornmeal cookies?"

"Were made from meal ground in this very mill." Jamie anticipated the question. "And the waitresses have all been instructed to mention that fact when they're serving."

"And the oyster stew?"

"Ready to go up in about three minutes. Everyone is sitting down." A waitress appeared upon the steps that rose from the other doorway. "But we have a real problem here."

Gwen Ivy was instantly alert. "What's going on?"

"It's impossible to carry trays up and down these steps wearing long skirts. And they can't be hiked up and tucked into our aprons—not everyone is wearing dark opaque stockings."

"In fact, Carla's wearing red stockings embroidered with tiny little Santas," someone called out.

Gwen walked to the bottom of the steps and looked up. "They're steep. This should have been checked out before." In the silence of her pause, Susan wondered whether everyone in the room was thinking that if Z had been alive, it would have been done before this.

"We'll have to set up a relay system. The food will have to be taken to the top of the stairway by someone who is not wearing these ridiculous costumes." She looked over at Susan speculatively. "I don't suppose there are other members of the historical society who are willing to work tonight?"

"I don't believe so. Everyone else is expecting to be waited on," Susan said honestly. "But I don't mind helping out." Actually, she wasn't looking forward to the idea, but it would give her an excuse to hang around. She certainly couldn't go upstairs and sit down with the expected guests. But Gwen Ivy was speaking.

"I don't think you should trot up and down those stairs carrying trays—you're not used to it. Why don't you station yourself at the bottom and pass things up to Stefan. He'll supply the women at the top. But don't do anything until you're done there," she added as Susan made a move to hop up. "We don't want that damn meat to burn up after all the work it's taken to get it nice and crispy.

"Well, good luck, everyone. We're working under difficult circumstances, and I appreciate your competence. I'll be back in a little while."

As Gwen left, there was a general shuffling and a sound of chairs being scraped across the floor. The waitress dashed up the steps, and the young man that Susan was waiting to speak with turned out to be the Stefan who was stationed on the stairs.

"If you can help me get this thing off the spit, you'll be free to help out over there—and get away from this fat. You really volunteered for a miserable job."

Susan did as she was asked, relieved to get away from the fire—until she realized how drafty other parts of the room were.

Stefan noticed her discomfort. "You should have been here when we were setting up. This place is a sieve—no storm windows and cold air pouring in around that waterwheel," Stefan said, handing a large platter of homemade crackers over his head to whomever was waiting above. "Even the head of the historical society insisted that we ignore historical accuracy and ring both floors with electric heaters."

"Really?"

"They're hidden, of course."

"Of course." And that was the last chance she had to chat. First, deep bowls of steaming oyster stew were handed up the stairs.

"Oysters were practically free during Colonial times. The settlers kept them alive in barrels of cold saltwater, feeding them cornmeal like they were pets," Stefan commented. "Of course, I don't know how much heavy cream they had available back then or whether the fresh thyme sprinkled on top is absolutely authentic."

Susan passed on tiny crocks of butter and some sort of cheese spread, amused by his chatter.

"Wonder who spent the afternoon at the old wooden churn to make these?" He chuckled at Susan's startled look. "Not a chance. Probably the best New York City's gourmet stores had to offer. Actually, the first edible thing I ever made was butter—whipped it up in the old Cuisinart."

Stefan amused the room through the rest of the meal, from stew to the currant fool, crisp cornbread heart cookies, and warm (and slightly smoked) gingerbread with nutmeg sauce. His lively chatter kept Susan from thinking about how hard she was working.

Loud scraping of the chairs announced that the meal had ended, and Susan sighed and leaned back against the wall. "I'm glad that's over. I didn't realize how much work catering a party would be—and this is your third party today."

"None of us worked all the way through all the parties, believe me," Jamie said. "But it is hard work." She passed Susan a steaming glass. "Have a hot toddy—just like in the Dickens stories. You deserve it."

"I have to drive home," Susan protested, sipping and realizing how strong the drink was.

"Don't worry. Someone else can drive you home. You've done more than enough for us—you deserve it," Jamie said.

"Actually, I wanted to talk with—" Susan began.

"Maybe Stefan would drive you home," Jamie interrupted.

Susan looked up at the handsome young man. "That would be very nice," she agreed.

"I'd rather be with a lovely lady than cleaning up any day."

"When you're done chauffeuring, you can come back to the carriage house and do your share of the dirty work," Jamie insisted.

"They don't appreciate me," Stefan said, grinning at his coworkers. "Where did you hang your coat?"

They gathered their belongings and walked out into the freezing cold to Susan's car.

"You did some good work tonight," Stefan complimented her, accepting her car keys and sliding into the driver's seat. "Why were you there?"

"You mean you didn't believe that I was the only member of the historical society doing volunteer work tonight?"

"It seems a little unlikely."

"It is. I came to the mill looking for you."

"Me? Why? Has something happened between your daughter and my brother?"

"Your bro—" Susan had a revelation. "That's who you remind me of . . . Klaus Hoffmann."

"My beloved younger brother." He started her car before asking a question. "You mean you didn't know who I was? Then why were you looking for me?"

"Because Jamie Potter told me that you knew Z Holly better than anyone else."

"Gwen . . ."

"Gwen only tells me what a wonderful person he was. . . ."

"Because he was truly a wonderful person. I don't think you'll find many people who say anything different than that."

"But . . ." Susan began to protest that no one was completely wonderful—no one who would inspire a murder. "What about all the people I've met this week who seemed to have good reason to be mad at Z?"

"Who?"

"Like men whose wives have fallen for Z. And men whose daughters Z seduced . . . ," Susan began.

"I'll bet if you look closely at those situations, you'll discover that Z didn't seduce anyone. Z wasn't like that."

Susan glanced over at her driver, a suspicion sneaking into her mind. "Are you saying that Z was gay?"

Stefan chuckled. "No, Z was definitely heterosexual. He loved women. That was the problem. He loved them, but he didn't understand them—actually, that might have been part of his charm."

Susan, who believed that the most charming (and rare) attribute a man can possess is a deep understanding of women, wondered just how well Stefan knew Z. She asked that question.

"I was his roommate for two years in college. I introduced him to Gwen as a matter of fact. She was in one of my classes, and when she found out who my parents are—"

"The food stores—"

"And the cookbooks, the articles in food magazines, the products that they produce under their own label. All that stuff. I was busy rebelling against that. I was determined not to be a foodie—classic adolescent response to having famous parents, I'm afraid.

"Anyway, Gwen was already interested in food back then, so she sought me out, and we became friends."

"Was Z interested in food then, too?"

"Not that I knew about. He knew how I felt about my parents, so he wouldn't have talked about it."

"But he was popular," Susan suggested.

"Yes, very. Especially with women. At one point, half the women in our dorm were in love with him."

"And how did he handle that?"

"Same as always. Z didn't know how to turn anyone down, so he didn't."

"He was promiscuous?"

"Well, this was before AIDS, remember. And he didn't use these women. He just didn't want to disappoint anyone. I hope I'm not making him sound like an idiot."

"No, just sort of shallow."

Stefan nodded. "He was—that's exactly the right word. He was shallow. He loved material things; he loved giving parties, giving other people pleasure, but he didn't have any depth. And he knew it."

"He did?"

"Yes. He used to say that he wasn't someone to depend on—that he was only good at the little things in life."

Susan thought about the elegant parties, the sophisticated apartment, the boyish charm . . . It was all beginning to fall into place. "But why kill someone like that?" she asked, thinking out loud.

"Well, he did tend to fall into and out of relationships pretty easily. That made some people furious."

"Enough to kill him?"

They were pulling up in front of Susan's house. "I can't quite imagine that. Most people knew exactly what Z was about—at least since he graduated from college. Back then, the women were younger and more likely to take him seriously. But most women knew exactly what they were getting when they got involved with Z—a fine romance, but no one was going to overdose on reality."

"Unless they were still young—like those women back in college," Susan suggested, thinking of Cameo Logan.

"Maybe." Stefan turned off the engine and turned to Susan. "Do you mind if I come in and call a cab? I have to get back to the carriage house."

"Why don't I drive you?"

"I thought—"

"It was strong, so I didn't drink it. I just wanted the chance to talk with you."

"But—"

"And now I want the chance to talk with Gwen. If you think she'll be back there."

Stefan frowned. "She must be. In the past, either she or Z would close up after a busy day like this one, but now that Z's dead . . . Well, it's too much of a job for just one person."

Susan looked at him. "She is around more, isn't she?"

"That's just it," Stefan explained. "She seems to be around less—but that might just be a faulty impression. It might be that she doesn't happen to be where I am."

"Is that possible?"

"It's more than likely. We're doing three or more jobs each day. The chances of two people being together much is probably fairly rare.

"You're sure you want to go back with me?" he asked, reaching out to start the engine.

"Yes. Let's give it a try," Susan insisted, sitting back and watching one of her neighbors turn off the candles in her windows, one by one. "Who do you think Gwen will choose for a new partner?"

"I'm not sure, but I think she'll be looking for someone who can fill Z's shoes—someone to take care of the more public details of the business, someone with style and charm, probably good looks. And, of course, someone who can afford to buy into the business. I haven't seen the books of The Holly and Ms. Ivy, but I would think it would take a large chunk of cash to buy half of the business."

"Any idea of a name?"

"Well, if my parents will finance it, I'm hoping it will be me."

Susan was quiet the rest of the drive.

"Why don't you drop me off by the curb," Stefan suggested. "I have to get a change of clothing from my car. I don't want to go home wearing my uniform, and I don't think there's anything clean in my locker."

Susan did as Stefan asked and then pointed her Jeep into an empty parking spot. The lot was still full of cars, but not so full that she couldn't see that Stefan Hoffmann was removing a gym bag from a white Range Rover. Deciding to ask that question later, she followed the walk to the carriage house.

Jamie Potter was carrying a large pile of tablecloths down the center aisle as Susan walked into the room.

"Phew. Everyone you meet will wonder what you've been doing," she commented.

"They'll think she's a volunteer firefighter after a busy day," another chef, busy scrubbing a large slab of marble with vinegar, suggested.

"I smell like the fireplace," Susan said, suddenly realizing the truth of that statement.

"You reek," Jamie agreed cheerfully. "I thought you'd be home showering by now. What's up?"

"I was hoping to see Gwen," Susan admitted. "Everyone keeps talking about how she's around when you're closing up. I thought if I came here I couldn't miss her. But I did, didn't I?"

"Yup. She left about ten or fifteen minutes ago."

"Why are you still here?" Susan asked, glancing over at Jamie's work area: It was immaculate.

"Gwen asked if I would help put away some of the linens. I don't have to be in until noon tomorrow."

"No parties scheduled?" Susan couldn't believe it.

"There are never many parties the day before New Year's Eve. Sometimes none. This year we're doing one. A sweet-sixteen party for some girl named Finn or Sawyer . . . or something Mark Twainish . . ."

"Courtney Sawyer!"

"You know her?"

"My son is going to that party. In fact, I understand Chad has a real crush on Courtney Sawyer."

"You must have a good relationship. I certainly would never have let my parents know about that type of thing when I was a teenager." Jamie sorted and folded clean napkins as she spoke.

"My daughter told me about it."

Jamie chuckled. "In my case, my brother was the family blabbermouth."

"I understand Courtney's party is going to be very elaborate," Susan said, not mentioning that what she had actually heard was that The Holly and Ms. Ivy had, according to her daughter, "messed up" the reservations for the place where the party was to be held.

"Not for The Holly and Ms. Ivy. We're used to doing

these extravagant events for children. I don't think the kids like them as much as their parents do, but they are fun to arrange. If your son is going, you might want to stop in sometime during the evening."

"He'll be disappointed if there aren't lots of desserts," Susan said, as Jamie folded the last napkin and got up.

"There are lots—an excess. But no elaborate cake decorating. I'm going to be spending tomorrow working on the New Year's Eve parties we're doing. Remember, I promised you something special."

Susan grinned. "I'm looking forward to it." She glanced at her watch; it was almost one A.M. "Look, could you tell me where Gwen lives?"

"It's a little late for visiting, isn't it?"

"I won't stop in if it's dark—don't worry."

"And you won't mention my name when she asks how you know where she lives?"

"I could say I looked it up in the phone book. . . ."

"Won't work. She's unlisted. She always says that she works sixteen-hour days and has an answering machine on for the other eight, so she deserves some privacy. Well, maybe she won't ask how you know," Jamie said, frowning. "Anyway, I know you won't get me in trouble. It's 18 Applejack Lane. It's one of those cul-de-sacs down by the river—a tiny house that looks like it should be in Sweden or someplace."

Susan knew the area, and she thought she might even know the house. She made her excuses, stifled a yawn or two, and drove right over to the address she had been given. There were lights on inside the charming cottage, but despite her intentions, Susan didn't knock on the door. She had noticed that Gwen drove a silver BMW convertible. Parked in her driveway was a white Range Rover with a soiled tux tossed over the backseat.

TWENTY

Jed wandered into the living room. His wife was standing in the middle of the carpet, staring straight ahead. "What are you doing?"

"Do you think the tree looks dead?" Susan asked, not bothering to answer his question.

"It's the most beautiful tree we've ever had." Jed repeated his annual Christmas mantra.

"It's awfully dry, and I don't think it's absorbing any water."

"Well, it's been in the house for almost three weeks. But it will look beautiful tomorrow night. Everything will be just fine."

Susan sat down on the edge of the coffee table. "I'm usually frantically busy today."

"I know what you mean. I miss all the hustle and bustle myself. About now, I'm usually standing in line at the liquor store for something we forgot. It's not a bad way to visit with people you haven't seen in a while. . . ." He sat down next to his wife and put an arm around her shoulders. "Next year, we'll do the party oursel—"

"Mom's always telling me not to sit on the coffee table. And you're both doing it." Their son stood in the open doorway, a smirk on his face. "This might cause me to wonder what else you do when I'm not around."

"Are you here for any reason other than to hassle your hardworking parents?" Jed asked.

"I need a ride to Courtney's party this afternoon."

"When?"

"I don't want to be too early, and I should shower and shave. In an hour," Chad decided.

"I'd be happy—"

"I'll do it," Susan interrupted her husband. "I have to go out anyway," she added.

"And you'll nag me the entire way," Chad said, turning and leaving.

"What was all that about?" Jed asked his wife.

"He has a crush on Courtney Sawyer. He's nervous."

"Why don't we drop him off, and then go out for lunch? We could try that new Indian restaurant downtown."

"I was thinking that I might stop in at the party."

"Are we planning to go? Chad might not appreciate our presence."

"No, but . . ."

"I gather The Holly and Ms. Ivy are doing the catering."

"I'm actually getting somewhere—I think."

"You're awfully involved in this investigation, hon."

"But, Jed, I'm getting somewhere."

"You know who killed Z?"

"No, but I know that something strange is going on, and I may even know what it is."

"So what's wrong?"

"I woke up in the middle of the night, positive that if I knew why Brett and Kathleen were leaving me out of this investigation, I'd be a step or two ahead of the game. I mean, if you and I are right, and Kathleen and Brett aren't romantically involved . . ."

"Kathleen . . ."

"Won't tell me anything."

"Brett . . ."

She nodded. "That's exactly what I was thinking. I should talk to Brett. The question is, should I talk with him before or after I check out Courtney's sweet-sixteen?"

"Well, it sort of depends on when he's around, doesn't it?"

"You're right. You drive Chad. I'll check out the police

station, and then head over there. Thanks." Susan kissed her husband on his forehead and stood up. "You'll walk the dog, too?"

"I'll bet no one has ever bought a dog in the middle of a snowstorm," Jed muttered, looking out the window at the snow.

"Probably true," Susan agreed, leaving the room without a backward glance. She had things to do.

She had awakened early this morning and filled two pages of her ever-handy notebook with questions that she needed to answer. She ran upstairs and grabbed it, stashing it in her large purse, putting on her long wool coat, and heading out the front door. Brett Fortesque might not be in his office, but Emily Benson was bound to be around.

The roads were slushy, and Susan was thankful for four-wheel drive; she passed two fender benders before following a snowplow to the municipal center.

Emily Benson was standing in the portico by the door, scattering bread crumbs on the ground. "Hi!" she waved, and metallic stars bobbed around her head. "Where's your dog?"

"My husband is taking care of her today. I'm here to see Brett—if he's available."

"You're in luck. He's in his office. And that's rare these days. Go on in. Tell the guy at the desk I saw you—I'm on my coffee break."

"Thanks. I'll talk with you later." Susan waved and hurried out of the cold. She was soon knocking on the door to Brett's office.

"Who's there?"

Susan opened the door a crack and looked in. "It's me," she said unnecessarily. "Do you have a few minutes?"

"No, but I could use a break. Come on in." Brett smiled.

"How are things going?" Susan said, sitting down in the chair he indicated.

"No more murders and, so far, no recent cases of food poisoning. And I had understood that you were staying out of this investigation."

"That's what Kathleen thinks."

"No, it's not what she thinks, it's what she knows would

be best for you and your family," Brett said seriously. "And I agree with her."

"And does that mean that you're not going to tell me anything?"

"Susan, you've helped in the past, but this investigation is different."

"Why? Why is it different? What's going on that no one is telling me about?" Susan's voice rose in anger. "I thought you were my friend! And Kathleen . . ." She was suddenly too angry to speak.

"Susan . . ." Brett reached across his desk and patted her hand.

"Don't try to calm me down. I have every right in the world to be mad."

"Susan! Damn it! We're protecting you!"

"No, you just think you are. I'm going ahead and asking questions and gathering information—"

The phone on Brett's desk rang, and Susan stopped talking.

He grabbed the receiver. "Fortesque here."

There was a long silence during which Susan looked around the room. File cabinets covered one wall and on top of them were piles of papers, falling into each other and off onto the floor. Brett's conversation continued on its unintelligible course, and Susan stood up and stretched. She had seen a book on top of a particularly precarious pile that she wanted to look at more closely. She walked casually in the direction of the files.

"Susan, would you mind getting me a cup of coffee?"

Brett's voice stopped her progress across the room. What could she do but agree? She smiled weakly in the direction of his desk and left the room, heading for the small coffee room just off the lobby.

"Done already?" asked Emily.

"Brett's on the phone, and he wants coffee."

"You know where it is. And there are pecan bars that someone sent in as well. Have some yourself. I have two calls on hold for him when he's done with this one—unless you were doing something in there?"

"I was trying to get a peek at some books and papers on

top of the file cabinets when Brett asked me to come down here."

"Ah. Well, come on out and keep me company." She looked over her shoulder to see if they were alone before continuing. "If you bring me a cookie or two, I might have some information."

Susan hurried to do as requested, and minutes later, the two women were huddled together behind Emily's desk, drinking coffee and chattering.

"I keep wondering why they won't let me help out with this investigation—what's so different about it," Susan explained.

"I don't know exactly, but it has something to do with the mayor's daughter."

"Cameo? What about? And what does that have to do with me? I don't think I've even seen her since she and Chrissy graduated from high school last spring."

"I don't know about that. Let me tell you what happened."

Susan nodded and leaned even closer.

"The chief and Kathleen Gordon were together in his office yesterday around noon when Mayor Logan wandered down from his end of the building."

"Does he do that frequently?"

"Constantly. If he's not napping in his office, he's wandering the halls, wasting everyone's time. Ask in any office. No one seems to know why he doesn't just go home. He's always talking about this big new house he has; why doesn't he spend more time there?" She pursed her bright red lips over the mystery and continued. "But that's neither here nor there, is it?"

"Brett and Kathleen were together in his office," Susan prompted.

"Well, Mayor Logan started talking to me about how noisy the snowplows are going back and forth in front of his house in the middle of the night. . . ."

"He should try being a private citizen—we barely get plowed in the daytime," Susan said.

"I know. People are always calling the police department to complain about it. But the mayor's so boring, and he's always here, and I guess I was just in a bad mood, so I told him I was busy and sort of walked away down the hall, claiming that I had some things that needed to be distributed. But he followed me, so I went into Brett's office. Well, what happened next was really embarrassing. . . ."

"What?"

"Kathleen and Brett were talking about Cameo Logan. She evidently made something of a spectacle of herself with Z last year—following him around and stuff like that. Kathleen was actually reading a report about it from a notebook when Buck followed me into the room."

"Oh, no. I know how he feels about his daughter. What did he say?"

"He didn't *say*, he roared. At first he was so furious he could only sputter. When he got his voice back, he threatened lawsuits. Then he talked about firing Brett for incompetence. I don't think he would have ever calmed down if Kathleen hadn't spoken up and said that everything she had read was confidential and was only being mentioned because Z had been killed."

"But Cameo was in Switzerland when Z was murdered," Susan protested.

"That's what Mayor Logan said. And Brett assured him that she was certainly not being considered as a suspect. Everyone was looking at me as though I didn't belong, so I left the room at that point. But I sort of hung around in the hallway, and no one bothered to close the door, so I heard the rest of the conversation, too."

"And?"

"And Brett said that the only reason Kathleen had been talking about Cameo is that they didn't want you to be involved in this particular investigation."

"What sort of sense does that make?"

"None that I know about, but I know that's what Brett said. Nothing else happened. The mayor muttered something about privacy and stormed out of the room. I couldn't keep hanging around in the hallway. The phone was ringing, and besides, someone closed the door."

"But you're sure that's what Brett said."

"Definitely."

"Then maybe I'm asking questions in the wrong office."
Emily shrugged. "It's probably his nap time, but go right
ahead. If Brett asks, I'll tell him you had to leave. . . ."

"Tell him I'm in the ladies' room—I'll probably want to
talk with him, too," Susan called over her shoulder as she
walked down the hallway toward the rest of the municipal
offices.

The holiday decorations were looking worse for wear as
Susan crunched through fallen pine needles to the mayor's
office. She was prepared to knock loudly on the door jamb,
but Buck Logan was awake. And pacing.

"Buck? It's Susan Henshaw," she continued when he
looked at her with a blank expression on his face. "I
wanted to talk with you for a minute or two—if you don't
mind."

"About what?"

Susan had known Buck Logan to be boorish, but never
outright rude. She didn't know what to say so she just
asked her question. "What connection does Cameo have
with my family?"

"Excuse me?"

"Why would Kathleen and Brett be talking about Cameo
and then connecting that with me?"

"Why would I know? All I care about is keeping the
name of my little princess clean. Ask Brett if you want to
know."

"I guess I will. And maybe," she added, spinning on one
heel, "I'll ask him to tell me if Cameo seduced Z or if Z
seduced Cameo!" And she strode off down the hall, mutter-
ing curses under her breath.

Brett was out in the hallway looking for her. "Susan!" he
called out.

She took a deep breath to calm herself down. "I was just
going to get your coffee," she lied.

"Why don't you just go back to my office, and I'll get
a cup for you? I called Kathleen, and she's on her way
over. We want to talk with you."

"About . . . ?"

"About why we've been trying to keep you out of this
investigation. Obviously, it's not working." He smiled

weakly. "Go ahead and sit down. We have a lot of talking to do."

Kathleen didn't live far, and Susan knew she wouldn't have long to wait. The papers in Brett's office hadn't been hidden, and she saw that they were copies of the admission sheets from the Hancock hospital. She thumbed through the sheets. All the preliminary diagnoses were food poisoning, type to be determined by further testing. She read through the pile quickly, but the record of Dan Irving's admission and death must be somewhere else. Hearing footsteps in the hallway, she straightened the papers and resumed her seat.

"Susan . . ."

Susan was surprised by Kathleen's entrance. "Hi. How are you?" she asked politely and formally.

"Dreading this conversation," Kathleen admitted, sitting down on a wooden bench that was fastened to the wall. "In fact, I've been dreading this conversation since Z died," she added, unwinding a long orange scarf from around her neck. "Did Brett tell you anything?"

"No." Susan leaned closer to her friend. "But you do believe that Z and I really weren't involved romantically, don't you?"

"Yes. I believe you."

"And you're not involved with Brett either, are you?" Susan whispered.

"What?" Kathleen shrieked. "How did you—? That's what you thought?" Her large eyes opened wide. "And that's what my mother-in-law has been worrying about, isn't it? Oh, my god! I can't tell you how much that explains. I've had such a strange week." She flung herself against the hard seat back. "How could you think Brett and I . . ."

"Well, it made as much sense as Z and I," Susan explained as Brett walked back into the room holding a tray of cookies and coffee.

"None of this makes a whole lot of sense," Kathleen said seriously, taking the mug Brett offered.

"So you're going to tell me what's been going on," Susan prodded, accepting a full mug and setting it on the desk untouched.

Brett and Kathleen exchanged serious looks. "Why don't you . . . ," Brett began.

"I'll do it," Kathleen said reluctantly. "But you have to understand, Susan, that we never wanted you to know any of this. We didn't think there was any reason you would have to know. We hoped . . ."

"Please tell me before my imagination takes over—I'll end up thinking the worst."

"This may be the worst," Kathleen said so quietly that Susan almost didn't hear her. She took a deep breath and continued. "You have to let me tell you everything without interrupting, otherwise I might end up leaving something out."

"Fine. Just get on with it." Susan realized that her hands were beginning to shake.

"We think . . . ," Kathleen began and took a deep breath before continuing. "We think Chrissy may have been involved with Z."

"Chrissy? No," Susan protested. "She's in love with Klaus Hoffmann. I told you about him. Okay, I'll let you finish, but it isn't true."

"First, you should know that we've checked and double-checked—and you can go over everything again. And our information is that Chrissy was involved with Z. It has nothing to do with her current young man—this was last year. Over the holidays last year," Kathleen continued to explain.

Susan thought for a moment. She didn't know that Chrissy had dated anyone seriously in her senior year. Susan had been particularly pleased with that, hoping her daughter would play the field before settling down. She certainly hadn't been aware of anyone special in her daughter's life at that time. And neither had her son, she remembered. "Who . . . ?" she began her questioning.

"Let me start at the beginning," Kathleen said. "We thought there was some connection with your family almost immediately after finding the body."

"How did you come to that conclusion?" Susan asked angrily.

"He had your address in his pocket."

"We were working together on my party tomo—"

"Susan, we're not idiots, and you know us well enough to know that we would check this out carefully," Brett said.

"I know. I'll stop interrupting," Susan promised, knowing that she had to get the entire story.

"I checked out the contents of Z's pockets myself as soon as the body was ready to be moved," Brett explained. "And there was a note inside that said 'Two o'clock in the afternoon, three days after Christmas. No one will be home but us. I love you.' That was all, except that your address was at the bottom of the page."

"Naturally we didn't think of Chrissy right away," Kathleen jumped in. "To be honest, we assumed that the note was written by you. You had been working with Z on your party, and you were . . . Well, Z could be pretty difficult for women to resist—everyone knows that."

"But Kathleen insisted that, if you were going to have an affair, you wouldn't have it in your own home," Brett added.

"Whose handwriting was it?"

"It was typed. . . ."

"You're kidding!" Susan exploded, some of her pent-up energy needing to be released. "No one types notes to a lover!"

"This person did," Brett argued. "This note is proof."

"But we didn't believe it at first ourselves," Kathleen reminded her. "Initially, all we did was try to keep you out of the investigation."

"So I wouldn't be hurt by the information that Chrissy was involved with Z."

"No, so we could get to the bottom of the note without anyone accusing us of trying to protect you or any member of your family. You know us better than that."

"Okay, I do. I'm sorry I keep interrupting. I'll shut up and listen."

"We checked it out thoroughly—sent it off to the lab immediately. It was not written recently—the tech said nine months to a year ago. It was printed on a Hewlett-Packard laser."

"We don't have one," Susan insisted.

"The high school has a couple of dozen," Brett explained.

"And you weren't home for the three days after Christmas last year," Kathleen reminded her.

"And Chrissy was," Susan said slowly. "We left her home alone for the first time. But I can't believe she would have been involved with Z back then. We didn't know either Z or Gwen at that time!"

"It's been years since you knew all of the people your children know," Kathleen reminded her quietly. "You told me that yourself just the other day."

Susan pursed her lips. "None of this is proof."

"She went to a party Z was at—a party in New York City. It was a party for foodies. It was where she met Klaus, in fact," Kathleen said.

"And Chrissy told you about that?" Susan asked.

"We heard about it first when we were questioning Gwen. She admitted meeting Cameo and Chrissy in New York City last winter. She didn't mention anyone else."

"Klaus confirmed that he was there and that he had met Chrissy there," Brett said.

"You interrogated Klaus Hoffmann!"

"I spoke with Klaus the other night at the hospital ball. I just asked some questions about how they met, and he told me. He didn't know that I was questioning him. He was very open about everything," Kathleen said. "And then, of course," she continued slowly, "there was that note in your hallway."

"The note?"

"The one that accused you of having an affair with Z . . . ," Kathleen reminded her.

"But that's not what it said . . . ," Susan began.

"No. It said, 'I know about the affair with Z,' " Kathleen said.

"It couldn't have been Chrissy," Susan protested, trying hard to believe it herself.

"It could have been. But it may have had nothing to do with his death," Kathleen reminded her.

"We have been waiting to talk with Chrissy about this,"

Brett said. "We hoped, in fact, that it wouldn't be necessary."

"Chrissy never said anything about Z," Susan said quietly.

"This may all have absolutely nothing to do with his murder," Kathleen reminded her.

"But it may," Susan said very quietly.

"Yes, it may," Brett agreed.

TWENTY-ONE

COURTNEY SAWYER'S SWEET-SIXTEEN PARTY MADE COT-
ton candy look like diet food.

Susan didn't know whether or not The Holly and Ms.
Ivy had originally booked a different location, but this restaurant had been transformed into a nightmare of pink ruffles and lace. At least that's what Susan thought. Courtney
evidently agreed; she was wearing a black Lycra sheath,
black stockings, and well-polished army boots. She was
sulking in a receiving line between her parents, telling everyone who would listen about her "new Christmas tattoo."
Her father looked like he would like to kill her. Her mother
was hoping Courtney wouldn't tell anyone exactly where
the tattoo was located.

Susan exchanged what-can-you-do-with teenagers? looks
with Courtney's parents and headed over to the dessert buffet. She knew her son well enough to assume that's where
he would be. At least, she hoped she knew her son well.
Apparently she didn't know Chrissy in the least. She took
a deep breath and continued. Her daughter hadn't murdered
anyone, and Susan wasn't going to let her be accused of
anything so absurd.

Chad wasn't by the long table of pink-sugared food, but
Susan spied him across the room, leaning against the walnut bar. He looked so grown-up, so comfortable standing

there that she rushed to his side, determined to find out what was in the tall glass he was sipping. Surely the bartender wouldn't serve liquor to anyone so young. . . .

"Chad."

"Mother."

Susan was stopped in her tracks by the formal greeting. She glanced at the other young men standing around her son. She had known many of them since they were in nursery school. They all nodded at her with less than remarkable enthusiasm. "Your mother's here," a young man whom Susan had once transported, bleeding and with a broken ankle, from a soccer game to the hospital emergency room informed Chad in a flat voice.

"I see her," Chad answered, not moving.

"I wanted to speak to you for a moment, Chad. It's important." Would she kill him if he emitted one of those bored sighs?

She didn't. He reluctantly put down his glass and walked over to her side.

"I have to ask you some questions about Chrissy. It's important," she repeated.

"It depends on what you want to know. Well, Mom," he continued, sounding more like himself, "if I tell you things about her, she could tell you things about me. Not that my life isn't an open book, as they say. But, you know."

She did. "This is important, Chad. It has to do with the murder."

He didn't say anything, so Susan continued, after looking around to make sure they weren't overheard. "Do you have any idea if Chrissy was ever involved in any way with Z Holly?"

"She's been in Boston."

"Last year. I'm asking about last year. Around this time—Christmas."

Chad looked puzzled. "I don't think I'd even heard of Z Holly until you started talking about your New Year's party."

Susan frowned. "Do you remember at all who she was dating over the Christmas holidays last year, Chad? It's important!"

"I'm thinking." He leaned back against the wall and furrowed his brow. Susan thought how cute he looked, but she had the good sense not to say anything about it. "She was going out with that guy who played the French horn in the school orchestra. I remember that. . . ."

Susan did, too. He had once spent an afternoon in her kitchen eating half a batch of chocolate-chip cookies—before they were baked.

"And she was hanging out with the Casella twins—I never could tell those guys apart. I really don't remember anyone else. She wasn't mooning around in love with anyone that I remember. Unless she had some reason to keep him hidden. Do you think that could be it?"

"It doesn't sound like Chrissy . . . Does it?" she asked, seeing the look on her son's face.

"Mom, you're not supposed to know everything about your children—we're almost grown up, for heaven's sake."

"You're right," she lied. "But I'm not prying for the sake of prying. Do you happen to remember her going into the city to a party over the holidays? I think it was around the time we were up in Vermont."

"The party in Greenwich Village! I didn't think you knew about that. Okay. It wasn't a big deal, really. But I heard about it because Chrissy tried on every piece of clothing in the house before deciding to wear black leggings and some huge shirt of yours—and then she went out and put a green rinse on her hair."

"I don't rem—"

"She did it at a friend's house. And then it didn't wash out, and she thought she was going to have to spend the rest of her life away from home."

Susan's brow was furrowed. "Did this all happen the night before we left for Vermont?" She remembered that she had been forced to talk to Chrissy about staying alone early that day because the girl was "going to a movie" with friends and wouldn't be home until late. "But she was in bed when we left in the morning!" Susan protested. "I remember her talking to me when I stopped in before we left. I'm sure of that."

"She may have talked to you, but I'll bet she kept her

hair under the blankets. My friends who saw her were still talking about it when we came back home a few days later."

"But this doesn't have anything to do with Z," Susan muttered to herself.

"The party in the Village was where Klaus met Chrissy. He said he didn't mind her hair color—that it reminded him of lettuce. You can tell he's a foodie, not one of those artistic guys that she usually likes."

Susan got the impression that her son approved. "Chrissy must have thought that it was a different type of party than it was—artists, not people in the food business."

Chad nodded.

"So how did she get invited? If she didn't even know what sort of party it was."

"I know that," Chad said confidently. "She went with a group of friends from the high school. They weren't even invited to the party. Someone knew about it, and they decided to crash. Neat, huh?"

"Cra— I really don't think that shows very good manners, Chad," Susan started, biting her lip. Like sitting on coffee tables, she wasn't going to be able to protest against this type of thing—not after this week. "But that doesn't matter now," she added quickly. "Do you happen to know which friends she went with?"

Chad frowned. "Probably that art class group she used to hang out with. You know, the dyed-hair, earring-in-the-nose clique."

"Chrissy didn't look like that in high school. She doesn't look like that now," her mother protested.

"Chrissy wasn't allowed to look like that. She and the mayor's daughter—what's her name . . . ?"

"Cameo Logan?" Susan said, thinking she was finally getting somewhere.

Chad shrugged. "Maybe. I don't remember. The girl with the terminal case of the preppies—worse than Chrissy. Well, the two of them used to stand out in that group like two virgins among the whores—I didn't call them that!" he added quickly. "That's what some of the kids used to say."

"And Cameo went to this party in New York with Chrissy and the rest of that group?"

"I don't know. I didn't stand at the door and wave good-bye. I'm not even positive about any of this!"

"Well, you've been very helpful, Chad." Even if you didn't mean to be, she added in her head. "I'll let you get back to your friends." She glanced toward the group that was still holding up the heavy walnut bar. "How are you getting home?"

"I can hitch a ride with someone," he answered, moving back across the room without waiting for more questions.

Susan let him go; she had probably already damaged his social standing beyond repair. Things were beginning to fall into place, she thought, accepting a glass of something pink from a strolling waiter.

"Wow!"

"Knocks your socks off, doesn't it?" the waiter said, smiling. "It's an old family recipe that we were given by the host. It contains dark rum, light rum, brandy, peach liquor, sugar, and grenadine. It's the grenadine that makes it pink."

Susan looked doubtfully at her glass.

"There's an open bar where you can get something else," the waiter added. "And a tray next to the wall for empty—or almost empty—cups."

Susan looked in the direction he indicated and saw a few dozen crystal cups, most containing substantial amounts of the Sawyer's family tradition. "Thanks. I think I will get something a little less sweet." She wound her way through dozens of young people, who seemed to think it "cool" to hang out around a bar, and got her drink. A band (punk? heavy metal? grunge?) was beginning to warm up on the platform to one side of the bar, and most of the adults were fleeing toward quiet corners.

Susan followed the general exodus, hoping to find the better half of the Logan marriage—preferably after that half had consumed three or four of those pink abominations. If they didn't make her sick, they'd surely eliminate any inhibitions Camilla might possess. And Susan hadn't witnessed any undue restraint on Camilla's part when it came to alcoholic beverages.

Susan didn't find anyone from the Logan family, but she was almost instantly greeted by parents of children she had known for years—many wanting to know where she had managed to procure a "real" drink. Susan made the rounds of the room, hoping to run into someone whose child might have been part of the group Chrissy used to spend time with in high school. But one of those people found her.

"Susan Henshaw. You are so lucky!"

The lottery? Maybe the Publisher's Clearing House sweepstakes? There must be something that was causing Evelyn Montiagne such excitement. Susan hadn't seen Evelyn so happy since they had found two other suckers to take over the Brownie troop they had run for three years.

"Why?" she managed to ask.

"Your daughter's boyfriend! He's wonderful. How did Chrissy manage to meet such a wonder?"

"Where did you meet Klaus?" Susan asked, sitting down next to Evelyn.

"Let's see . . . First I met them together in Bloomingdale's. Chrissy was shopping for a Christmas gift for you, and he was helping her. Your daughter has such lovely manners. She introduced him immediately. But, of course, department stores are no place to chat—at least, not the week before Christmas.

"Then they came over Christmas evening. Chrissy had called before that and talked with my daughter, of course—talked for hours and hours just like they used to. But Klaus and she stopped in with some friends, and we all had a lovely time. It's so nice when your children are grown-up enough to talk with, isn't it? And I can't tell you how impressed my husband is with Klaus. They talked like old friends. Jed must just adore that young man!"

Susan smiled weakly. What could she say? "And you've seen them since then?"

"Why, they're here. Didn't you know? They were heading off to dance the last time I saw them. Klaus was telling me how much he's looking forward to your party tomorrow night. And we are, too, of course. It's the best way we know to start the year."

Susan was glad Klaus and Chrissy were planning on coming to her party, but she had a more immediate problem. "Did you say they were heading to the dance floor the last time you saw them?"

"Yes. He's a wonderful dancer, isn't he?"

Susan seemed condemned to compliment a man she had met only once. She just smiled and, with promises to talk longer tomorrow night, hurried back to the bar area. Klaus and Chrissy were dancing energetically to music loud enough to cause the pink ruffles to jump up and down. Susan got into a position to catch her daughter's eye, but immediately realized that Chrissy wasn't helping out. Finally, Klaus stopped dancing and spoke seriously to her daughter, and Chrissy reluctantly allowed him to lead the way to her mother.

"Mrs. Henshaw, nice to see you again."

Chrissy didn't look as though she agreed with Klaus. "Hi, Mom."

Susan greeted Klaus, and then asked if her daughter would help her out in the ladies' room for a few minutes. "I think my slip . . ." She left the statement unfinished, knowing there was no way her daughter could refuse such an oblique request.

"The ladies' room is over there." Chrissy pointed. "The door with the picture of the heifer on it."

"Cute." It wasn't, but Susan was so pleased that her daughter had followed her lead that she didn't criticize. She was also pleased to discover that they were alone in the room. She started to ask questions immediately.

"Chrissy, I really need to talk with you." She stopped. "I know these question sound like prying, but I'm not. This has to do with the investigation."

"Mother, I have to get back to Klaus. Could you just get on with it?" Chrissy pulled a comb from her purse and started to touch up her hair.

"Okay. As long as you understand . . ."

"Mother!"

"Okay. You met Klaus at a party last year."

"Yes, in Greenwich Village. We crashed the party—sort of." She shrugged. "We were in high school and thought it was cool. What can I say?"

"How did you hear about the party?"

"Someone . . . I don't know who knew about it. I thought it was going to be this really artistic thing. You know, down in Greenwich Village and all. As though any artists can afford to live in Greenwich Village. I had this beatnik image from stuff I'd read."

"But it wasn't a party of artists."

"No. It was given by a Frenchman who runs a cooking school in the city, and his friends were mostly food people. Klaus was there with his mother. . . . His father was in Europe at the time, and she asked him to accompany her. I thought he was nice, but I had this weird outfit on, and I had put this rinse on my hair, and I looked a little strange. I wanted to hide in a closet, but everyone else thought it was so cool to be there that I couldn't talk anyone into leaving. Cameo acted like she was going to spend the night. Of course, we all knew how she felt about Z. . . ."

"How? Were they going together?"

"Mother, he's got to be at least ten years older than Cameo. And I don't think anyone believed that it was anything other than a high-school crush."

"So Z didn't reciprocate her feelings?" This was serious stuff to Susan, so she didn't have to work to keep from smiling at her daughter's newly found perspective on her past.

"Did they have an affair? Is that what you're asking?"

"Well, I guess that's what I am asking."

"I don't know. There were lots of rumors, but Cameo may have started them herself." Chrissy shrugged. "She's like that, you know. Hates to have the attention directed at anyone else. Probably the result of living with such awful parents," suggested her psychoanalytical daughter.

"She might have told people that she had slept with someone even though it wasn't true?"

"She might have. It's status conferral. After all, Z was a very sexy guy. Cameo might have decided that it would help her reputation if people thought they were having an affair."

".Was Z at that party?" Susan didn't ask the question that she wanted to ask.

"Yes. Gwen Ivy too. She wears wonderful clothing, doesn't she? I wonder where she shops."

"I've wondered about that myself." Susan returned to the subject. "Do you think Cameo was the person who knew about the party—because she had heard about it from Z?"

"It's possible. I remember that The Holly and Ms. Ivy were catering some sort of annual dinner party that Cameo's parents were giving. She seemed to think it was a big deal that this famous caterer was being hired by the mayor of a suburb. That's Cameo. She crabs about her parents and what jerks they are, and then, without taking a breath, she's bragging about them. She'll be shocked when she comes back from Switzerland and discovers The Holly and Ms. Ivy working for us, too.

"Come to think of it," Chrissy continued. "You're probably right about Cameo knowing about the party. It certainly wasn't a group that anyone else I used to hang out with would have known about."

"And do you remember if Z looked happy to see her?"

Chrissy frowned. "I don't remember. Z was always so polite and, well, so enthusiastic about people that it would have been hard to know if he wasn't pleased. He always looked happy. Didn't he?"

"I guess so." Susan was going to have to ask the question. She tried to phrase it as gently as possible. "Chrissy, you were a lot younger then . . ."

"Definitely. I can't believe the way I used to act."

"And you might have done things that are embarrassing to you now . . . ," Susan continued.

"Like dying my hair green, I know."

"Did you have a crush on Z back then, too?" Susan asked, looking intently at her daughter. Was she going to embarrass her?

"Z? You're kidding! Even then, I could see through him. Z was charming, but shallow. Not," her daughter added, tucking her comb in her purse and snapping it shut, "my type at all!"

"Chrissy." Susan put a hand on her daughter's arm. "Just two more questions. I promise."

"Okay. What?"

"Is it possible that Cameo met Z at our house last year?"

"No, of course not." Chrissy paused, and then continued more thoughtfully. "You know, you may be right. All my friends knew you were out of town, and Cameo actually asked if she could use our house to meet someone. I refused, of course. I didn't like her that much—and I knew you wouldn't approve of people being in the house when there weren't any members of the family at home. But she could have met him there while I was at the beauty parlor having my hair dyed."

"I thought you dyed it green with a friend."

"I had it dyed back to the original color by a professional. And, you know, I used Cameo's hairdresser. She recommended the man highly—almost insisted on him." Chrissy paused and thought for a minute. "She even called and made the appointment for me."

Susan was so relieved that she didn't bother to wonder about Cameo's own blonde locks. She didn't have to worry anymore. The note on Z's body must have been written last year by Cameo Logan, and then put in his pocket after his death—by the murderer. But it had nothing to do with Chrissy or any other member of her family. She took a deep breath.

"Can I go now?"

"Just one more question," Susan insisted. "Why didn't you introduce Klaus to us earlier this week?"

TWENTY-TWO

"Don't you ever get tired of Christmas carols?"

"Don't tease your mother, Chad," his father insisted. "She's busy resting up for her party. It's tough being a lady of leisure, you know."

"She wasn't this crabby when she was doing all the work herself," Chad said, leaving the kitchen with a plate piled high with food.

"Who does he think cooked the goodies he's been eating all week long," Susan muttered, leaning down to scratch Clue's belly. "This dog needs to go on a diet."

"We'd all be better off if we lost a few pounds," Jed suggested, taking a large cinnamon roll from the microwave. "These are really good. When did you bake them?"

"Last night. I needed some time to myself, and baking seems to—what's the new phrase?—to center me."

"I thought I heard you banging around down here pretty late."

"Yeast dough takes a while to rise," Susan said, not admitting that she had also cleaned out all her kitchen cupboards to prevent anyone from The Holly and Ms. Ivy seeing them in their usual state. "I suppose I should take a bath. I want to be ready to get dressed before anyone from The Holly and Ms. Ivy arrives."

"What are we going to do about Clue?" Jed asked, finishing the sweet roll himself, much to the animal's obvious disappointment.

Susan looked down at the drooling dog. "I never thought about it. I guess we're going to have to lock her up somewhere. Otherwise she'll be jumping on everyone and stealing food."

"How about the basement?"

"I suppose so." She looked down at the retriever's sad eyes and told herself that she had to be projecting her own feelings onto the animal. There was no way Clue could know what was being talked about. "Why don't I take her for a long walk? The party doesn't start till nine, so I have lots of time, and this may be the last time everyone will have their houses lit up this year."

"Fine. I'd better go pick up the basement. We don't want to discover that Clue whiled away the evening by chewing up your ski boots."

"Good thinking." She reached out for Clue's leash. That was all it took. The animal forgot her stomach and jumped up on Susan, tail banging hard against the kitchen cabinets. "Okay, Clue, let's try to get out of here without destroying the furniture."

"I'll open the door," Jed offered, and Susan and Clue were soon traveling down the street, bounding between patches of yellow snow. It was a lovely night (despite the pollution underfoot), and she paused about halfway down the block and turned to look back at her home. Clue sat obediently at her side.

The house looked lovely in the snow. Lights shining, ribbons blowing in the crisp breeze. "We're pretty lucky to live in such a nice place with such a nice family, Clue," Susan said quietly, looking down at the dog. Clue leaned against her leg and sighed. Susan would have been more impressed with the animal's sensitivity if she hadn't had a pocketful of dog biscuits. Clue could smell a biscuit through many layers of wool. "Come on, puppy. We don't have all day."

It was over an hour before The Holly and Ms. Ivy were due to arrive, but Susan was determined to be ready ahead of time. She wasn't going to miss this opportunity to ask some questions.

They were walking by the Kent house, and Susan couldn't help thinking about her encounter with JoAnn a week ago. What had JoAnn said? That The Holly and Ms. Ivy had started a fire in her kitchen? Susan continued on around the block, thinking about all the disasters that had happened to the catering company starting Christmas Day—starting, in fact, with that fire.

Susan turned around so quickly that Clue, trotting by her side, barked in surprise. The light over the Kent's front door was on, and Susan took that as an invitation. "Come on, Clue, let's go for a neighborly visit." They hurried back down the walk and up the driveway to the front door.

JoAnn Kent opened the door at the first knock. "Susan. Hi. Aren't you supposed to be getting ready for your party?"

"It's all taken care of. I wondered if you had a few minutes? I need to talk with you."

"I guess so." JoAnn looked down at Clue. "Can you tie your dog up outside?"

"Of course," Susan agreed, glancing around. "I'll just wrap her leash around this lamp," she said, spying a cast-iron light that rose about a foot out of the snow next to the sidewalk.

"Good. Tell me," JoAnn said, leading the way into her home, "have you actually heard anything about who killed Z yet?"

"Actually, I wanted to ask you some questions about that," Susan admitted, taking her coat off and draping it over the banister. "You know, you gave the last party that Z was personally involved with."

"And don't I regret that! I'd probably still have a kitchen if it hadn't been for Z Holly. Have you seen the damage the fire did?"

"No."

"Well, come on in. The contractors can't start working until the middle of next week—they're vacationing somewhere warm. All that's been done is that the burned area was cut out, thrown away, and the holes patched up. I was assured that would get rid of the scorched smell."

"And has it?"

"Breathe for yourself," JoAnn offered, flinging open the swinging door between her dining room and the kitchen.

"Phew."

"You can say that again."

Both women stood in the doorway and stared at the mess. The far wall of the room was naked, stripped of its cabinets, furniture, and wallpaper. New wallboard was protected behind sheets of heavy plastic. Quarry-tile flooring covered only half of the room, and the rest was encased in plastic. Everything reeked of smoke.

"You're not doing much cooking these days, are you?" Susan commented, aghast at the sight.

"None. I wanted to move to a hotel—preferably a nice suite at the Plaza, but my cheap husband wouldn't hear of-it."

"The holidays are so expensive," Susan murmured diplomatically. "But tell me, how did this fire get started?"

"The small oven blew up," JoAnn said abruptly.

"During your dinner party?"

"Right in the middle of it. We were just starting on the main course when there was this terrible bang."

"It must have spread very quickly," Susan said, looking at the large area of damage.

"I don't know about that. Apparently there was no one around when it happened."

"But you were eating in the dining room. Right next door. How did it have time to spread?"

"Well, we just kept on eating," JoAnn admitted. "We assumed that someone in the kitchen would take care of whatever had made the noise. Of course, we had absolutely no idea that it was a fire until smoke started seeping out under the closed door. . . ."

"But who was in the kitchen?"

JoAnn nodded. "Now you know why we're suing. Apparently there wasn't anyone in the kitchen when the explosion occurred."

"You're kidding!" Susan was stunned. She had spent the last week in kitchens where The Holly and Ms. Ivy were producing a party; there were always lots of chefs and workers around. More than enough, considering the size of the parties, it had seemed to Susan. "Do you know how many people were working here that night?"

"When I spend the money to get one of the best caterers on the eastern seaboard, I assume that I'm paying for competence—that they know what they are doing, and I don't have to do anything but enjoy myself. And I was busy getting ready for my guests. I didn't stand in the kitchen and count as people walked through the door."

"But you must have noticed something. Was Z here? Or Gwen Ivy?"

JoAnn smiled for the first time. "Z came by with the setup crew. . . . Oh, all right, I remember four people who arrived around noon. They set the table, started cooking, put out canapés, and arranged a portable bar by the tree in the living room."

"And Z?"

"He brought a bottle of champagne with a tiny sprig of mistletoe tied around it." She smiled again, and Susan remembered the rumor about JoAnn and Z. "But he had to go on to another party—he worked so hard—and then, I suppose, only four of his employees were here."

"Do you remember any of them? What they were doing?"

"Well, the bartender was in the living room until dinner was served around three in the afternoon. There was a cute young woman who offered appetizers before the meal, and then she put the meal on the table. My husband is very old-fashioned, and he likes to pass food around the table."

"So you might not have seen anyone else from the company until after you had eaten."

"True. But I didn't expect to be left alone. What if someone wanted something? Or if the kitchen appliances exploded?" she added sarcastically.

A loud shout from outside interrupted before Susan could ask more questions. JoAnn hurried to the nearest window.

"It's my husband. He seems to be yelling at our front door."

"Clue!" Susan cried, and ran to the door. She pulled it open and discovered her pet jumping up and down and preventing David Kent from entering his own home.

"Where did this mongrel come from?"

"She's mine," Susan said indignantly. "And she's a golden retriever from one of the best kennels in the country—and I'm sorry she ate your doormat. I'll buy you another one."

"She growled at me!" he stated, getting to what he considered the point.

"She does that sometimes when she's playing," Susan explained, patting her dog's head and accepting her coat from her hostess. "You've been a big help, but I'd better get going," she added quickly. "See you both later!"

"Later?" David asked.

"At my New Year's Eve party," Susan explained.

"Is that beast going to be there?"

"She'll be locked up," Susan insisted, untangling Clue's leash, waving good-bye, and hurrying back to her own home.

"Where have you been?" Jed asked, as she reentered her kitchen.

"Talking with the Kents. Did you finish up down in the basement?"

"Sure did. Are you going to take a bath?"

"I'm on my way upstairs," Susan said, suiting the action to her words.

There was loud music coming from her children's rooms. It was so nice to have the entire family together, she thought, hurrying on into the master bedroom.

Her new dress was hanging on the closet door, and Susan caressed it as she passed. She loved this dress with its full skirt and gauzy gold vest. But, right now, she had other things to think about. She hurried into the bathroom, tossed some mimosa-scented oil into the tub, and turned on the tap. While the tub filled, she returned to the bedroom and grabbed a pen and her trusty notebook. A warm bath was a great place to do some serious thinking.

Half an hour later, she was clean, she smelled good, and she was ready to give Brett a call. It was important that he attend her party for professional, if not personal, reasons. As if on cue, she heard her husband greeting people at the back door, joined by the tinkling of glass as Clue, barking, jumped on someone‾ carrying a load of glassware. Jed yelled. Susan tightly tied her robe around her waist and ran downstairs. Gwen was standing at the foot of the stairs. Finally. This is what Susan had been waiting for. And now she knew what questions to ask.

TWENTY-THREE

CANDLELIGHT IMPROVES MANY THINGS. IT HIDES THE DOG fur on the carpet and the wrinkles around middle-aged eyes.

"This is your best party ever," Jerry Gordon said, coming up to where Susan stood by the doorway, watching her guests.

"But we miss some of your specialties," Kathleen added tactfully.

"You're a good friend to lie so well," Susan said. "I appreciate the thought, but The Holly and Ms. Ivy did a beautiful job. Their food is fabulous. I really think it's the best I've had at any party all week long."

"And she's been to a lot of parties this week," Jed said, joining the group. "But not all of them were catered by The Holly and Ms. Ivy."

"Oh, yes, they were," Susan contradicted him. "The Logans' dinner party was and, of course, the hospital ball. And The Holly and Ms. Ivy catered both Gillian's and Alexis's parties. And they did all three parties on Thursday night— even the historical society dinner at the old mill, and I'll bet they don't usually do dinners like that. And there was Courtney Sawyer's sweet-sixteen yesterday. Every single one of them was catered by The Holly and Ms. Ivy. And they worked on others in town that I didn't get to," she added. "That's what finally tipped me off."

"What do you mean, tipped you off?" Jerry asked.

"Susan did it again." They had been joined by Brett Fortesque.

"Did what?" Jed asked, looking at his wife.

"I solved the murder," Susan said, grinning at the surprised looks of everyone around her.

"Mrs. Henshaw!" Jamie Potter interrupted before Susan could explain further. "When do you want dessert served? It takes some last-minute preparation, and I want to get the timing right. I couldn't find Gwen."

"How about at eleven-fifteen? Then there'll be time for everyone to serve themselves before champagne at midnight. I can't wait to find out what it is."

"And don't worry about Gwen Ivy," Brett suggested. "She was called away. I think she put that young man . . . Stephen . . ."

"You mean Stefan?"

"That's right. Stefan Hoffmann. That's what she said. She put him in charge."

"No problem," said the ever-obliging Jamie. "And thanks for inviting my aunt to your party, Mrs. Henshaw. She's found someone who tats, and she's having the time of her life—of course, we'll all probably be getting tatted toilet-paper holders sometime later this week."

"I'll look forward to that. I'm really glad she could come." Susan smiled.

"So Gwen Ivy did it," Jed said, after Jamie disappeared into the crowd that was standing around the dining room table. "You're saying that Gwen's the murderer."

Susan nodded yes.

"But how did you catch on?"

"Because she organizes the schedule for The Holly and Ms. Ivy, and why else would she only accept jobs in Hancock, Connecticut, during the busiest week of the year? And remember, we're talking about a very well-known catering company. One that has been entertaining famous people for years. Hancock is a nice town, but it's not New York City."

Kathleen blinked. "You know, I wondered about that, but it didn't seem significant. After all those years in the police department . . . I must be losing it. Nothing is insignificant in a murder investigation."

"You weren't running a house, raising a preschool child, and entertaining your in-laws when you were a detective," Susan reminded her.

"And you weren't two months pregnant," Jerry added, grinning broadly.

The Gordons had to accept congratulations all around before the conversation could continue.

"What did Bananas say when you told him that he's going to have a little brother or sister?" Susan asked, hugging her friend.

"We have over six months to discuss that. Why don't you tell us about the murder before it's next year," Jed insisted.

Susan waved at a neighbor. "Happy New Year! Have you tried the duck pâté?" She called out before turning and smiling at her husband. "We are giving a party here, you know."

"A party where the owner of the catering company was just arrested," he reminded her.

"And much to the credit of my people, no one's good time has been interrupted," Brett added.

"Maybe Susan should tell us about all this . . . ," Jerry suggested.

"Okay, but let's keep it down. I don't want to ruin anyone's good time," she insisted, moving back and sitting down on the stairway to the second floor.

"First tell me why she did it," Jerry asked. "Kathleen told me that Gwen and Z weren't romantically involved anymore."

"If they ever were," Kathleen added. "Even though they lived and worked in the same house at one time, there was never any hard evidence that they were more than friends and colleagues."

"The motivation was professional," Susan explained. "In fact, Gwen told me why she did it when she was explaining the origins of The Holly and Ms. Ivy. Remember, they went to New York City to raise money. Gwen failed to convince a completely disinterested venture capitalist to invest in them, but Z got money—as well as their first job—from his aunt. The business was completely funded by Z. In fact, it really was Z's company."

"But he was doing less and less of the real work," Brett added. "That was obvious to Kathleen at the beginning of the investigation."

"True." Susan nodded. "People overheard Gwen claiming that she was happy to leave all the schmoozing of the clients to Z—and she probably was—but that didn't mean that she enjoyed being left to plan all the details of each and every party. Every time I asked a question about who did what, the answer was Gwen. Selecting the food, talking to suppliers, ordering everything from staples, to seafood, to toothpicks, and flowers fell into her lap more and more. And she did all the paperwork for the company as well."

"And Z?" Jerry asked.

"Z did the fun work. Anyone who has planned anything can tell you that the broad outline and the concepts are exciting to develop. Z met with clients and suggested English tea parties in homes where the first floor could be turned into a Victorian conservatory. Z planned miniature rodeos in rooftop gardens and toga parties in swimming pools under apartment houses. He convinced hostesses that balloons and a circus theme would be fun, and that they would be remembered more for the wine tasting they gave if their guests were entertained in a mock-up of a French wine cellar built for the day in the middle of the lawn.

"And then Z was always around to take care of the hostess right before the party began, going so far as to bring champagne to toast the success of the event before it actually happened. But while all this was going on, Gwen was back in her small office doing the hard work. And knowing that if Z got bored, it could all change in minutes—and that was more and more likely all the time."

"Why?" Kathleen asked.

"Because Z didn't have to work anymore. His wealthy aunt had died, making him a wealthy person in his own right. Remember, he was her only heir."

"But even if he left, and The Holly and Ms. Ivy folded,

couldn't Gwen have just started another company and gone on without him?"Jed asked.

"Probably not in the style that they had developed over the years—with the carriage house and all. And, in fact, the reputation of The Holly and Ms. Ivy was that Z was a wonderful party planner. I'm not sure that Gwen could have done it without him. At the very least, she would have spent years building up a reputation. And everyone talks about how much competition there is in their field. If The Holly and Ms. Ivy ever folds, there will be a lot of people prepared to step into the void.

"But, with Z dying unexpectedly, the company can survive for a time on its reputation. They're fully booked for months to come, and it's too late to hire someone else. Gwen planned on handling the upcoming parties, and if they were as good as in the past, she could have continued on without much more than a pause for Z's funeral."

"But what did all this have to do with the parties in Hancock this week? Why Hancock?" Kathleen asked, sticking to the point.

"Gwen is no slouch either when it comes to planning, remember. It was what she did sixteen hours a day, seven days a week," Susan explained. "And she planned this murder so that she wouldn't get caught. If Z had been killed in New York or somewhere in Westchester County, she would have been the only suspect—being the one person closely connected with the victim. But in Hancock, things were different. Z was romantically involved with women in town. He worked out at a popular club, jogged with friends, lived with the relative of a fellow worker. He was a part of the community. There were bound to be more suspects here than any other place."

"So Gwen murdered Z here in Hancock to muddy the waters, so to speak. That makes sense." Jerry nodded.

"And she made a bunch of quote mistakes unquote that confused things even more," Susan continued. "Gwen claimed it was a mistake that she scheduled Gillian's party for the same day and identical time as Alexis's party. And the mix-up wasn't discovered until both sets of invitations were in the mail, and it would have been difficult to correct the problem. So it was logical that each party would go on as planned—with each woman competing to be Hancock's hostess with the mostest. And then Gwen actually encouraged the two women to compete with each other over every detail by telling one that the other was trying to surpass her. She made a mistake there—Alexis told me about that.

"And Gillian and Alexis had both spent a lot of time with Z as well, planning the parties and, probably, flirting like crazy. When Z was murdered, naturally they became primary suspects—under the circumstances."

"Circumstances that Gwen Ivy created," Brett added.

"Was the fire at the Kent's party a planned mistake, too? Was it set?" Jerry asked.

"That was an accident. An accident that almost ruined Gwen's plans," Susan said.

"You see," Brett explained. "Gwen killed Z during that party. She strangled him—probably getting a black eye in the process. Susan talked with JoAnn Kent today and realized that Gwen must have sent all her employees to another party or back to the carriage house. That's the only reason that no one was in the kitchen when the stove caught fire."

"On the other hand, what I was thinking about wasn't the logistics of the fire and Christmas Day, but that JoAnn had been involved with Z. I wasted a lot of time looking at the wrong things," Susan admitted. "Of course, if I had been thinking, I would have started out wondering why Gwen wanted to work for me so much."

She frowned and continued. "Gwen was lucky that I got the flu early in the fall. Normally, I wouldn't have been anxious to give up planning this party, but when I ran into Gwen in New York, I wasn't feeling well. I was vulnerable. Her kindness was so welcome that when she suggested that The Holly and Ms. Ivy could take over my party, I felt only relief. And, looking back now, I realize that she actually pressured me to hire the company, telling me that she had heard of my parties, even exchanging recipes. It was flattering to think that she had heard about my parties or that it would help the reputation of her company to work for me—but completely foolish of me to believe it for a minute. The Holly and Ms. Ivy are a big deal. They have pictures of the rich and famous on their walls. Under normal circumstances, they wouldn't have been interested in this type of party—or working for most of our friends in Hancock.

"I must have been feeling dreadfully ill. It never even occurred to me to wonder why the most popular caterer on the East Coast was free for New Year's Eve. A few days ago, Jed mentioned that a colleague couldn't hire The Holly and Ms. Ivy to cater his daughter's wedding—a wedding that's still over six months off. I should have realized then that there was something strange going on. Normally The Holly and Ms. Ivy are booked solid months in advance."

"That's true," Brett added. "When my men started checking things out, they discovered that Gwen had canceled all their events for this past week. If we had checked into that earlier, we would have known something was up." Brett shook his head regretfully.

Susan nodded. "And that wasn't all. Gwen had another ace in the hole, so to speak. You see, Cameo had a crush on Z. She even tried to seduce him in her parent's kitchen with other people around. Gwen certainly knew about it. She even got hold of a note that Cameo had written to try to convince Z to meet her at our house last year. So she put the note in Z's pocket after she killed him, and she dropped a note of her own in our mail slot on Christmas Day. She knew I would get involved to protect my daughter—and of course, I didn't understand any of this.

"But Gwen had made a huge production out of a simple murder. She was relying on me not being able to untangle all the elements, not being able to separate the fact from the fiction."

"And then there was the food poisoning. That confused things all the more," Brett explained.

"I don't understand about that yet," Susan admitted. "I know Cameo's behavior was so outlandish at this time last year that her parents sent her off to Europe so The Holly and Ms. Ivy could cater their party without risking a repeat of last year's kitchen antics. And Gwen must have known that both of the Logans would be suspected of murdering Z. But Gwen was trying to protect the company's reputation, and the food poisoning threatened to shut it down. . . ." She stopped talking, a confused expression on her face.

"Maybe we can help you there," Kathleen said, looking to Brett for confirmation.

"He admitted it—privately. I don't think we'll ever get him to admit it publicly," Brett said, nodding. He leaned closer to his audience and spoke quietly so he wouldn't be overheard. "I just found out the truth a few minutes ago from Buck Logan himself. Once Gwen was arrested, he was ready to talk about what he and Camilla did."

"And you are going to tell us, aren't you?" Susan insisted.

"Apparently the Logans blamed Z for Cameo's behavior last year, and they decided to get revenge by ruining the reputation of The Holly and Ms. Ivy."

"Are you saying that the food poisoning wasn't an accident?" Susan asked.

"Can someone intentionally cause food poisoning?" Jerry asked. "I wouldn't think it's like adding rat poison to someone's food. And Kathleen did say that your lab had done tests. . . ."

"That's true," Kathleen said. "But the Logans weren't trying to kill anyone. They wanted to make one or two of their guests sick. So they chose the only guests they didn't care about—Dan Irving and his vegetarian friend—and offered them special 'healthy' canapés. They weren't healthy at all, of course. They were full of bacteria that made the couple ill."

"And they knew that Dan Irving and his guest were the only people who would be ill," Susan said, nodding slowly. "I didn't understand that immediately, although I thought it was strange when I went to see Buck in his office the day after the party, and he didn't ask me how I had been feeling. If I gave a dinner party where some of the guests became ill, I'd certainly be concerned about everyone else who ate the same meal." And she looked through the hallway into the living room, hoping there was nothing prophetic about any of her words.

"But, of course, Buck was sure I hadn't been ill—he didn't even bother to act as though it were a possibility," she continued. "Which it wasn't. Dan and his guest hogged those particular canapés."

"What about the next night at the hospital benefit?" Jed asked. "Chrissy told me that a lot of people were ill."

"And wasn't Dan Irving murdered in the hospital that night?" Jerry asked. "Smothered? People don't accidently suffocate in a hospital bed, do they?"

"It's not unusual," Brett said. "But people who know too much about one murder are, unfortunately, known to end up being victims of another. Sadly, it happens over and over. People never seem to learn how dangerous it is to keep secrets during murder investigations. It really is a waste," he repeated, a serious look on his face.

"Gwen killed him, too? I don't understand," Jed said. "Why, if the food poisoning had nothing to do with The Holly and Ms. Ivy?"

"Because it did have to do with them ultimately," Brett continued to explain. "It was the salt substitute that was full of bacteria. And Buck broke into the carriage house while his wife kept all the employees busy after the party; he put the poisoned salt substitute on the shelf there, too. Of course, he couldn't know that Susan would appear at the carriage house before anyone else."

"Or that I would see his white Range Rover and confuse it with the one that someone else drives," Susan added.

"And so poor Dan Irving was poisoned with the same salt substitute again," Brett said. "But this time the stress was too great for him, and he actually did have the heart attack that he had been expecting for so long. It was bad luck in more ways than one. He was also the only person who might realize that it was the healthy appetizers in both places that were making people sick. Gwen had already killed Z to get control of The Holly and Ms. Ivy; she killed Dan Irving to protect the reputation of the company."

"What a sad story," Susan said.

"I guess it is, but it's all over now. It's been one strange holiday season, but Gwen is going to be locked up for a long time. And I think we can safely say that there are a lot of talented chefs around to take up where The Holly and Ms. Ivy leaves off."

Susan looked around at the bright decorations, the wonderful food, and her happy guests. "I guess this is The Holly and Ms. Ivy's last affair."

"And everyone seems to be enjoying it," Kathleen said.

"What's that ringing?" Jerry asked, turning around.

"It seems to be coming from the dining room," Jed said, getting up.

Susan glanced at her watch. "It's eleven-fifteen. I'll bet that's Jamie letting us know dessert is ready."

"Then we'd better go gather our guests," Jed suggested, helping his wife to her feet.

TWENTY-FOUR

"IT's FANTASTIC!" SUSAN EXCLAIMED.

"It's symbolic," Jamie explained.

"It's beautiful," Kathleen said.

"Let me explain it," Jamie suggested, standing beside the large oval table she had set up in the dining room. "There are three levels." She pointed to a towering display. "And each symbolizes a part of our world. The bottom is the sea. The middle area—the largest one—is the earth. And the top is the sky.

"Now, for the sea level, I made cookies shaped like shells and coral. The sand is colored sugar, and the fans of sea grass are royal icing—edible but not terribly interesting."

"There's even a treasure chest full of candy jewels," Susan said, looking more closely.

"That was great fun to make," Jamie said enthusiastically, displaying the smile of an appreciated artist. "The first one I ever did was my graduation project at cooking school.

"The middle level is the largest," she continued. "That's the earth. That was easy. Lots of fruit—tarts, candies, fruit-flavored mousses, fruitcakes, and puddings. All good food comes from the earth, so I just produced lots of my old favorites.

"But the sky is the most interesting. . . ."

"And the most impressive," Jed insisted. "Look at those cookies shaped like tiny moons and comets, and the yellow meringue stars are amazing. And these little gold chocolate things . . ."

"That's real twenty-four-karat gold on the chocolates," Jamie said. "Completely edible, and nothing else looks like it. They symbolize the planets in our solar system. See, there are even little rings around Saturn."

"Maybe we'd better stop admiring your work and let everyone sample some of it," Susan suggested, moving away from the table.

"And I should get back to the kitchen." Jamie leaned closer to Susan. "We're trying out your new cappuccino machine in there if you'd like some before the champagne."

Susan smiled and looked around the room. Everyone was having a good time. "Go ahead and enjoy yourselves," she insisted. "You all deserve it."

"So why," Kathleen asked, coming up behind her as Jamie hurried off, "didn't Chrissy introduce us to her charming young man before now?"

"Because Klaus is such a nice open person that she knew we would find out about her going into the city last year if we started talking to him. She thought we wouldn't approve of her crashing an unknown person's party." Susan chuckled.

"If only she could have known how you were going to be spending this week."

"True. Well, it's probably better that our children don't know everything about us. I'm glad we finally did meet him. He's a fine young man, isn't he?"

"Yes. They're serious about each other, aren't they?" Kathleen asked.

Susan nodded. "I think so."

"Did he get her a ring that day in New York?"

Susan laughed. "No. He got her a gigantic set of sable paintbrushes—and for an artist, that's the equivalent of a ruby surrounded by emeralds. He wasn't sure which manufacturer she preferred and . . ."

"That's why she had to pick out her own gift."

"Yes. And it's nice that he's encouraging her artwork," Susan said.

"He seems to be everything you could possibly want in a son-in-law," Kathleen said.

"She's much too young," Susan protested. "She hasn't even finished her freshman year of college yet. I know," she added, laughing at the look on Kathleen's face, "it's her life—and I have faith that she's going to make the right decisions for herself."

"You just don't want to start suffering from empty-nest syndrome," Kathleen said.

"There's still Chad. . . ."

"Who's looking pretty grown-up tonight himself. I just saw him in the living room. Who's the very sophisticated child in black that he's with?"

"Courtney Sawyer. She's something, isn't she?"

"Sure is. She was telling him about getting a tattoo. She claims it didn't hurt at all."

Susan sighed. "When you have children, if it's not one thing, it's another."

"At least you don't have to worry about diapers anymore. . . . What was that noise?" Kathleen asked as a scream followed by loud laughter floated out of the dining room.

Susan hurried toward the commotion without stopping to ask questions. Only one thing in her house caused shock and laughter simultaneously. She yelled as she went, "Clue! Sit!"

"Actually, she's already sitting," explained the first guest she ran into that wasn't choked with either laughter or food.

That was true, Susan discovered. Clue was sitting right in the middle of the tablecloth she'd pulled from the dessert table, lapping up every goodie she could find. "Oh, no! What are we going to do?" Susan wailed.

"Why not have a glass of champagne?" Jed suggested, handing her one, "and then we can wish all our friends a very happy New Year."